L.A. MCBRIDE

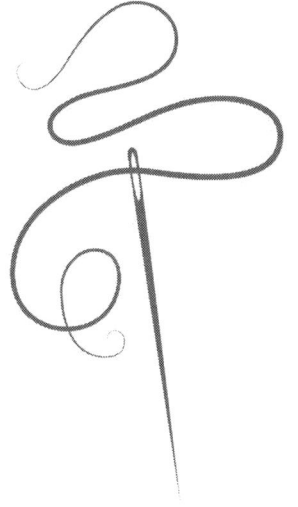

FASTENING THE GRAVE

A KALI JAMES NOVEL: BOOK ONE

For my sister Amanda, who didn't get enough time to live out her adventures.

NEWSLETTER SIGNUP

Subscribe to my newsletter for updates, announcements, and bonus content: lamcbride.com/newsletter/

CHAPTER 1

*I*f there were two constants in my life, they were death and illusion. In the year since I'd opened the Costume Shoppe on Kansas City's haunted house row, I'd outfitted more zombies, vampires, and ghouls than a Hollywood special-effects team. Most of my clientele were what I called the working dead—actors who worked weekends at one of five massive haunted houses that made up Halloween central.

The towering industrial warehouses that had once been notorious for frequent flooding and a burgeoning rat population had been transformed into multi-story scream factories. From the beginning of September through the end of October, this part of the city became an over-the-top gauntlet of theatrical haunts. Around here, there was fierce competition to become the most gruesome show in town. And people couldn't get enough of it, swarming to Kansas City to be seen and to be scared.

Although I loved creating elaborate costumes for the

actors, this was my first time seeing the full production in person.

"Aren't you cold?" Emma asked, her hands disappearing into the oversized sleeves of her Royals sweatshirt. Even though we were the same age, twenty-six looked a lot younger on Emma.

"Nah," I lied.

Some things were worth suffering for, and tonight's ensemble was one of them. I was Bettie Page in sensible shoes. I'd pinned my dark curls back, securing them with a sheer red scarf to show off my latest creation: a form-fitting black polka dot top with a sweetheart neckline. Paired with a flared skirt with pockets, a chunky red belt, and matching red flats, I was rocking my inner 1950s pinup. Sandwiched between girls waving pastel phone cases and guys sporting obnoxious t-shirts and too much cologne, I was happy to stand out.

I scanned the growing crowd. "Where is Riley?"

There were a lot of ways I'd rather spend a Friday night than paying people to scare me, but Riley was hard to say no to. After using up my allotment of excuses, Riley convinced me and Emma that free tickets to Howl, one of the premiere haunted houses, would be worth suffering the late September lines.

It wasn't Riley who caught my eye. In the sea of twenty-somethings, the man watching me stood out as much as I did. He was as still and unnatural as a wax sculpture. His clothes, too big for his lanky frame, were straight out of a 1920s gang-ster movie. His fedora was tilted low and cast most of his face in shadow. Although I couldn't see his eyes, I knew from the angle of his body and his complete disregard for the people moving around him that they were locked on me. My shiver had nothing to do with the cold.

"Are you alright, Kali?" Emma waved a hand in front of my face.

I blinked. "Yeah. Sorry, just got distracted."

I wiped my now clammy palms on my skirt and swallowed. This wasn't the first time I'd seen the man. Last week, I spotted him standing across the street from my second-floor apartment. He was watching me then, too.

It had been fourteen months and six days since I'd seen a ghost. Naively, I thought I had put that behind me when I'd packed up and moved halfway across the country. Here, the only ghosts were supposed to be the ones I costumed.

There were perfectly ordinary reasons for him to be here, I reminded myself. Perhaps, he worked at Howl. Actors did wander among the crowd to heighten anticipation for the show. Of course, that wouldn't explain his appearance outside my apartment. He could just be a run-of-the mill creep who was stalking me. Plenty of explanations didn't involve a ghost, but even so, I couldn't make myself look away.

I was so focused on the man that I hadn't noticed Riley until she was standing beside me, craning her neck to see what had my attention.

"What are you looking at?" she asked.

"Who is that guy over there?" I asked her, still staring at him.

Among her collection of odd jobs, Riley worked at one of the other haunted houses. If the man was an actor, chances were she would know him.

She snorted. "You're going to have to be more specific."

"Tall guy, sickly looking, dressed like Pretty Boy Floyd."

"Who?"

"Seriously?" I turned my head to look at her. "How long have you lived in Kansas City?" It was true that I loved digging into area history more than most, but Pretty Boy Floyd was famous. "You know—1920s mobster who went out in a blaze of bullets."

She stared at me blankly before turning her attention back to where I had been looking. "I don't see anyone like that."

I couldn't make out what she said next because the crowd noise closed in on me. This wasn't my first panic attack, but it was my first in years. I shut my eyes and concentrated on deep breathing until the sounds receded. By the time I was calm enough to check, the man was long gone, and both Emma and Riley were watching me with concern.

Riley touched my arm. "Hey, are you okay?"

"Yeah, of course." I smiled, hoping it looked more genuine than it felt. "Just got light-headed there for a minute. I shouldn't have skipped supper."

Emma dug around in her purse and handed me a granola bar. Out of the three of us, Emma was definitely the Girl Scout. She never left home without snacks and emergency first aid supplies.

I wasn't hungry, but I took the bar anyway. "Thanks." I choked down half of it, the texture like sawdust in my mouth, before wrapping it back up and putting it in my pocket.

Seeing the lingering concern on their faces, I wanted to tell them about the ghosts that latched on to me like a lifeline. For a moment, I imagined the conversation going differently than it had with everyone else I had confided in.

Since moving here, Riley and Emma had become my closest friends. Both of them walked into my shop on opening day as strangers. Riley, lacking the patience or desire to put together her own costumes, quickly became a regular. Emma, I'd hired as a part-time employee, so I didn't spend all my time bent over a sewing machine or waiting on customers.

Our friendship was rooted in a shared appreciation for the dramatic, love of bad movies, and a healthy appetite for bacon and chocolate. Normal things. But if years of therapy had taught me anything, it was that my particular brand of drama was a surefire way to alienate the people around me.

Even if the man was a ghost, it didn't mean I had to acknowledge him. I smiled at my friends. Then I turned my back on the spot where he had been standing and focused on what was in front of me. "Finally, this line is moving!"

As we neared the front of the building, I distracted myself by studying Howl's impressive facade. Five stories tall, the daylight version—one run-down, crumbling brick warehouse among a line of them—became something else entirely at night. The streetlights on this block were old and sparse, and the light here was dimmer than the rest of the city. None of the streetlights quite reached Howl's entrance. Instead, a lone flickering bulb lit the massive metal-studded doors. Billowing smoke spilled out of the entrance and rose to the roofline.

One door was propped open against the side of the building, funneling high-pitched screams and heavy bass into the street. Next to the door, a burly sentry stood with his arms crossed over his massive chest. As we got closer, I noticed the pair of wicked-looking fangs he flashed periodically at the crowd.

Emma nudged us and gestured with her head at the black-clad man, rolling her eyes. Riley laughed, pulling us with her as we reached the door. The man flashed us another fang-filled grin before he lifted the rope to let us inside.

The leggy redhead taking tickets was far less friendly than the guy guarding the door. Despite the autumn chill, the woman was dressed simply in a black ribbed tank top tucked into dark-washed blue jeans. She had arms that rivaled the bouncer's, testament to a serious CrossFit addiction.

The redhead narrowed her eyes at Riley and leaned toward her. "Did you get lost, kid?"

Despite the hostility rolling off the woman, Riley smiled sweetly before blowing a fat pink bubble in her face. When it popped, the woman flinched.

"Nah," Riley said. "Just checking out the competition. You got a problem with that?"

Riley handed her a crumpled ticket and stepped past her without waiting for a response. The redhead sneered but made no move to stop her. She gestured for me and Emma to move, forcing us to shift sideways to squeeze past her.

"What was that about?" I asked, not caring that we were still within earshot.

"Haters gonna hate." Riley started up the stairs that led to the first room of the haunted house. "You ready for the second-best show in town?"

"Ready as I'll ever be," I said.

We climbed the long staircase and passed through an archway into the first room. Stepping across the threshold, we were immediately enveloped in darkness, the faint light from the entryway below dimming at our backs.

Emma groaned. "Why did I let you talk me into this?"

"Come on. It'll be fun." I nudged her with my hip and then took the lead. "Just stay close. I've got you."

Emma scooted closer. "Shut it," she snapped as I started making "ooooohoooooh" sounds under my breath, and Riley poked her in the side.

Before we took more than two steps into the first room, a middle-aged couple and their bored teenager filed in behind us, followed by a group of frat brothers who had been standing near us in line outside. Together, we all shuffled across the room and made our way deeper into the haunted house.

The rooms were laid out like a maze, with entry and exit doors scattered throughout. While the haunted house was five stories, there were no stairs beyond those in the entryway. Instead, the bigger rooms angled upward, making our ascent slow and slightly off-balance. We fought our way through chainsaw-wielding lumberjacks, Dracula wannabes, and a sizable zombie horde in the first few rooms. Make-believe or not, the feeling of half a dozen hands grasping at your arms and legs was enough to make anyone jumpy.

By the time we stepped into a long, mirrored hallway, the crowd had thinned, leaving the three of us momentarily alone. There was little room for the spook-and-grab patrol to leap out at us, but the mirrors reflected small bits of our movement as we walked. Mirrors in a dark room were terrifying in their own right.

The hallway was quiet except for the in and out of our breathing, which was amplified in the tight space. When the remaining light suddenly snuffed out, we were stranded in darkness. We felt our way along the narrow hallway, but it was slow going.

The light came back on just as quickly as it went out, illuminating a man dressed in head-to-toe camo blocking our path. He grimaced and brandished a realistic-looking assault rifle. The mirrored walls caught his reflection and splintered it, creating a kaleidoscope of soldiers.

There must have been speakers in the ceiling because the sound of gunfire exploded and echoed down the hallway. It was realistic enough to make me crouch down with hands over my head, elementary school tornado-drill style. Emma

7

was right there with me. Riley, however, was still on her feet, shaking her head at us.

"Ha!" crowed psycho Rambo, aka Bennie Walters. His war-painted face beamed down at me. "I told you this costume was better than a demonic clown."

He was right. When he wasn't smiling like a happy school-boy, which he had been when I had outfitted him, Bennie looked positively fierce. My makeup job had hardened his features. The football pads and quilt batting I'd wrapped him in earlier tonight had made his less-than-impressive five-foot-seven frame look downright stocky.

Bennie, like Riley, had become a regular at my costume shop. Most of the actors trickled in before the start of the spook season to have me craft them into gory characters, stopping back for costume repairs throughout the season. Scaring people in dark, smoke-filled rooms was hell on clothing.

Bennie came in almost every week. As someone who loved nothing more than to reinvent himself, he was a man after my own heart. He might be a zombie-apocalypse baby one week and psycho Rambo the next, which required frequent visits to my shop. And that made him my number one favorite customer.

I slow clapped. "Bravo, Bennie. You were epic."

Bennie bowed theatrically, which looked ridiculous, dressed as he was. He held out his hands to help us to our feet. Without the padding, Bennie was small and wiry, but he was surprisingly strong.

"Enjoy the rest of Howl. And a word of advice." He dropped his voice and leaned in for effect. "Not every door leads somewhere you want to go." He gestured to the two doors at the end of the hall before assuming his soldier stance and turning his back to us.

"What do you think? Door number one," I gestured toward the red door on the right, "or door number two?" I pointed to the black door on the left.

"Hmmm, red for blood or black for death," Emma said in her best dramatic voice. Because she spent most of her free time acting in community theater productions, she had that voice down.

Riley didn't wait for a discussion, reaching for the black knob before barreling into the next room. The room beyond the door was massive. It was forested with dozens of trees, thick vines dangling from their branches. Lit by flashing green strobe lights, every movement in the room had a herky-jerky quality.

"Cover me," Riley said, darting to one side.

I caught a fistful of her jacket before she could ditch us. "Wait. Where are you going?"

"Operation sabotage," she said, as if Emma or I had any idea what that entailed.

Emma scowled at Riley. "You're going to get us kicked out."

Riley scoffed. "They'd have to catch me first." She shrugged out of her jacket, leaving me holding it. She pointed across the room where a familiar redhead was looking right at us. Knowing the kind of trouble an unchaperoned Riley could stir up, it didn't surprise me that the redhead had abandoned door duties to check on her.

Riley winked at us. "Distract her for me." She snatched a fake fern out of a pot and stuck it on top of her head, weaving it into her pigtails to hold it in place. "Catch ya outside," she said over her shoulder.

Emma lunged for her, but I pulled her back. "Come on. Let her have her fun."

She put a hand on her hip and scowled at me. "Fine, but I'm not posting bail."

In the next flash of light, both Riley and the redhead were gone, and I was left holding Riley's jacket. It was a Riley Cruz wardrobe staple, so I couldn't exactly ditch it in the swamp room. I slid my arms in and tried not to think about how much this beat-up black leather jacket with too many zippered pockets ruined my carefully curated outfit. I grabbed Emma's hand and tugged her forward.

Across the room, a large swamp creature moved closer with each flash of the strobe light, the sudden movements building anticipation with every flash. I had to give it to the actors; they knew how to craft terror. Midway across the room, the swamp thing disappeared. In its place stood the man who had been watching me outside, his face ashen despite the sickly green glow of the strobe.

I stopped abruptly, Emma slamming into my back. When the light flashed again, the man was gone. I spun around.

"Did you see him?" My voice faltered.

"Um, yeah. Big, green guy. Hello."

I turned back to see the pale, slitted eyes of the Swamp Thing in the next flash of light. I didn't stick around for the next flash, dragging Emma back through the door we had just come through. "Let's try the red door instead!"

Emma laughed. "Are you actually scared of snake-face back there?"

I didn't bother correcting her. If I was the only one seeing him, it was better not to draw attention to it.

"Let me," she said, more than a little smug, as she reached for the knob on the red door.

That door was the first in a string of red doors, all of which led to what looked like the exact same room, causing us to wander back and forth, trying to find our way out. *This is what mice must feel like racing through their laboratory mazes.* I looked over my shoulder again before trying the next knob. The last thing I wanted to do was stick around long enough that my stalker caught up with us again.

"Okay, there has to be a frickin' way outta here." I tamped down my panic and forced myself to slow down. *Think.* "There must be several rooms that look alike, so we keep wandering back and forth through identical rooms and getting confused."

"You want to split up? We could each try a door and see if we end up in the same room," Emma suggested, her voice cheerful.

I didn't want to split up, but I also didn't want to be permanent residents. "All right. You go that way." I pointed to the door I thought was furthest away from the swamp room. "Just go in far enough that you can still hear me across the room, okay? If you see anything weird…"

"It's a haunted house. It's gonna be weird." She headed for the door.

I opened the other door just enough to peek into the room. "Same room over here," I called, still able to see Emma.

"Here, too," she called back.

"Okay, head through the next one and see if you end up back in the swamp room. If you do, come my way. If not, stay put, and I'll come to you."

The next door opened before I reached it, the frat boys rushing through.

"Woah," the one in a White Sox hat said, close enough that I nearly got a contact drunk from the alcohol on his breath.

I ignored him and pivoted, rushing back to Emma.

Emma's room was well-lit and remarkably normal, even if it was outdated. A pink tufted armchair sat next to an absurdly small footstool, and an ornate Queen Anne table was piled with old books. The walls were covered with portraits that would have made the couple in American Gothic look downright friendly. I watched the pictures, half expecting their eyes to follow me. But the eyes didn't move, and no one reached out from a gilded frame.

Emma scanned the room. "This may be the scariest room in the whole house."

"The pictures?"

"God, no." Emma pointed at the floral wallpaper and shuddered. "The decor. It reminds me of my great-aunt's house."

"Terrifying," I agreed, trying to keep the agitation out of my voice. "Let's get out of here." I looked over my shoulder to make sure she was following.

As soon as we stepped into the next room, the light went out, and the sound system shut off, as if someone tripped a breaker. *She wouldn't.* After a minute, the light came back on, along with the sound. "Who Let the Dogs Out" blared through the room at full volume.

"Oh shit, Riley," I laughed, looking at Emma, who had her hand over her mouth. "I think that's our cue to get out of here."

Someone must have reached the sound system because the song stopped abruptly, and the normal soundtrack came back on. The room we had entered was styled like a medieval dungeon, with old metal bars lining the left side of the room. Hooks hung from the ceiling, high enough that we wouldn't walk into them but low enough to cast shadows.

The only light in the room came from a single bulb

dangling above a rolling table that held an array of instruments for torture. Blood covered the rusty saws, pliers, and knives.

A mannequin was shackled to the wall across the room. At least I hoped for his sake that it was a mannequin because standing in that position for hours would be torture itself. His clothes were in tatters, and his arms were secured in metal cuffs high above his head. Between the low light and the distance, it was impossible to tell for sure whether he was a live actor or a prop, but he didn't move as I made my way deeper into the room. I kept my eyes fixed in his direction and edged to the other side of the room, just in case.

"Stay to the right," I told Emma.

The faint light didn't reach the edges of the room, so I put my arms out in front of me. I made my way to the wall furthest away from the shackled man. I was almost there when I stumbled on something solid. My slick flats slid out from under me, proving they weren't so sensible after all. It was too dark to see what had tripped me, but there had been enough give to tell me it wasn't the furniture.

"You okay?" Emma asked from behind me.

"Yeah, hold up. I fell on something." Feeling around, I made out the solid shape of a person—a bent arm, long torso, and matted hair that clung to my fingertips. The body was warm, which ruled out a dummy. I sat up and waited for the person to twitch to life, for a strong hand to grasp my ankle where it rested against the prone body. I prepared for a jump scare, but it never came.

"What is it?" Emma asked.

Against the rules or not, I fished my cell phone out of my pocket. I pressed the flashlight app and held the phone in front of me, spilling a beam of light across the man lying at my feet. The thick red blood that covered the man's throat and pooled next to his body looked pretty damn real. If this was fake, it was the best makeup job I had ever seen, bar none.

I heard Emma's scream, but my attention remained riveted on the face above that savaged neck, the man's soft, brown eyes vacant. I pulled my hands back and quickly scooted away from his body, leaving a trail of blood in my wake.

CHAPTER 2

J was still on the floor when the group of frat brothers piled into the room behind us, stopping short when they spotted the body.

"Dude."

Several of them pulled out their own cell phones, aiming the lights at the body on the floor. As they waved their phones around to get a better look, the lights glinted off a penny. The coin gave me something to focus on besides the dead man next to it. It was untouched by the blood pooling around it. Before I could stop myself, I reached for it, my bloodied fingers muting the shine.

The guy in a White Sox cap almost knocked Emma over as he jostled for position. "He looks real."

"He is real," I assured him.

The kid in the cap laughed, clearly thinking I was pulling his leg. "No way."

I kept my eyes focused on White Sox because when I looked at the dead man, I couldn't help but see my sister Claire's brown eyes staring back at me. Although she'd been dead for years, the image of her lying broken on the pavement, her beautiful eyes flat with death, was one I still carried with me. I swallowed.

This was not Claire, I reminded myself. I could fall apart later; right now, I was the only thing standing between the crime scene and a pack of drunk college kids angling for morbid selfies. Whoever this guy was, his chance for justice would likely depend on the evidence found within a few feet of where he was killed. I shifted, putting myself between them and the body. The frat guy's buddies, who must have had a little less to drink, were more cautious as they peered around me to get a good look.

"Is that fake blood?" the skinny one in the back asked hopefully.

White Sox stepped past me before I could stop him, nudging the victim's leg with the toe of his sandal. He wobbled as he tried to hold his balance.

"Get back!" I snapped, throwing my arm out to block him from trying it again. When he opened his mouth to argue, I did the only thing I could think of to shut him up. I dragged my finger through the blood pooling on the floor and brought it to my nose. The telltale metallic scent made my stomach flip flop.

"Sick." He stumbled backward into his friends. "Did you just smell that fake blood?"

I wiped my finger on my stomach, ignoring the dark smudge it left. It wasn't like I'd be wearing this outfit again. "Sorry to break it to you, but that's not fake blood."

At that, several of them grimaced. One bolted for the door he'd just come through. Emma looked at me like I was Jack the Ripper.

I'd worry about my inability to fit in later; for now, I did my best to channel my father.

"Look, this is a crime scene. Stop before you walk all over the evidence." I used my best no-nonsense voice. Growing up in a family of cops did, in fact, come in handy at times.

Of course, instead of clearing out the room as I had hoped, my announcement made the men lean over me to get a better look. Apparently, the pinup girl outfit undermined whatever authority I managed to put in my tone.

The guys were still craning over each other when Bennie arrived with a giant of a man. Even in the half-light, the man looked dangerous, but if the security t-shirt was any indication, he was on staff at Howl.

"Kali?" Bennie reached for my hand and pulled me to my feet, quickly taking stock of the scene. "Are you okay?" To his credit, he didn't flinch at the touch of my blood-covered palm against his.

"I'm good." I wasn't good, but my well-being wasn't actually important at the moment.

Bennie turned his attention to Emma, who was still pressing her body tightly to the wall across the room, as far away from the dead man, and from me, as she could get.

"Come on, darling," Bennie coaxed. "Let's get some fresh air."

Bennie put himself between Emma and the body. He discreetly wiped his palm on the back of his camouflaged fatigues before placing his hand on her arm and leading her out of the room.

The man with Bennie was all business. He flipped on a light switch that was concealed mid-wall, and light flooded the room, giving me a clear view of him. Unlike Bennie, this man didn't need any padding to look intimidating. He was tall, well over six feet, and to borrow my dad's favorite phrase, built like a brick shithouse. His hair was shaved close to his scalp, the kind of purposely bald that pro wrestlers and bikers favored. On his face, he sported a five o'clock shadow that did nothing to soften his features. His expression was more intimidating than his size; his dark eyebrows flatlined over hard eyes and a clenched jaw.

"Get back," he barked at the group, and for him, the men scrambled. He glanced at me, then pulled a walkie talkie off his belt. "Ruby, it's Craig. Call the cops. We've got a dead body in the green room." He said it as if finding a dead body was a normal occurrence. "And lock down the building. No one leaves until they get here."

After a long pause, a woman's voice answered. "You got it, boss."

I would've thought a dead body would cause a little more panic. I studied Craig, mostly because looking at him meant I didn't have to look at a dead man. If Craig's stance didn't out his military background, the scuffed black combat boots would have been a giveaway. Probably not his first rodeo.

White Sox edged toward the door, but Craig sidestepped to block the exit. "Everyone is staying put until the cops get here," he growled. To the walkie talkie, he ordered, "Cut the sound." This time, the only response was the abrupt stop of the house's sound-effect system. Once it was off, I heard staff in the next room directing bystanders away from the door. No one else came in as we waited.

Now that Craig had control over the room, I took a few steps away from the body, trying not to look too closely at the dead man's face. Instead, I studied my palms, the blood on them drying. I tried wiping them on my skirt, but it was already slick with blood from where I'd fallen. I covered my mouth with the back of my hand and closed my eyes.

"You okay?" Craig's voice was close, even though I hadn't heard him cross the room. He moved quietly for such a large man.

"Yeah," I lied. "I'm okay." I forced my eyes open, looking at his face, which hadn't softened at all.

He gave me a quick once over, taking in the bloodbath that was my clothes and skin, before looking directly into my eyes for several seconds. He probably thought I'd go into shock or dissolve into hysterics at any moment. And okay, my hands might be shaking a bit, but I wasn't going to fall apart.

"Do you know him?" I gestured toward the man at our feet, trying to redirect Craig's attention.

It was hard to gauge a man's height when he lay sprawled on the floor, but the dead man looked tall. He wore simple clothing: tan dockers, a maroon short-sleeved polo, and loafers, all of which screamed, "I work in an office." I knew a lot of blue-collar workers, and not one of them wore loafers. Or maroon shirts.

The man's hair was ruddy brown and short, and he had a neatly trimmed beard that glinted red under the bright fluorescent lights. If I'd had to guess, I'd have put him in his mid to late thirties. No wedding ring. I hoped that meant he wasn't a father with two toddlers and a young wife waiting at home for him.

Craig leaned over the man to examine his throat, blood still seeping from the wound. "Jack Gates," Craig said, as if I should know who that was. Craig was all business again, looking over the victim before turning his attention to the room.

Now that I was standing, I could see bloody weapons scattered on the other side of the body. From the empty spaces on the torture cart across the room, it wasn't hard to imagine where they came from. I could make out a pair of steel shears, an assortment of serrated knives, and vise grips. I didn't dwell on which was the most likely murder weapon. Instead, I watched as Craig quickly walked the perimeter, eyes searching the floor and walls. I wasn't sure what he was looking for, but his facial expression didn't invite questions.

One of the guys cleared his throat. "Who's Jack Gates?"

Craig didn't answer immediately. Instead, he bent down to get a closer look at the soles of the dead man's shoes. He was careful not to step in the blood or to touch anything.

"Reporter for *The Kansas City Star*," Craig finally answered.

Before anyone could ask another question, the distant sound of police sirens closing in registered. We all waited for the cops and the long interview that was sure to follow. On TV, police questioning might take ten minutes, but in real life, there was a whole lot more repeating yourself. It'd be after midnight before I got to sleep, assuming, that is, I could sleep at all. Finally, the low murmur of voices started making their way to us.

The uniformed officer who stepped into the room was young; he barely looked old enough to drive. "Is this the crime scene?" he asked.

Given the man lying in a pool of his own blood, it was an absurd question. Not that the officer had bothered to look down. The possibility of quick justice for Jack Gates wasn't looking particularly promising.

Before the officer could say anything else, a second man came into the room. This one was older, with graying hair and a weathered face. He gave the younger officer a disapproving glance before walking over to where Craig, the four remaining frat brothers, and I all stood staring pointedly down at the body.

"My name is Detective Woodson, and I'm with the Kansas City homicide unit," he said, flashing a badge. "And this is Officer..."

"Dodd," the younger officer said, standing up a little straighter.

"Officer Dodd here is going to help secure the room until our coroner and forensic crew get here."

Officer Dodd nodded but made no move to secure anything.

"While we wait, I'd like to ask you all some questions," Detective Woodson said.

Craig nodded and stepped forward, extending his hand. "Craig Ward."

They shook hands as if they were meeting at a community fundraiser rather than standing over a murder victim.

"I'm the head of security here at Howl." Craig said.

Both officers looked expectantly toward me. "Kali James." I kept my blood-soaked handshakes to myself.

"And you?" Woodson asked the group of men, scribbling down everyone's names in his pocket-sized tablet. "Do any of you know this man?" he asked.

"I do," Craig said. "His name is Jack Gates. He is, he was, a reporter for *The Kansas City Star.*"

"How well did you know him?" Woodson asked.

"Not well. He did a feature on Howl about a month ago." Craig gestured to the dead man. "We gave him complimentary tickets as a thank you for the good publicity."

Some thank you.

Woodson turned his attention to Gates, hunching down to examine the body. "Who found the victim?"

"I did, but I didn't see him until after I tripped over his body." I held up my bloody hands.

"You didn't see him?" Dodd asked, his voice skeptical.

"It was dark."

"It is a haunted house," Craig reminded the officers.

"Yes, of course," Woodson said.

Dodd scowled at me. He probably thought the scowling made people take him more seriously. Unfortunately for Officer Dodd, it made him look constipated. Not that I was about to share that little observation with the group.

Dodd took a step toward me. "And you," he said, emphasizing the "you" like an accusation. "How well did you know the man?"

"I've never seen him before."

White Sox opened his mouth to say something, but Detective Woodson held up his hand. "Was there anyone with you?"

"My friend Emma came in right after I did." I pointed at the four frat brothers. "And they came in a couple minutes after us."

"Where is Emma?" Woodson asked.

"One of the staff walked her outside to get some fresh air," Craig answered. "I can take you to her next."

"Why did you come into this room?" Dodd asked Craig. It was the first good question he'd posed since arriving.

Craig pointed toward the frat brothers. "One of their friends came out the front screaming about a dead man."

Woodson nodded and turned back to me. "Was there anyone else in the room when you got here?"

"No," I said.

"If it was dark, how could you be sure?" Woodson asked.

"If someone was in here," I countered, "they couldn't have left the room without us noticing the door opening. It was dark in here."

Woodson walked over and examined the door frame

leading out of the room. "Are these the only two exits?" he asked, pointing at the door he came in and the one he stood next to.

"Just those," Craig said.

Woodson turned his attention back to me. "Where did you find the victim?"

"He was right where he's lying now," I said.

Woodson knelt again to examine Gates, careful to avoid stepping in the blood pooling next to the body. "Ms. James, can you describe what happened, starting from the moment you entered the room?"

After having listened to numerous interrogation stories from my dad and brother, both cops, over the years, I recounted my movements in as much detail as I could recall.

"And when you got here?" Woodson asked the group of men.

"I thought it was fake," White Sox said, glancing at me. "Until that freak sniffed his blood."

Everyone stared at me.

"Not ketchup," I volunteered.

Craig raised his eyebrow. Dodd turned red. Woodson just cleared his throat before turning back to Craig. "Who was the last person through this room before Ms. James?"

"I'm not sure. We can check with the staff who were working in the other rooms, but a lot of people come through here. Hundreds a night."

"What about the room after this?" Woodson asked.

"This is the last room before the slide out."

"Any security footage?" Woodson asked hopefully.

"Sorry, not in here," Craig said. "The only camera we have is in the front of the building."

"We'll need a copy of whatever footage you do have,"

Woodson said. "And any names of tonight's crowd that you might have, as well as a list of staff working tonight."

"Of course."

"You mentioned a slide out?" Dodd peered across the room.

"Yes. At the end of the haunted house, everyone goes down a giant slide to the outside of the building." Craig motioned for Detective Woodson to follow him into the next room, but we all trailed after them. There, he showed the officers the entrance to a large, twisting slide.

"Were there staff working this room?"

Craig shifted his weight. "Normally, there would be, but we were short-staffed tonight." He pointed at a sign directing guests to exit. "We had to make do."

"What about that door?" Woodson asked, pointing to the closed door behind the sign.

"That leads down to the gift shop." Craig walked over and turned the knob to show it was locked. "But because of the short staffing, it was closed off and locked."

"Then whoever came through here would have just slid out of this room and landed outside the building?" Woodson asked.

"Yes," Craig said.

Dodd stuck his head inside the opening of the slide, looking down, as if the murderer might still be wedged in one of its bends. "Where does this end?" His voice echoed off the metal sides.

"In the back alley," Craig said. "It ends about a foot off the sidewalk behind the building."

Dodd pulled his head out of the slide and faced us. "That's bad."

Woodson shook his head. "Yes, Dodd. That's bad."

CHAPTER 3

*I*t was long past midnight before the police were done with me. By then, Emma was already gone. Ruby, the redhead who had been working the door, told me that Bennie had taken Emma home. Although I couldn't blame Emma for running for the beige-walled safety of the suburbs, I would have felt better if I could have checked to make sure she was okay. I did have several missed calls from Riley, but I didn't have the energy to call her back. I sent her a quick text to let her know I was all right and that I'd check in tomorrow.

Craig lent me a spare t-shirt and pair of sweatpants, both of which were giant on me, so I could hand over my blood-soaked clothes to the police. The only piece of clothing I kept was Riley's jacket, which had miraculously survived without a speck of blood on it. Craig also insisted on walking me the two blocks to my place. For the first block, we walked in awkward silence. It was hard to make small talk after leaving the scene of a murder.

"Are you okay?" he finally asked.

"A lot better than the dead reporter back there."

Craig smiled, a small crack in his otherwise stoic face. "Fair point." As he walked beside me, his eyes scanned every direction as if the killer might be just around the corner. Not that I was in much danger with him hulking down the street next to me. "You know, it is okay to be shaken up."

I stopped and peered up at him. "I know you are trying to help, but I don't want to talk about it." When Craig stiffened, I added, "at least not yet."

He nodded and walked the rest of the way with me in silence, awkward or not.

It wasn't until I was alone in my apartment with the deadbolt latched behind me that I let the panic overtake me. I tried to slow my breathing, to inhale deeply, pause, and push the air back out of my lungs. Wouldn't the shrink that claimed my teenaged Tuesdays be pleased something stuck from those sessions? I sagged against the door and closed my eyes.

For the past year, I'd reveled in the fake monsters I crafted in the shop, believing myself far removed from the grim world of actual murders. I had moved five hundred miles from the place my sister had been killed for a fresh start. Here, I didn't have to live with constant reminders of her all around me—the route we walked every day for years, the colleges she would never attend, the places I'd now go alone.

Back home, I had looked into every car that passed me on the street wondering: was his the last face she saw before he ran her down? Did he wait, watching until she took her last breath, before backing up and leaving her body crumpled like trash on the side of the road? In Chicago, there was nowhere left for me that wasn't tainted with Claire's death.

Sometimes, I wondered if death followed me like a bad coin.

I pulled out the penny I'd pocketed at the crime scene, the small weight cool in my hand. I should have turned it over to Detective Woodson for the evidence locker, but the impulse to keep it had been too strong. Why I felt the need to collect a dead man's penny was a matter better left to psychotherapy, and that was something I ditched the day after my eighteenth birthday.

I'd been collecting things for years, starting with the button from my dead sister's jacket. I was fifteen the year my twin sister Claire was killed in a hit-and-run. While everyone else laid roses over her open casket, I twisted off the metal fleur-de-lis button, severing the loose string with my fingernail and hiding it in the folds of my dress.

Later, I told my shrink it was because I needed to hold on to a small piece of Claire's, a tangible connection to the sister I lost. The truth was, I didn't have a choice. The urge to take it was a compulsion, its metal like a beacon to me in that dimly lit funeral parlor. When I got home after the service, I hid it in my diary, hollowing out the book with a razor blade and spray gluing the pages until they formed a paper casket for my stolen button.

When you kept a token from your dead sister, you could convince yourself it was about connection. When you found yourself pilfering coins from a random murder victim, you were treading on serial killer territory.

I dropped the penny back into my pocket and headed for the kitchen. When I'd rented this place, a kitchen had been low on the priority list. As always with real estate, location was king. Of course, most people probably wouldn't understand the locational appeal of a row of run-down warehouses in West Bottoms, Kansas City, but for me, it was love at first sight. The retail space, complete with upstairs living quarters, may not have been a prime location for most business owners, but for a costume shop, it was ideally situated.

I'd scrimped and saved for five years, taking business classes at night and working dead-end retail jobs during the day to make my shop possible. A program that offered funding for young, creative entrepreneurs willing to move to Kansas and a misdelivered magazine that featured Kansas City were enough to set me in motion. The rest of my family didn't understand my need for distance, but I took the opportunity anyway. I'd rented this place sight unseen and moved a few weeks later.

The first time Emma visited, she had taken one look at the apartment's cramped galley kitchen with its peeling Formica counters and upper cabinets that looked like something the previous owner used for dart practice and declared it a room with potential. Over the summer, we'd removed all the wobbly cabinet doors. We patched and painted the cabinets a semi-gloss off-white and lined them with four rolls of contact paper patterned with faded yellow lemons that we found in a neighborhood thrift shop. When we finished, the kitchen was functional and cheery, a picture of normalcy.

Tonight, it would take a lot more than retro lemons to cheer me up. I pulled a chair over, so I could reach the cabinet above the refrigerator. I felt around behind the assortment of wine bottles with pretty labels to pull down my rainy-day bottle of tequila, not bothering to reach for salt or a lime. Tipping the bottle, I took a long swig before heading for the bedroom, bottle still clutched in my hand.

I rummaged through my nightstand for my prescription bottle of sleeping pills and washed a pill down with another sip. One swig too many later, and I was as convinced that Jack

Gates had nothing to do with me as I was that I'd never touch tequila again.

Despite the sleeping pill, I tossed and turned for hours. When I finally fell asleep, I dreamt of Gates. In my dream, he was still alive when I tripped over him, a pair of shears stuck in his neck. A pack of wild dogs circled him, growling at me as I edged closer. They waited until he took his last breath and then fell upon his body. The dogs ripped the flesh from his stomach the way my childhood beagle went after rabbits. I watched Jack's face morph into Claire's. Her eyes snapped open, and she locked her gaze with mine. No matter how hard I tried, I couldn't look away, and I couldn't save her.

Despite my pounding head, I forced myself out of bed early. A quick shower later, I pulled on the first thing I grabbed from my closet—a breezy floral midi dress with raglan sleeves and deep pockets. Even hungover, I didn't do sweats.

When I checked my phone, I saw a missed call from Emma. She kept the message short, her voice strained as she said she wouldn't be coming into work today. I called her back to check on her, but my call went straight to voicemail. I hung up without leaving a message. Then I texted Riley to let her know I was fine and that I'd fill her in when she came in for her costume appointment this afternoon.

I headed downstairs to the shop early, determined to put Jack Gates where he belonged: a passing obituary in the local paper. I threw myself into work, hoping if I was busy enough, it would keep the images of the crime scene at bay.

To an outsider, the back of my shop probably looked like an overstuffed mess, which is why I'd hung a curtain in the archway between the rooms to keep customers' eyes from wandering back here. Today, the rows of industrial shelving, bins of fabric, embellishments, and rolls of wire in assorted gauges were familiar and comforting.

Across the back of my work room were wall-to-wall racks of costumes, including my custom designs. In the front of the shop, I displayed no more than two costumes of the same type, keeping any duplicates in the back, out of sight. Even the customers who wanted cheap costumes demanded the illusion of uniqueness.

Early on, I realized that to succeed in the costume business, I couldn't just do monster balls and cosplay. Instead, I had to cater to young families, and I needed a slice of the sixteen- to thirty-year-old market of young women with money to burn. And that demographic wanted costumes in every flavor of sex-it-up. Mass-produced French maid costumes were perennial favorites, along with sexy nurses, cops, cheerleaders, and cats. Pair a hard hat with a short skirt and cleavage, and even construction workers were hot enough for masquerade parties. Those mass-produced costumes kept the lights on.

My specialty, however, was handcrafted, blending new fabrics and accessories with upcycled thrift store finds. The custom costumes I sold outright tended to be simpler, more assembly-line favorites: things like pirates, witches, and princesses. I invested more of my time and talent on the interesting creations that came in on special order and the ones that made up my rental inventory. The latter I reserved for customers with discerning tastes and a healthy deposit.

I wasn't as much a seamstress as I was an assembler. As a child, my favorite part of the garage sales my grandmother took my sister Claire and me to was the free box—that box of odds and ends that the seller recognized as absolutely, unequivocally unsellable. I, however, had a soft spot for lost causes. While Claire would search for name-brand jeans, I'd make a beeline for that box, digging through the knickknacks and self-help books to find the mismatched socks, the fake Mardi Gras beads, and the hand-knitted scarves. Occasionally, I'd hit pay dirt and find a tattered cowboy hat, a plaid vest, or a patterned curtain.

My grandmother claimed everyone had a talent. She said Claire's was bringing harmony to those around her, and mine was seeing a second life for what others discarded. Clothing, accessories, bottle tops, you name it. That plaid vest became a fat headband, the silk sock its flower. My room had always looked like a cyclone had blown through with fabric wedging like confetti in the nondescript carpet. Buttons were my Legos, and according to my barefoot mother, both Legos and buttons were the work of the devil.

As a kid, I waited for the air to turn crisp and the smell of cinnamon and pumpkin spice to fill our house, markers that meant I could start constructing Halloween costumes. While my friends donned cheap superhero costumes each year, I transformed myself into Boudicca and Claire into Amelia Earhart. I remade Claire into Diana, goddess of the moon and the hunt, while I became the god Saturn, wearing a headless doll strung on a rope around my neck.

By middle school, thrift stores had become my hunting grounds, an opportunity to reinvent myself. Each week, I blew my entire allowance on bits of lace, secondhand prom dresses, and retro curtains. My first intervention was about my vintage clothing "problem." My mother threatened to clear out my bedroom with trash bags if I brought one more article of old clothing into it. So I hid polyester pants inside my pillowcase and learned how to nest costume jewelry inside socks, shirts inside shirts, and bits of broken but colorful glass inside the sturdy pockets of my blue jeans.

Color drew me like nectar. Floral prints, jewel tones, and turquoise earrings were all hard to resist. The gaudier, the better. I cocooned myself in blues and greens, brilliant yellow, and aggressive orange. I changed colors like the seasons.

After Claire was killed, the winter before we turned sixteen, I couldn't bear color. For a year after her death, I layered black upon black. I still altered, cut, and stitched, but I did it all in shades of mourning, each outfit a penance. Claire had been the shining star in our family. Popular and kind, she had seemed destined for a gilded life. And when she died, the world went dark.

Although Claire came back, first in my dreams and later as a ghost who begged me to right the wrong done to her, she was never the same. After her death, Claire was muted. She was less than she had been but still enough herself that she could pull me along wherever she led. But no matter how many times I looked for the man who took her life, I couldn't find him. Gradually, she faded away, until all I had left of her were memories.

After I stopped seeing her, it took months before I could stand the brightness of color on my own body. Even then, colors were different. Red satin pooled like blood; icy blue was the color of the winter that took her.

Today, I shoved aside my memories of Claire and reached for the dove-gray hooded cape I'd been working on, the color fitting my mood. I donned my favorite work apron as I gathered supplies. After a bit of searching, I'd found a faux fur coat at one of the West Bottoms thrift stores. I'd already cut it into strips. All that was left was to trim the cape. I reached in my pocket for the measuring tape I thought I'd grabbed earlier but came up with nothing but lint and Gates' penny. I didn't remember bringing it with me.

As if he knew I was thinking about him, Jack Gates appeared behind the dress form, startling me. I jumped and clutched my chest as I took a step away from him. I dropped his penny as if burned.

I kept my eyes trained on the cape, doing my best to avoid looking at Jack Gates, because I knew what he wanted. He was a stranger, and while I felt bad for him, the police could find whoever was responsible for his death. The last thing I needed was the ghost of a murder victim taking up residence in my life. Claire taught me that once I acknowledged a ghost, the visits would become frequent and the demands more insistent. I'd moved halfway across the country to build a life untouched by the dead, so I did my best to ignore him.

I reached inside the container for a pin, my hand only shaking slightly. Keeping my gaze fixed on the intersection of dark fur and misty gray fabric, I pinned the next stretch of hemline. I pricked my finger reaching for another pin. When I lifted my finger to my mouth, the bead of blood was another reminder of last night. Although I had skipped breakfast this morning, an empty stomach didn't stop the wave of nausea that hit me. I tried to ignore it, continuing to work until the cape was finished, and I had nothing else to distract me.

When I finally forced myself to look again, Jack Gates was there, waiting patiently beyond the dress form as if he had all the time in the world. He opened his mouth to speak but paused, reaching for his throat. From the way he ran his fingers over his neck, I knew he must still feel the wound tearing at the delicate skin of his throat. Although his neck appeared smooth and tanned without the gaping wound that had stolen his life, he didn't seem to know that. I couldn't look away, watching as he worked the muscles of his throat, then flexed his jaw and attempted speech. He was as silent as if his vocal cords were still severed.

Suffering like his was difficult to ignore. Without meaning to, I leaned in, opening my lips to speak first. By the time I found the words, however, Jack Gates was already gone.

CHAPTER 4

*a*side perk of costuming half of West Bottoms was that I didn't have to go chasing after information; it came to me, whether I wanted it or not. As I rotated through my regulars and a steady stream of Halloween shoppers, I learned that Jack Gates had been making the rounds of the haunted houses before his death, asking a lot of questions. I also learned that he wasn't exactly well-liked. On the coasts, people expected reporters to be pushy, but here in Kansas City, there was an ironclad expectation of Midwestern courtesy that Gates had apparently lacked. People resented that sort of thing.

By the time Riley showed up, I'd given up on talking about anything other than Jack Gates' murder. Riley worked at The Dungeon, a haunted house just down the street from Howl. Today, she was here for mummification. I hauled out the strips of cloth I'd ancientified last week with a combo of tea stains and good old-fashioned fire. Mummies might be typical haunted house fodder, but if I was going to dress one, I was going to do it up right.

Riley didn't waste any time on small talk. "I heard you were the one who tripped over the dead guy."

"Lucky me, huh?"

"You okay?" she asked, looking me over as if she was searching for injuries.

I waved her off. "As good as can be expected."

Riley jumped up on the dressing platform, wearing nothing more than a nude unitard. If any other customers walked in, they'd no doubt think she was naked, not that it would phase her. Just the same, I positioned myself between her and the door.

She turned expectantly toward me. "Tell me everything."

Riley had more energy than a toddler on pixie sticks, which made dressing her something of a challenge. Whereas everyone else got the short version, for Riley, I drew the story out, hoping it would keep her still long enough for me to wind yards of cloth around her fidgeting body. Throughout the story, Riley begged for each and every gory detail. By the time I'd finished the retelling, only her eyes were visible.

I stepped back, giving her the full mirror experience. "All you need is blood-red contacts, and you'll rock this mummy costume."

She held her arms stiffly in front of her and mmmmmed through the fabric, doing her best mummy impersonation. Satisfied, she attempted a little happy dance. Hampered as she was by the cloth wound haphazardly around her body, the best she could do was an awkward series of wiggles.

"All set. I hope you're walking." Riley didn't drive, but I hated to think of her trying to climb on a city bus dressed like a mummy.

She nodded, or at least I thought she nodded. It was hard to tell in her current wound-up state.

"So back to Jack Gates," Riley said, dropping the mummy act, her voice still muffled by fabric.

I should have known I wasn't going to get out of the conversation that easily. I dropped into one of the chairs next to the changing rooms. "What about him?"

"I did some snooping."

I groaned. "Riley!"

"What? It's not every day some guy gets offed in a haunted house."

I couldn't argue with that. "What did you find out?"

"Apparently, he showed up yesterday afternoon and was grilling the actors."

"He was a reporter," I reminded her. "And he was writing a review of the place. It makes sense he'd want to interview the actors."

"True, but these questions came after the review was already out. I heard he was trying to dig up dirt on Howl's owner."

I leaned in, taking the bait. "Who would that be?"

Riley did her best to shrug, but the yards of fabric wound around her restricted movement. "Some richie-rich business-man." Her voice lowered to a conspiratorial whisper. "He runs the place like a mob boss. No one crosses him."

I wasn't exactly sure how someone would cross a haunted house owner. I tried to imagine the entertainment version of trade secrets. Actors double-dipping with a competitor? Spilling special-effects secrets? Stealing props and selling them on the haunted house black market?

"Cross him?"

Riley just nodded.

"Do you know him?"

She looked away. "I keep my distance from authority

types. Nothing worse than some self-important jackass trying to tell you what to do." She attempted to bend over to pick up her clothes, but bound up as she was, she ended up knocking them off the chair and onto the floor.

"Hold up," I said.

I grabbed the jacket she'd ditched last night along with a big plastic bag and stuffed everything inside. I worked the bag up to her shoulder, and she held her arm up to keep it from sliding off again. Before I could ask any more questions, Riley shuffled to the door.

"Gotta scoot. You call me if you need anything," she said on her way out.

I couldn't stop myself from fishing for more information during the rest of my afternoon appointments. None of the actors knew any more about Jack Gates than I did. They shared even less about the mysterious owner of Howl.

I stayed in the shop later than usual, trying to distract myself. When I did go upstairs, the apartment was quiet. I went to bed early, but every time I closed my eyes, I pictured Jack Gates' face. Even though I told myself it was none of my business, I lay awake, wondering who would have had it out for him enough to cut his throat in a crowded haunted house. How many enemies could an entertainment reporter for *The Kansas City Star* make?

After a couple hours of tossing and turning, I reached for my ratty terrycloth robe, the one concession in an otherwise fabulous wardrobe, and reluctantly climbed out of bed. At this rate, I wasn't going to get any sleep. I decided I might as well make good use of the time. What harm was there in satisfying my curiosity? I brewed a fresh pot of coffee and waited for my computer to boot up.

A quick search for "Jack Gates" revealed multiple pages of hits, which wasn't all that surprising, since he was a reporter. The first page was dominated by his death. Although KCMO was no stranger to murders, this one was splashy enough to garner a lot of local media attention. I waded through a few articles and video clips. The clips were variations of the same theme. A perfectly manicured woman, usually blonde, held a microphone in front of the hazy entrance to Howl and narrated the few details they knew, all while a professional-looking headshot of Gates was inset on the screen. The haunted house, the reporter would announce, had "no comment," and the investigation, according to police, was "ongoing." Standard murder fare, followed, of course, by a lineup of eager customers clamoring for ten seconds of fame. Sometimes, people were gross.

Rather than get bogged down in his death, I turned my attention to Jack's life. Whether I wanted to admit it or not, I was looking for potential motives for his murder. I found the published review of Howl easily enough. "Kansas City is known for two things: Barbecue and haunted houses," it read. He wasn't wrong. The review was what you'd expect of a profile of a haunted house. It was descriptive enough to pull in some new visitors and nostalgic enough to lure old ones back for a yearly reunion.

If I were the owner of Howl, I'd be pleased at the free advertising the piece provided. I scanned for an owner's name, but it wasn't listed anywhere in the article. The only names I could find were the names of customers providing feel-good quotes. Apparently, Howl was "world-class enter-tainment" and "the best show in town."

There was a photo of a forty-something-year-old man

with a receding hairline who was standing next to the entrance, looking up in mock horror at a looming werewolf on stilts. Next to the photo was a quote labeling him as a regular. Leon Matthews proclaimed Howl as "the only adrenaline rush in town that won't land you in prison."

I snorted coffee out my nose. *Not anymore.*

I looked through the headlines on the next couple pages, focusing on those authored by Gates. Most were fluff pieces: restaurant openings, wedding venues, the local music scene. Nothing remotely worth killing over.

Despite the second cup of Joe, my eyes were burning. It was going to take more than a thirty-minute Google search to give me a lead, not that I was looking for one. A case this sensational would hopefully find a quick resolution, one that didn't require anything more of me than the police statement I'd already given. I headed to bed, exhausted enough that I might actually be able to fall asleep and leave the sleuthing for the police.

The next time I saw Jack Gates, I was elbow deep in cantaloupe. Given the sad state of my nearly empty refrigerator, I'd made a run to the closest grocery store. I had one objective: to load up on fruits and vegetables that would slowly rot in my crisper drawer before I threw them out, then repeat the whole cycle again in a few weeks. While I'd never been the homemaker type, there was something about a crisis that sent me to the produce aisle.

As I diligently tap, tap, tapped the bottoms of the cantaloupe with my pilfered penny and lifted them one by one to my nose to sniff out the ripest fruit, I glanced up to see a familiar face hovering in the aisle. Startled, I dropped the cantaloupe but managed to hold on to the coin. Before I could catch it, the cantaloupe hit the polished cement floor, splitting the rind and exposing the light orange flesh inside, the stringy, slick seeds landing on my shoe.

The woman next to me looked at the fruit splattered across the floor and pursed her lips in disapproval. A little boy leaned out of the school bus cart his mother was pushing him in and laughed, his small hand reaching for the splattered fruit as he passed. I ignored them both, keeping Jack Gates in my sights. For his part, Gates' gaze never wavered, locked as it was on my own.

I knew that if I spoke to him, if I gestured for Gates to leave, the woman still glaring at the mess would give me that look of pity people reserved for the crazy and the homeless before walking away. The boy, still trailing his hand out the side window of his little school bus wouldn't so much as brush Gates' pant leg as he went by him. By now, I'd had plenty of practice learning why I should keep ghost sightings to myself.

Although my body was primed for escape, I stayed where I was, ignoring the fruit carcass squishing under my feet. I studied Jack Gates as intently as he watched me. I concentrated on my breathing, trying to maintain calm, and on the coin, pressing into my palm. I traced the familiar outline of Abraham Lincoln's face, the surface warming beneath my thumb. With the stand of fruit between us, I watched Gates as people milled around us.

The last year, devoid of dead people trailing after me, had lulled me into a false sense of security. I had thought, optimistically, that moving from Chicago to Kansas City had given me the possibility of a normal life. As I looked at Gates, I knew that some things were inevitable, and that death would always follow me.

For a second, I considered bending over and picking up the sticky fruit from the floor, smiling sheepishly at the other shoppers. I imagined turning my back on Gates and pretending I was like everyone else, that I didn't see him there in the grocery aisle. I thought about burying the coin inside the busted cantaloupe, shoving the metal so deep into the flesh that I wouldn't be able to find it again. I could walk away from this, from him.

But in the end, I did none of those things. I'd learned years ago that no matter how much I pretended not to see them, if they appeared more than once, they were likely going to stick around. Once the bond had been forged, most ghosts would stay tethered to me like a ball on a chain until I solved whatever kept them tied to this world.

Ms. Granger, the elderly neighbor who fell down a flight of stairs leaving her apartment when I was in tenth grade haunted me until I harassed the maintenance guy into fixing the loose board that had caused her fall. Others I acknowledged had wanted simple things: a retraction of words hurled in anger, a new job for a struggling mother, the completion of a half-done crossword puzzle. Given that I'd stumbled on Jack Gates' body nestled in a pool of his own blood, it didn't take a rocket scientist to figure out what he wanted. Justice was the long game.

Until now, the only ghost who had turned to me for justice was my sister Claire. In the weeks after her death, she'd show up in the bedroom we'd shared since we were kids or in the kitchen where we had bickered over the last bowl of cereal.

She didn't speak at first, either, just pleaded with those brown eyes that I knew better than my own. At first, I thought she stuck around because I hadn't been ready to let her go. When she finally spoke, though, it was to ask for the one thing that only I could get for her: justice.

Everyone else was content to believe her death a tragic accident, the product of a drunk driver. But I knew better. Over and over, Claire relived with me the moments before her death and the details about the man who had been driving. She told me how he waited until she was in the cross-walk to accelerate, how he swerved to make certain he hit her. She described the way he had smiled right before the grill of his SUV struck her body.

No matter who I told or how much I begged them to search for her killer, no one listened. I failed her, and eventu-ally, I lost her all over again.

Now here I was, looking at another pair of pleading brown eyes. Ignoring the man who bent down to clean up the cantaloupe, I watched Jack instead. Since we were going to be fast friends whether I liked it or not, I might as well drop the formalities and consider us on a first-name basis.

Although Jack still couldn't speak, I could read his lips: "Help me." He formed the words twice, and then waited, watching to see what I'd do.

I thought about all the reasons I should walk away: the fresh start I'd chased halfway across the country and the fact that I was the last person he should turn to for justice. But when I closed my eyes, it wasn't Jack's face I saw. Before I could second-guess myself, I answered him.

"I'll help you."

Jack stayed for another second before he nodded and disappeared.

The man still cleaning up the fruit looked at me, assuming I had been talking to him. Sighing, I dropped the penny back into my pocket and bent down to help him. Once the fruit was picked up, I left the store empty-handed. No amount of produce was going to help me navigate this crisis.

I wanted to believe this time would be different. No one doubted Jack was murdered. It was a high-profile case, and the police would probably announce an arrest soon. Worst case, I'd babysit a ghost for a few days while they wrapped up the investigation, and then I'd get back to my life.

I climbed in the driver's side of my 1979 Volkswagen Beetle convertible, a surprise gift from my grandmother's will. Although she had paid a mechanic for a rebuilt engine and a new lemon-yellow paint job, the car was as finicky as she had been, so I always held my breath when I started it.

My cell phone rang before I left the parking lot, the theme song from *The Wizard of Oz* announcing Emma's call. "Hey Em."

"Kali." Her voice sounded weird, tired and wary. "I should have checked on you last night. I'm sorry."

I didn't doubt her sincerity. Emma was a dyed-in-the-wool Midwesterner, the kind of Kansas nice that had become a Hollywood trope, except on Emma, it always felt believable. When I first met Emma, she had walked into my shop asking if I could transform her into a medieval fairy princess for the Renaissance Festival. With her golden hair, like wheat ripening in the field, and her bright blue eyes, all that was left for me to do was dress her in silk and gauze.

"It's okay. I'm okay," I assured her. "Are you all right?" I asked, even though I knew she wasn't.

Death rarely touched women like Emma. When death did come calling, it was a heroic boyfriend draped in the American flag or a great-grandmother who lay wrapped in talc and rose water, resting after a long and gentle life. It came as a condolence card, a version of sacrifice, or the natural order. It certainly wasn't like the death that kept finding me. I couldn't help but think that if it weren't for me, maybe she would have been untouched by this death, too.

Emma was quiet, as if she was searching for just the right words. She cleared her throat. "Do you want me to come over tonight?"

I didn't expect it. As soon as we found Jack's body, I recognized the shift, the inevitable pulling away point in our relationship. Ghosts were great for campfires and slumber parties, but when dead people started turning up in your life, it was only a matter of time before your friends ran the other direction.

It had happened with the theater kids I'd hung out with before my sister's death and with the hellraisers I befriended after. And it repeated with the business students I gravitated toward in college. Bonding over the hot guy in Business Math got you invited out for drinks. Mentioning the dead marketing professor who hung out by the vending machines was met with uncomfortable silence.

The only friendships that lasted were the ones I kept light-hearted, centered around girls' nights and pedicures, oblivious to the stench of death that clung to me like a rancid perfume. I didn't have a lot of practice with postmortem friendships, and it took me a second to respond.

"Are you sure?" I hated how my voice sounded, desperate and vulnerable, so I kept talking. "I mean, yeah. What time?"

"6:30," she said. "Order some pizza, double-cheese. I'll pick the movie."

"Deal."

I hung up, battling the stupid lump in my throat. I'd figure out how I was going to deal with Jack Gates later; for now, my priority was getting myself together enough to leave the grocery store parking lot. It had been a long time since I'd cried, and I wasn't ready to open the floodgates yet.

CHAPTER 5

*T*he quiet moments were the hardest. It was when the foot traffic died down, when I had nothing else to focus on, that the weight of what I'd promised Jack bore down on me. I coped the only way I knew how: by throwing myself into my work.

The back of my shop was set up for costume construction. After collecting what I needed, I got busy on one of the special-order costumes I was working on. My current project was a Queen of Hearts costume. By the time Bennie sauntered in, I'd sewn and ripped out the same seam three times. Clearly, post crime scene sewing wasn't my strong suit. I was happy for the distraction.

Bennie and I normally had a standing appointment on nights Howl was open. While he was perfectly capable of applying his own makeup, he preferred to have me do it. I welcomed both the steady income and the easy camaraderie we'd developed. He missed yesterday's appointment, but given the circumstances, I wasn't holding it against him. However,

Howl was still closed, with police tape stretched across the entrances, so I knew Bennie wasn't here for makeup.

Bennie wasn't in costume. Instead, he was wearing normal clothes: dark jeans and a forest-green shirt. He paused in front of me, putting his hands on my shoulders as if to brace me.

"How are you?" He didn't give me a chance to answer. "You look tired. Have you been sleeping?"

"Not really," I admitted.

Bennie guided me to a nearby chair. When I protested, he held a finger to his lips. "Why did you open the shop? You should've taken some time off."

"What would I do instead? Stay in bed?" I asked. "The show must go on, right?"

No way I was going to stay holed up in my apartment with only the ghost of a murder victim to keep me company, not that I could tell Bennie that. He frowned.

"Besides," I countered. "Did you take yesterday off?"

Howl was a side gig for Bennie, like it was for most of the actors. The rest of the time, he worked as a dispatcher for the police department.

"I wasn't the one who found him," he said.

I didn't know what to say to that, so I let it hang in the air between us. "Do you want a cup of coffee?"

"Sure."

I brewed the dark roast Bennie preferred in the coffee pot I kept in the back of the shop, handing him the cup and grabbing a second for me. We sat down in the cushioned chairs next to the dressing room, sipping our drinks.

I broke the silence first. "What do you know about the mysterious owner of Howl?"

It took him a while to answer. "Other than his name?"

Bennie avoided eye contact. "Not much. Craig runs everything at Howl."

"Which is?"

"Which is what?"

I tried to keep my frustration out of my voice. "His name?"

"Why are you asking?" His voice was wary.

"Just curious. Is it a secret?"

He leaned back in his chair but didn't answer me.

I tried again. "You've never met the man?"

"I didn't say that." He set his half-empty cup on the small table between us. Two things were clear. One, Bennie knew his name, and two, for whatever reason, he wasn't about to share it with me.

That didn't stop me from trying. "How well do you know him?"

"Well enough to know he's not involved, if that's what you're asking," Bennie said. "Why are you digging?"

"You saw Jack Gates, Bennie. His throat was cut."

"Yes, and that's a tragedy. But it's a tragedy for the police to solve."

I sighed. "I know that."

"Have you talked to Emma?" Bennie asked.

"Yeah. She's coming over later, so we can bond over pizza and our shared trauma." I tried to make light of it, but Bennie wasn't fooled.

"Listen, it's normal to be upset, Kali. What you saw, that would traumatize anyone."

"You seem okay."

He grabbed my hand. "I spend forty hours a week navigating this shit. After a while, you either develop some armor or a drinking problem."

I squeezed his hand and smiled. "I'll be okay."

"I know you will."

Bennie changed the subject before I could. "Emma mentioned that you were acting weird before you found Gates."

"What do you mean?"

"She said you kept seeing someone, and you seemed scared of whoever it was. Why didn't you tell me?"

"I didn't want to worry you." That was mostly true. Of course, I couldn't get a close enough look at my stalker to be sure he wasn't already dead. Dead men, while annoying, didn't seem to be particularly dangerous to anything except my sanity. "Besides, I'm probably overreacting. He's just a guy who keeps showing up."

Bennie leaned forward, his eyes sharp with interest. "What did he look like?"

I hesitated, not sure how to describe the man.

Bennie snapped his fingers and motioned for me to pony up a description. "You know, I might be able to help. I do have connections." As a dispatcher, those connections might come in handy, if my stalker turned out to be alive. Otherwise, I was on my own.

I started with the obvious. "Male, around six feet tall, white."

"Well, that narrows it down."

"No. I mean really white. Almost albino white. And gaunt, like his cheekbones could cut the air, gaunt."

Bennie had grown still, all trace of sarcasm gone. "Go on."

"He wore a black hat, like a fedora, and a suit that hung off him. His hair, what I could see of it, was white."

"He was old?" Bennie asked.

"No," I said. "Not that kind of white."

"How did he move?"

It was an odd question, but I answered him. "Unnaturally."

He didn't ask what I meant. "Stay away from him, Kali."

"You know him?" I asked, trying to keep the relief that the man was a living, breathing stalker out of my voice.

Wrangling one ghost was one too many. I was glad I didn't have to add another to the fray. My relief was short-lived though. If he wasn't a ghost, then he hadn't been there for me. Maybe he had come for Jack.

"He's not the kind of man you want to know," Bennie said, making me even more uneasy.

"Who is he?"

For a second, I thought Bennie was going to tell me. Instead, he said, "I don't know. I've just seen him hanging around the haunted houses."

We both knew he was lying.

"Promise me you'll call me if you see him again."

"Yeah, sure," I said.

Bennie leaned in for our usual quick hug. "I mean it. And I'll check on you next week."

Emma showed up at the shop just as Bennie was leaving. I flipped the closed sign around. She stood in the doorway, one foot inside and the other paused on the threshold, as if she couldn't quite decide on whether to come in or not. I pretended to wipe away a smudge on the window, giving her ample time to change her mind and retreat.

Bennie didn't give her the same opportunity. He pulled her into the room, hugging her as if they were old friends, murmuring soothing words like he was comforting a frightened child.

"I'm fine," she told him, her voice soft but steady.

I was glad he was here, a buffer against the awkwardness

of it all. He didn't stay long, however, and soon enough, it was just the two of us in an empty shop.

"I'm almost done. Just have to close out the till. I'll be up in a minute. Pizza should be here in ten," I said, buying myself a few more minutes. "I left cash on the table."

She nodded, her shoulders relaxing as she headed outside to the stairwell that led up to my apartment. I took my time counting the money and putting it in the safe. When I was finished, I thought about sweeping or arranging the pins by color, but there were some things procrastination couldn't fix.

"Hey," I said as I walked into the apartment.

Emma had already kicked her shoes off by the door, hung her coat on the back of a chair, and taken up residence on the couch. Pizza boxes were stacked, unopened, on the coffee table in front of her. I'd ordered enough pizza that we'd have leftovers for a week. Emma had one foot tucked under her and was tapping my behemoth all-in-one remote against the palm of her hand. She looked up as I walked in.

"The remote isn't working. Batteries?" And just like that, we were back on familiar ground.

"Let me check," I said, rifling through kitchen drawers. "Damn."

Emma laughed. "No worries. We'll just do this old school." She walked across the living room to push the TV's on button.

"What movie did you pick?"

She waved a tattered VHS case. *Hocus Pocus*.

I was likely the only VHS owner in a hundred-mile radius, but that had its perks. What I couldn't get for free, I could pick up for pennies from secondhand store movie bins. I'd built an impressive collection of 80s movies that way. On the downside, there was always the risk of a twisted tape wrecking the end of a movie.

When I first moved in, I thought about trading my clunky VHS player for a streaming device, but I couldn't bring myself to ditch the box of old movies Claire and I had watched growing up. The tapes had been my mother's, squirreled away in the attic where they gathered dust alongside broken furniture and my grandmother's antique steamer trunk. Claire and I had smuggled the movies out of the attic, stuffing them in the waistbands of our pants and tucking them under our shirts like contraband. We spent whole weekends on movie marathons, rolling our eyes at the cheesy dialogue in *Sixteen Candles* and mocking the special effects in *Nightmare on Elm Street*.

My mother would shake her head and frown at us, and as soon as she left the room, Claire and I would burst out laughing. Back then, I could laugh so hard my stomach hurt and tears ran down my cheeks. I'd kept the movies, got a can of compressed air, and did my best to blow out twenty years of dust from the VHS player I had shared with my sister since elementary school.

"Good choice," I said, grateful for a light-hearted, campy Halloween tale. We made it through a third of the movie and a box and a half of pizza before we talked about anything other than how fabulous Sarah Jessica Parker was back in the day.

I broke first. "How are you holding up?"

Emma shifted toward me, her face pinched. "I don't know," she admitted. "I just keep thinking about that poor man." She got up and paused the movie. "Do you know who he was?"

"Jack Gates. All I know is he was a reporter for *The Kansas City Star*." I shut off the movie. *Hocus Pocus* would have to wait for another night.

Emma was quiet for a minute. When she did speak, her voice was sad. "I'm sorry I left you there alone." She turned, shifting closer to me. "I guess I freaked out. After I talked to the cops, I just wanted to get out of there."

I pulled her in for a hug. "It's okay, Em. I'm glad Bennie took you home."

"Bennie was great. He stayed with me the whole time. I think I would've fallen apart without him."

It didn't surprise me that he was as good at his day job as he was at his side gig. As a dispatcher, Bennie was used to dealing with trauma. I was glad he had been the one with Emma. I somehow doubted Craig's presence would have been quite as comforting.

Emma pulled back and wiped away the tear sliding down her cheek. She shook her head as if to will the sadness away. "Do you know that even that crazy redhead who took our tickets was nice to me?" She laughed. "She bought me a Coke."

"Ruby?" I tried to picture her non-aggressive.

"I know, right? I think it really got to her too," Emma said. "She was pretty shook up, which must have been out of character for her, because Bennie seemed surprised."

"Really?"

"Oh yeah." Emma reached for a tissue to blow her nose. "Her hands were shaking when she was on the phone with her boss."

"Her boss?" I asked, confused. "I thought Craig was her boss."

"No. I don't think so. Ruby called whoever she was talking to on the phone boss."

"What did she say?"

"Well, she told the person they had a situation, that a man had been killed in the haunted house. Other than that, she did more listening than talking."

"Did she say a name?"

"Gates, you mean?"

"No, no. I mean, did she call her boss by name?"

"All I heard her say was 'boss.'"

Emma and I spent the next hour trading notes about the aftermath. Even after hugging her goodbye, I kept thinking about the anonymous owner of Howl.

I replayed the conversations with Bennie and Emma most of the night, and I kept coming back to two things: Bennie's reaction to my mention of the guy lurking around and the secrecy with which everyone seemed to guard the name of Howl's owner. Jack hadn't made another appearance, so I couldn't grill him about either. But I couldn't shake the feeling that those details were important.

I waited until morning to call the police. The number on the card Woodson had left me turned out to be the general non-emergency police number rather than his direct line. "May I speak with Detective Woodson, please?"

It took several seconds before the call was transferred, and he picked up the line. "Detective Woodson here."

"Hi. This is Kali James. We met Thursday night at Howl. I was the woman who discovered the dead body." I introduced myself as if Woodson might not recognize my name, despite my starring appearance in a homicide investigation.

"Of course, Ms. James. I remember you. How can I help you?" he asked.

"I was just curious if you had made any progress on the case." I doubted he'd tell me anything, but I took a shot, anyway.

"It's early yet, Ms. James." Woodson sighed. "We gathered a

lot of evidence, but it takes a long time for the crime lab to analyze everything."

"And interviews?" I asked, well aware that the response would be the standard, police issue "we have no information at this time" line.

Woodson didn't disappoint. "We are continuing to interview customers and employees to gather evidence and identify suspects. Is there anything else, anything that you thought of, that might be helpful to us?"

"That's why I'm calling. It might be nothing." I stumbled, even though I'd rehearsed how to say this without sounding crazy. "It's just that I did see something odd that night. I didn't think it was connected at the time, but now I'm not so sure."

"What did you see, Ms. James?"

"I saw a man outside the haunted house. He seemed to be loitering around, out of place." I didn't mention that I'd first seen him outside my apartment or that he appeared to be following me. "He seemed," I paused, "off."

"What do you mean?"

"I'm not sure how to explain it. He didn't seem to be there for the haunted house. It's like he was watching and waiting." That much was true, even if I did leave out the bit about him watching and waiting for me.

"For what?" Woodson asked.

"I'm not sure," I hedged.

"All right. I'll make a note of it. Thank you for calling."

"Wait! I also saw him inside the haunted house."

"Okay." Woodson was displaying the kind of patience people offered children when they were humoring them.

"Look, I really think you should look into this guy."

Woodson cleared his throat. "We questioned everyone at the scene, so if he was there, we should have his information."

"Yes, but..."

"If you think of anything else, Ms. James, please give me a call." He hung up before I could argue.

Let the police do their job. They were the ones with the resources and connections to solve this murder. They knew what they were doing. But I battled back the sense of déjà vu.

Stay in your lane, K. It was my brother Drew's voice I heard in my head, the refrain one I heard often in the months after Claire was killed. Everyone except me, my father included, was content to accept her death as the unfortunate accident it had been ruled, a classic drunk driver hit-and-run. While the police had investigated, they had more high-profile murder cases competing for attention. A hit-and-run didn't warrant the kind of resources or time it took to find the driver. But I couldn't let it go.

In the aftermath of losing Claire, we'd all channeled grief in our own way. My mother fractured, day by day. Three months after we put Claire in the ground, I came home from school to the somber faces of my dad and brother standing in the empty spot where my mother's car should have been. By then, it hadn't been much of a surprise.

Since learning about magnets in fourth grade, I understood what my mother and I were. As a child, I drew her to me, the pull undeniable. And as I grew up, the poles flipped, and no matter how much I reached for her, we couldn't touch any more. After Claire died, the gulf between us grew, the chasm so wide, it swallowed her whole.

Dad, for the most part, lost himself in other people's tragedies. As a homicide detective, he'd always been dedicated to his work, but after losing Claire, it seemed to be the only fuel he had. Our dining room table changed from a gathering place for holiday dinners to a surface to spread out crime scene photos.

My brother Drew turned his bedroom into a weight room, spending hours pushing his body to the edge of its endurance. Although only a year and a half separated us, the gangly seventeen-year-old who used to tease me about my crushes became a younger, harder version of my dad. One more person to warn me to leave the investigation to the actual police.

I hadn't listened then. But I hadn't found the man who killed her, either. This time, I reminded myself, I wasn't searching for the person who left my sister broken and dying on the pavement. Jack Gates was a complete stranger. Maybe this time, I should heed the voice rattling around in my head. I could still walk away, leaving the investigation to the people who got paid to do it.

I had a long day of sewing ahead of me, and keeping the lights on was higher on my list of priorities than hunting down some creep who may or may not have killed Jack Gates. I bypassed my open laptop, resisting the temptation to spend the next hour digging into Gates' past and headed for the bathroom.

I opened the shower doors and turned the water on hotter than usual, hoping the heat and steam would unknot the tension I'd been carrying around. I shrugged out of my pajamas, Gates' penny falling out of my pocket. Despite my best intentions, I kept carrying it around. I dropped it on the counter along with my jewelry and stepped into the steamy shower.

I stood under the almost scalding water for several minutes before reaching for my pricey splurge shampoo, breathing in the scent of sweet orange and vanilla. By the time

I finished, the water had turned cold. I opened the shower door and reached for a towel, feeling more relaxed than I had since stumbling into a crime scene.

It didn't last long. There, in front of my vanity, stood Jack Gates. I screamed and clutched the towel to my body. Jack jumped, his eyes going wide before he disappeared.

One thing was clear: Jack Gates had no intention of parking himself anywhere other than in smack dab in the middle of my lane.

*N*o matter how many times I told myself to walk away, I couldn't stop replaying the look on Jack's face when I said I'd help him. After checking the news on the slim chance that an arrest had already been made, I took matters into my own hands. I messaged Emma to let her know that I wouldn't be in until this afternoon. I was going back to ground zero.

None of the haunted houses, Howl included, operated during the week, but I hoped that the bare bones office staff worked weekdays. With any luck, I could catch Craig there. Despite Emma's tale of bonding with Ruby, I doubted Ruby would be forthcoming. Even with his hardcore exterior, the odds of getting Craig talking seemed infinitely better. I considered calling Howl first to make sure he was there, but I was banking on the element of surprise to help loosen his guard. I was willing to risk a wasted trip.

First, I had to dress for success. I rifled through my closet and settled on a pair of curve-hugging indigo pants, a scoop-necked, ribbed black sweater, and red kitten heels. I rarely pulled out the heels, but this little reconnaissance mission required a certain balance of everyday casual and power pumps. I pulled my hair into a no-nonsense ponytail, balancing it out with soft pink lip gloss and a double coat of mascara. I was as ready to take on the intimidating head of security as I'd ever be.

It didn't take long before I was rethinking the heels. I could've made short work of the two blocks in running shoes, but I was already committed, so I soldiered on.

In the daylight, Howl looked like what it had been for decades before the spooks moved in: an old run-down warehouse among a row of old warehouses. Everything looked remarkably normal despite the recent murder.

I tested the heavy metal door handle, and when it wouldn't budge, I pounded on the front door. "Hello!" When there was no answer, I put my weight behind my next blows. I was mid-fist when the door swung open.

Ruby stood in the doorway, her expression anything but welcoming. "We're closed." She started to swing the door shut again, but I wedged a foot in the opening.

"I'm here to see Craig."

She paused, inches from smashing my foot. "Is he expecting you?"

"Not exactly."

Ruby leaned close enough to me that I could smell her peppermint gum and kicked my foot out of the door. "Then we are closed."

Before she could slam it shut, Craig's voice interrupted.

"It's okay, Ruby. Let her in."

I didn't know if he had already been hovering near the door, or if he just had really good hearing. Either way, I sidled past Ruby before she could respond.

Craig must have had a wardrobe full of black t-shirts and broken-in blue jeans because he was dressed similarly to what he wore the night Gates was killed. In the light of day, without the distraction of a murder victim between us, I could take in the view. Craig was tall, six-two at least, but it wasn't his height that I appreciated. Crossed over his chest, those arms of his warranted attention. Some women got hung up on washboard abs or boy-band hair. Me? I was all about a good set of biceps, and his strained the tight sleeves of his t-shirt in all the right ways. Not that the rest of him was half bad either. He even made bald look hot.

By the time I finished my visual inventory, Craig had one eyebrow raised. "How can I help you?" He sounded amused.

It would take a lot more than getting caught appreciating the male anatomy to embarrass me. But I reminded myself that I was here to gather intelligence, not enjoy the scenery. "Is that offer to talk still open?"

Craig's stance relaxed. "Of course. Let's go back to my office."

I followed him through the main room. The last time I was here, I'd been too focused on the climb up the beautiful old staircase into the haunted house to note much else. I'd missed the black curtain at the back of the room. Craig held it for me, and I stepped into a hallway. I moved aside, letting him take the lead. We passed a door on the left before he entered a room on the right side of the hall.

It was a small room with a large, no-nonsense oak desk that dwarfed the space. Two mismatched chairs were pulled up to it. Craig pointed to an upholstered chair that looked like it escaped from the '80s. I sat down. Instead of moving to the business side of the desk, he seated himself in the chair next to mine, his long legs crowding me.

I spoke first, trying to break the ice. "Do you know when you'll be able to open back up?"

"No. Hopefully, we'll get the all-clear any day now." He waited expectantly for me to switch from idle small talk to what brought me here.

"Have the police told you if they have any suspects?" I watched his facial expression close down. "Besides me, I mean." I shifted in my seat.

"I doubt they think you are a suspect," he said, eyeing my fire-engine red kitten heels and smiling. I tried not to bristle. Just because a woman put on a nice pair of shoes didn't mean she was harmless. Maybe I didn't look like a walking menace like he did, but I hated being dismissed.

My face must have telegraphed my feelings because Craig cranked down his smile. He didn't backpedal, though. "It takes a lot of strength to overpower someone and cut his throat." His gaze swept down my body, a hint of a smile returning. "Besides, Gates was tall. Unless you were standing on a step stool, I'm not sure how you would have managed it."

He had me there. "True," I conceded. *But you could.* My instincts told me he hadn't, though. I went with my gut for now, hoping my attraction and instinct wires hadn't gotten crossed. "Have you heard if the police have any leads?"

"No. I haven't. Without a murder weapon, I'm sure the investigation will take a while."

I frowned. "I don't understand. I saw them bag those knives and shears that were next to the body."

He nodded. "They did. But the initial forensics showed that the blood on them was fake. They were just props from the room. Whoever killed Gates must have dumped them there as a decoy."

Shit. There went my hopes of a quick arrest. Whoever

killed Jack had the sense to cover their tracks. High profile or not, the longer it took to identify his killer, the higher the chances that this case would go unsolved.

Craig must have noticed my distress because he tried to reassure me. "Hey, they're going to catch this guy."

"I hope so," I said.

I wished I had the same faith he did in the system, but I knew firsthand how much fell through the cracks. But then, that's why I was here. Right now, I had two leads—a stalker and a secretive haunted house owner—both of which I doubted the police were following.

I started with the most likely suspect. "I wanted to ask you about someone I saw that night. It's probably nothing, but the guy freaked me out."

"Was this guy harassing you?"

"No, not really. At the time, I thought he might be following me."

Craig sat up straighter. "Where did you see him?"

"I saw him outside while I was in line. He kept staring at me, but then he disappeared. Then I saw him again in the swamp room."

Craig relaxed. "You're a beautiful woman. I'm sure he wasn't the only one in line staring."

I felt the little thrill that came from a well-placed compliment. As much as I wanted to follow up on that compliment, I corrected him. "I might believe that if I hadn't seen him a week before Jack was killed. He was hanging outside my apartment one night, staring up at my window."

Craig dropped all pretense of flirting. "Did you tell the police about this guy?"

"I tried, but they didn't seem interested." Of course, I'd left out the bit about the guy showing up at my apartment.

"What did he look like?" Craig asked.

When I described the man, I saw the recognition on Craig's face.

"Does he work here?"

"No," he said quickly. "But I've seen him hanging around the area. He's the kind of guy you want to stay away from."

"What if he's the killer?"

Craig shook his head. "I doubt that. The guy you're talking about might be dangerous, but no way he leaves a bloody mess like that."

"What does that mean?"

Craig shifted uncomfortably, as if he'd given something away he hadn't intended to. "Just that the guy you're talking about stands out. People would have noticed if he'd come out of Howl covered in blood."

"Do you know who he is?"

Craig didn't answer right away. "I know where to find him. He won't bother you again."

I ground my teeth in frustration. What I wanted was a name, not a protection detail. But if we were going down the damsel in distress route, I might as well use it to my advantage. I crossed my hands in my lap and softened my expression into one that I hoped passed for vulnerable.

"I can't stop thinking about Jack Gates," I said, willing a slight tremble into my hands. I looked at my lap, mentally counted to five as if I was gathering my courage. "I'm afraid that whoever killed him will come after me." Seconds stretched out uncomfortably between us, but I refused to break first.

Eventually, Craig patted my hand, trying to comfort me. Even though I'd expected the gesture, I wasn't prepared for the zing of chemistry that passed between us.

"You're safe, Kali," he assured me, squeezing my hand. "The murderer is long gone. I'm sure it was personal; most murders are, and you have no connection to Jack Gates."

"But I found him." I widened my eyes and held them open without blinking, a trick I learned in middle school drama class. My eyes started to water, and I sniffed. "What if the killer thinks I saw something?"

"Did you?"

"Nothing," I insisted. "But people have been talking."

"Who?"

I didn't want to name Riley, so I kept it vague. "An actor from one of the other haunted houses came into the shop, and she said all the actors were talking about the murder, about Jack Gates. She said that people were also talking about the owner of this haunted house who no one seems to know much about. The rumor is that it's crime-connected, maybe gang or mafia even." I had no idea if Kansas City had a mafia, but it sounded appropriately threatening. I paused, as if catching myself. "Oh, I didn't mean..."

Craig released my hand, but his voice, when he spoke, was still comforting. "I can assure you that Max is in no way connected to the mafia. In fact, he's about as far away from a mob boss as you can get. And there is no way that he is connected to Jack Gates' murder."

I was careful to keep my eyes locked on my lap so that I wouldn't give away my excitement at his casual name drop. "Max?"

He paused before responding. "Max owns Howl."

I'd hoped for a last name, but the silence that followed made it clear that Craig wasn't going to be forthcoming with that particular detail. I tried another tack. "Well, how can you be sure Max didn't kill Jack Gates?"

"I've known Max a long time. Now, about you feeling afraid," he said, shifting the conversation back to more neutral ground. "Do you have someone who can come stay with you? A male friend or a boyfriend?"

After his earlier compliment, I didn't know if this was him flirting or simply asking. "Actually, I just got out of a relationship. I could ask Gavin, I guess, but I'd hate to send mixed messages."

Craig smiled. "Wouldn't want that. How about family then?"

"My family is all in Chicago." Not a chance in hell I was calling my brother or dad about this. "I'm sure I will be fine. I'll invest in some mace." I stood up, and he followed. "Thank you for reassuring me." I leaned in and gave him a quick hug. From the sudden tensing of his muscles, the hug was unexpected, but he recovered quickly enough, wrapping me in those arms of his. I let go first. "I don't want to keep you." Before he could object, I bent down to pick up my purse.

"Listen," he said, touching my arm. "If you need anything, anything at all, you give me a call. I live nearby and can be at your place in minutes." He reached for the yellow sticky pad on his desk and scrawled his name and phone number across it.

I slid the note into my pocket and gave him a full-wattage smile. "Thank you. Now, I better let you get back to work." I took a step toward to the door, but Craig stood up, effectively blocking my exit.

"Did you come here alone?" At my nod, he said, "Let me walk you home."

Given my I'm-scared-of-my-own-shadow routine, I couldn't easily turn him down. "Thank you. I'd appreciate that."

We walked out of the office into the entryway where Ruby was standing by the door.

"Leaving so soon?" Her voice was saccharine sweet.

When she spotted Craig's hand pressed lightly against the small of my back, she narrowed her eyes. I wondered if it was because she disliked me or if she had a thing for Craig.

Before we could get out the door, Craig's office phone rang. "I need to get this. I've been expecting a call. It'll only take a minute."

"No problem," I assured him.

Left alone with Ruby, who was still glaring at me, I decided to make the best of the opportunity.

"So, how well did you know Jack Gates?" I asked.

"What kind of question is that?" she snapped.

"Just making conversation."

"Well don't."

Thankfully Craig's call didn't take long, so I didn't have to spend much time alone with the piranha. He must have noticed the rising tension because he frowned at Ruby.

"I'm going to walk Kali home," Craig said. "If you need anything, I've got my cell." He ignored Ruby's sputtered protest and pushed open the heavy door.

As we stepped outside, we were greeted by a handful of people loitering in front of Howl. A young couple was posing in front of the building while another woman held up a phone to take their picture. It was like a gruesome tourist attraction, with everyone wanting their very own memento of a man's murder.

I shook my head. "That's messed up."

"People are drawn to death."

Didn't I know it? I shivered, looking over my shoulder as

we walked away, half afraid that I'd see Jack Gates standing among the rubberneckers.

We walked the two blocks to my apartment in relative silence, the only noise the clip-clop of my heels. By the end of the first block, my feet ached. How women wore stilettos, I had no idea. Although tempting, I resisted the urge to slip them off and walk barefoot.

Once we arrived at my shop, I headed to the front rather than upstairs to my apartment. Craig stopped behind me, close enough that he blocked the wind at my back. I fumbled with my key before sliding it in the lock and opening the door.

"Thank you for walking me home." I turned to Craig. "Please don't mention the mafia gossip to Mr...." I paused, making one last attempt to get Craig to tell me Max's last name.

"Max," he answered, giving me nothing.

It had been worth a shot. "Right. Max." I let out a small sigh. I was getting the hang of this acting business. Emma would be proud. "I usually don't spread rumors," I confided. "It's just, well, these are unusual circumstances."

"Nothing you said will go beyond me," Craig promised. Looking into his eyes, I believed him.

CHAPTER 7

*W*hoever the mystery man I saw outside the haunted house was, I'd now been warned twice that he was dangerous. Despite Craig's assurance that the man wouldn't bother me again, my stalker seemed to have other ideas.

My living room window gave me a bird's-eye view of the street and the sidewalk in front of my shop. I stood there a long time, the moonlight and lone streetlight casting the area in a hazy glow. The street was still, without so much as a leaf blowing down it, which made his presence that much more ominous. As I watched, he stepped out from the shadow cast by the building across the street.

He took his time crossing the road, pausing beneath my window. The man tilted his head up, locking gazes with me for several seconds before touching the brim of his hat and leaving the way he came. I stayed at the window for a long time, scanning every nook where the streetlight didn't reach. He didn't return.

My phone rang, startling me. Detective Woodson's name came up on the screen.

"Hello?" I asked, stepping away from the window.

"Ms. James, we are going to need you to come to the station," Woodson said.

A request like that this late at night couldn't be good. "Why?"

"We need to do a second interview," he said.

I tried to keep the nerves out of my voice. "Am I a suspect?"

"Just standard procedure." His voice was calm. "Now that you've had some time to think about it, we need to make sure we didn't overlook any important details."

I recognized the kind of details he was looking for—the kind that would incriminate me. "Like the guy I told you about who was lurking outside Howl that night?"

He cleared his throat. "Sure. You can tell me all about him when you come in."

"Of course. When?"

"First thing tomorrow morning. Nine o'clock."

Better to get this over with quickly. "Tomorrow at nine," I agreed, not that I had much of a choice in the matter.

The last time I woke up with a man in my bed, I was much happier to see him.

Jack was stretched out on the mattress beside me; he must have been watching me as I slept. After I got the scream out of my system, I settled down enough to scold Jack. "Dead or not, you can't just pop up in a woman's bedroom while she's sleeping."

Jack didn't look even a little sorry for his early morning drop-in. He fidgeted like he had something to say, but he didn't attempt to speak. After a few minutes, I gave up and grabbed my clothes.

"Don't you dare follow me," I said as he moved to get up.

I took my clothes in the bathroom. I changed as quickly as I could, in case Jack decided to join me, but he didn't make an appearance. By the time I ventured back into my bedroom, Jack had already left.

Thanks to the slow-moving line at the coffee shop and the even slower traffic, it took me over an hour to get to the police station. Now that the caffeine had hit my system, I regretted it. I was already on edge, and caffeine was not helping.

"Hi," I greeted the uniformed cop at the front desk.

He held up his finger to shush me, his eyes glued to the TV in the corner. I looked over my shoulder. Jack Gates, it seemed, was going to be my constant companion. The TV volume was turned down, but the subtitles rolled. *Grisly murder in a local haunted house*, it read, Jack's face filling the screen. The picture wasn't a particularly good likeness; it was slightly out of focus and faded, as if it was a photocopy of a newspaper photo. *KC mourns the loss of award-winning local reporter*. I snorted. I didn't even know they handed out awards for entertainment writing. There was a pause, making even the subtitles dramatic. *His killer is still at large*.

The cop cleared his throat, dragging my attention back to the task at hand. "Can I help you?"

"I'm here to see Detective Woodson."

"Name?" he prompted.

"Kali James."

He nodded and wandered out of sight, coming back a few

minutes later to usher me back into a plain Jane conference room where Detective Woodson was already seated with a yellow legal pad in front of him. Although the table was surrounded by chairs, only the two of us were in the room. Detective Woodson stood up and went through the standard niceties.

Then he asked me to recount the events of that night in excruciating detail. Again. I made sure to add the sightings of my potential stalker.

"Where did you see him last?" Detective Woodson asked.

"In the swamp room, a few rooms prior to where Jack Gates' body was. He came up behind me."

"If he was behind you, he couldn't have gotten to Gates before you, could he?" Woodson's voice was patient but more than a little patronizing.

"That's the thing. The lights flashed, and he was gone. Vanished. I assumed he went back out of the room, but the more I thought about it, the more likely it seemed that he passed me and went to the next room."

"Still," Woodson said, his voice polite. "A few minutes' head start doesn't seem like enough time for someone to kill Gates and escape out the next room."

"That's true," I said. "But Emma and I got mixed up in the next rooms, which were set up to look identical, and spent a good ten or fifteen minutes trying to find our way out."

"Fifteen minutes?" Now that there was a plausible time-line, Woodson grabbed his pen and wrote on his legal pad.

I held my breath, hoping this time he'd take the lead seriously enough to investigate the man.

"Would you be willing to work with a sketch artist so we could get a rendering of this man?" he asked.

"Yes, of course. When?" I asked, hoping it wouldn't be on one of the shop's busy days.

"Let me see if she's available today." Woodson stepped into the hallway to make a phone call. When he came back, he was more relaxed than he had been when interviewing me. "We're in luck. Our sketch artist can be here in thirty minutes."

Woodson led me back to a cluttered office with a large desk and a couple of uncomfortable-looking chairs.

"Can I get you something to drink while we wait?"

The last thing I needed was another shot of caffeine. I started to decline until I spotted a brand-spanking-new folder labeled "Howl visitor log" lying dead center on his desk.

"Coffee would be great." I smiled at him, hoping he wouldn't notice my heart rate kicking into high gear. "Sugar and creamer if you have them," I added, even though I took my coffee black. A sugar rush was a small price to pay to buy me a few more minutes alone in his office.

If this was some kind of test, I was going to fail it. After he left, I counted to ten before lunging for the folder. I glanced over my shoulder before sliding it closer and opening it. The visitor log was dated Friday, September 26, the night Jack was killed. Knowing Woodson would be back any second, I didn't bother reading the pages, just snapped pics with my cell phone as quickly as I could.

Stealing police evidence might be a felony, but taking photos of the evidence seemed more like misdemeanor territory. At least that's what I told myself as I listened to Woodson's footsteps coming down the hall. I fished around in my purse for some lip balm and tried to look nonchalant as he returned.

None the wiser, Woodson handed me a white Styrofoam cup of coffee. The next twenty minutes were some of the slowest of my life. I tamped down the guilt I felt rising every time Woodson attempted small talk.

Finally, the sketch artist showed up. She was younger than I'd imagined, with harsh bangs and an ill-fitting suit.

"Kali, this is Violet March, our local sketch artist."

I stood up, and she shuffled the portfolio she carried to her left hand before shaking my hand briskly. She didn't waste any time, settling into the chair next to me and arranging her charcoal pencils along the edge of Woodson's desk.

"Can you describe the man you saw?" Woodson asked.

"Be as detailed as possible," Violet added, her hand now poised above a blank page.

"He was white. Not Caucasian white," I corrected before she could object to my vagueness. "White, white. Like an albino, except not."

Violet looked at me, her expression telling me I'd have to do better.

I started again. "His skin was pale."

"Yes, yes," she said, irritation creeping in. "I've got that. Was he old or young?"

"Hard to tell," I said, not earning any brownie points with Violet. "His face looked late thirties or early forties, but the way he dressed and held himself, much older."

"What do you mean?" she asked.

"His clothes were old and too formal."

"Old like worn out?"

"No. Old like 1920s. The suit itself looked new and expensive, but it hung off him."

Violet furrowed her brow, still not sketching. Woodson jumped in to try to help. "Ok, late thirties and pale. Tall or short? Thin or fat?"

"He was tall and thin, gaunt even," I said. "With white hair and dark eyes."

Violet nodded and set to work, prodding me at intervals for more details. A few minutes later, she held up the sketch. Even with my bungled descriptors, she'd captured him pretty accurately.

"Close," I said. "But his face was leaner, his cheekbones more prominent, and his eyes were not that friendly." A few corrections later, and we were all satisfied.

Woodson walked me out. "Thank you for coming in. I will circulate this and see where it leads."

When I reached the lobby, I avoided looking up at the TV in the corner and made a beeline for the parking lot.

Meeting with the sketch artist took so long that I went straight to work from the police station. It was almost closing time before I got a break long enough to view the photos of Howl's visitor log. I squinted at my too-small smart phone screen for a few minutes before deciding that the task warranted printouts. A printer wasn't high on my list of necessary business supplies; electronic records suited my needs and my bank account just fine. Fortunately, there was a print shop a few blocks away.

After closing, I welcomed the brisk walk on the quiet weekday street. The only people I crossed paths with were a couple of business owners heading home for the day and a woman dressed in clothes better suited for the dog days of summer than a crisp autumn night. To each their own.

Before I got to the print shop, my phone vibrated in my pocket. I pulled it out, and Emma's name popped up. I let it go to voicemail, unwilling to hear her inevitable lecture about walking by myself in a dicey neighborhood.

When I looked up, I was no longer alone. Jack stood

blocking the sidewalk in front of me. I thought about crossing the street, pretending not to see him, but by now, I was so far in, there was no point in pretending that I wasn't at his beck and call.

"I'm working on it."

He nodded and stepped aside, gesturing for me to follow him down a side alley. Although I may not have feared walking alone in a questionable neighborhood, I certainly wasn't brave enough to follow a dead man down a dark alley.

"That's so not happening," I mumbled under my breath.

Jack stepped in front of me again, and I was forced to stop or walk right through him.

"Look," I reasoned. "I can't help you if I'm murdered in that alley."

He gaped at me like I was crazy, but he let me pass. I kept trudging toward the edge of the neighborhood, where the businesses were well-lit and ordinary.

Forty-five minutes and twenty bucks later, I was back home with a white envelope stuffed with my stolen information—information I hoped would give me a clue as to who killed Jack. I laid the photocopies out on my coffee table, pulling my floor lamp close enough to read them.

Whether a result of the overload of caffeine or nerves at swiping evidence from the police, my photography skills left something to be desired. The first and last photos were too blurry to make out much. Fortunately, the remaining photos were in better focus.

Some of the names I recognized, my own among them. There was Emma and Riley, along with the names of the frat boys from the crime scene. I scanned the list, looking for one that looked like it could belong to a stalker, but it was hard to tell much from a name alone.

I grabbed a notebook and made a list. A few names were vaguely familiar, probably people who worked in West Bottoms, people I may have met in passing or that my customers mentioned while being fitted for costumes. One name, however, I kept coming back to. It seemed more familiar than the rest: Leon Matthews.

I powered up my laptop and looked through my book-marked articles until I found the picture of Leon Matthews, haunted house superfan. Because there was a photo with the article, I knew this guy wasn't my stalker.

A quick internet search turned up another mention of Matthews. I clicked on an article about a local factory that gave ex-cons a second chance. The photo of the man standing next to a t-shirt assembly line was the same guy. It was entirely possible that as a regular, Matthews' appearance on the list was nothing out of the ordinary, even if he was an ex-con. However, I starred his name anyway.

On my last pass through the list, I noticed something else. Jack Gates' name was conspicuously absent.

CHAPTER 8

*T*here was one surefire way to identify a murderer: ask the victim. Unfortunately, that whole dead and buried thing typically got in the way. The only avenue left was the one I'd spent the better part of the last decade avoiding at all costs.

Standing in front of Old World Occult & Curiosities, I wiped my sweaty palms on my wool trousers and took a deep, shaky breath. In the year I'd lived and worked in West Bottoms, I'd explored nearly every thrift store, flea market, gallery, and artisan shop. I'd spent hours rifling through vintage fabrics and handcrafted soaps.

For months, I had forced myself out of bed early on Fridays and Saturdays and joined the throng of suburbanite shoppers who took over First Weekends, celebrating the slow crawl through unique local shops, many of which seemed to spring up overnight. I'd risked food poisoning to eat fish tacos out of a food truck idling in a land-locked Midwestern parking lot. I'd even spent an entire morning talking antique pocket watches with the man who dressed in twill vests and ran the old timey clock maker's shop around the block from the haunted houses.

What I hadn't done was step one foot in this occult shop, knowing instinctively that once I welcomed the dead into my life, I would never stand a chance of getting them back out again. Before I could change my mind, I pushed open the heavy wooden door and stepped inside, the small bell above the door announcing my arrival.

Inside, the occult shop was like something out of a Pinterest spread—all old wood and leaded glass. A counter stretched across the room, its wood polished to a rich, soft sheen. Behind it were floor-to-ceiling shelves that ranged from open shelving at the top to four rows of small wooden drawers below, their fronts hand-labeled with beautiful calligraphy. Some of them, like sage, lavender, and St. John's Wart, were recognizable. They were herbs you'd find in your local natural foods store and were therefore reassuring to me. I tried to ignore the more exotic and strange labels, refusing to consider that eye of newt might be anything other than retail appeal for the season. I admired the small amber glass jars lined up on the shelves, each one boasting a faded label.

A woman stood behind the counter, a pair of thin-rimmed reading glasses perched on her nose as she wrote in a leather ledger, presumably tallying the sales like it was 1940.

She smiled. "I've been expecting you."

"Excuse me?" I looked around to make sure she was speaking to me. We were the only two people in the store.

She repeated herself but didn't elaborate. Had she been dressed like a run-of-the-mill fortune teller, I could have accepted her odd proclamation without the shiver of unease that danced up my spine. Instead, she was dressed for a high society fundraiser, with her smooth, silver hair styled perfectly to her shoulders. She wore a charcoal gray sweater and tailored black pants, understated and elegant. Around her neck hung a delicate half-moon, dangling from a long silver chain. Her nails were painted a barely-there peach, a color that upper middle-class women her age seemed so fond of. In any other occult shop, she'd look out of place. Here, she looked like she owned it.

"I think you've mistaken me for someone else."

She studied me for several seconds before shrugging. "Suit yourself." She pulled the glasses off her nose, letting them dangle on the cord around her neck. "What are you searching for today?"

"Just browsing," I said, even though I most certainly was not here just browsing. I turned around, forcing myself to move leisurely to the shelves lining the far wall rather than performing the clutch-and-run that would get me out of here as quickly as humanly possible. There was something both comfortable and unsettling about this shop. I didn't dwell on my conflicting emotions, scanning the shelves along the back wall.

The first shelves held rocks and crystals nestled in velvet-lined baskets. Above them were artfully arranged books on rock collecting and the miraculous healing benefits of crystals. There were neat bundles of incense and small ceramic incense holders. A whole section of the shelves was devoted to candles. The tension I'd been holding in my neck and shoulders relaxed as I picked up a vanilla scented candle. These were all things I could get at most big box stores.

As I made my way further into the store, the unease crept back in as the contents went from general purpose to oddities: shrunken heads, fake fingers with nails yellowing from whatever brine they were soaking in, and cow eyeballs gazing back from their murky jars. At least, I told myself they were fake fingers and cow eyeballs. Nearby, stone mortar and pestles, decks of Tarot cards, ceramic knives, and plush fabrics were arranged on tabletop alters.

I glanced up. The shopkeeper was focused on her ledger, those glasses perched precariously on the bridge of her nose again. I kept going. In the back, there were old leather volumes with embossed titles like *The Devils and Evil Spirits of Babylonia*. That book I granted a wide berth.

I didn't pause until the display of Ouija boards, none of which resembled the mass-produced versions sold in the game stores of my childhood. Instead, these appeared to be handcrafted, made of old wood and hand-lettered. Their finders were the color of ivory and heavy in my hand as I cradled them one at a time. I looked over my shoulder to see the shopkeeper was still engrossed in her bookkeeping, a faint smile playing across her lips as her pen scratched across the page.

I had only toyed with a Ouija board once as a dare at a preteen slumber party. Even as a twelve-year-old, I recognized a hack when I saw one. Misty Reynolds had been an obvious hack, wielding the board like a Magic 8-Ball, asking it if I'd lose my virginity soon. Then, she demanded it declare the name of the boy who would take it. Her fuchsia-tipped fingernails trembled before they pushed the plastic finder across the board to spell out N-O-A-H, my nerdy neighbor who lived in *Star Wars* t-shirts and wore his dark hair in a cowlick. As if.

This time would probably be just as disappointing, but it was the only way I could think of that might give Jack a voice. Claire had been the only ghost I'd encountered capable of speech. She was also the only ghost that could affect the environment around her. Although she hadn't been able to move large objects, she could shift papers and put out candles. She had also been able to touch me, the feeling whisper light against my skin. My theory was that the strength of the bond determined how corporeal the ghost became. After Claire, I'd avoided prolonged contact with ghosts, so I hadn't exactly tested the theory. For Jack, I'd rather go the direct route.

There were several Ouija boards to choose from, and each of them was a work of art. I picked up a board crafted from walnut, its edges beveled. The letters and numbers were burned into its surface. In the center was a compass, and in the four corners were triangles, their edges burrowed deep into the hard wood. The whole board had been stained rich and dark like molasses and then covered with lacquer, so its surface felt like satin under my fingertips. I didn't bother flipping it over to look for a price, taking it to the counter before I changed my mind.

"You don't need that," the store clerk said without looking up from her ledger.

Perhaps she was shop sitting for her daughter or a friend. Because if she was working on commission, she was bound to starve, based on her customer service skills. I doubted that the store had many repeat customers.

I stiffened. "Maybe not, but I'm buying it just the same."

She sat her pen down on the table and slid her glasses off her nose. "Women like us have no need of such trifles."

"Women like us?" As far as I could see, the only thing I had in common with this woman was the location of our businesses.

"Do you even know what you are?" she asked, one eyebrow arched.

"Taurus?" I shot back, the board still clutched in my hands.

"You are a necromancer." She studied me, her eyes softening with something that looked suspiciously like pity. "Do you even know what that is, child?"

"Of course." I made a mental note to ask Siri as soon as I got home.

"You raise the dead." It wasn't a question.

"If you mean talk to ghosts, yes. That is what I'm trying to do." I squared my shoulders. I was walking out of this store with this Ouija board, whether she thought I needed it or not.

"You, my dear, do not need props to speak to the dead."

"How much?" I countered, setting the board next to the cash register but keeping one hand on it lest she snatch it away.

She sighed, but she rang up the purchase. "That will be $153.24."

I stifled the urge to leave the board, even though that amount meant I'd probably be breaking out the ramen noodles by the end of the week. I handed her my credit card. "No bag," I said when she reached under the counter.

She handed me a business card along with the receipt. "Come back when you're ready."

"Ready for what?"

The woman smiled. "Ready to take the training wheels off." She turned her attention back to her ledger.

I tucked the board under my arm and walked out of the store without responding. I regretted forgoing the bag almost immediately, the curious looks from fellow shoppers making me self-conscious. I flipped the board around, so the side with the carvings was pressed against my ribs. As I walked back to my apartment, I kept my pace steady, all the while imagining each letter on the board heating up like a brand and burning its way through my clothes.

For the first time in my life, I was purposely going ghost hunting. Tentatively, I ran my hand along the grain of the board, the wood warming beneath my fingertips. I touched the planchette. I'd learned the name for the pointer when I'd looked up the rules. Apparently, calling on the spirits with a Ouija board didn't have many rules. I closed my eyes and took a steadying breath.

"Oh spirits," I said, improvising from what I remembered from my junior high days. "I mean no harm."

Speaking to an empty room felt just as stupid now as it did in seventh grade, but I powered on.

"I wish to speak to Jack Gates."

I cracked one eye open, squinting to see if he had appeared. He hadn't. I tried again, this time pressing the planchette more firmly into the board. No screwing around this time.

"I must speak to the spirit of Jack Gates."

Despite the urgency I'd pushed into my second try, he was a big, fat no-show. I wondered if Ouija boards worked solo. Maybe you needed the wild energy of a room full of hormonal teenagers to spark the thing. I debated rounding up teenagers, but since I didn't know any in Kansas City, the only avenues open to me would land me in jail.

I needed a connection. I got up and grabbed Jack's penny from the ceramic dish where I'd dropped it. I put the penny in my left hand, closing it into a fist and holding it next to my heart. With my right hand, I touched the planchette again, willing it to move without words this time. I closed my eyes and thought of him, imagined his body as I had found it.

When I opened my eyes, Jack was standing in front of me.

His clothes were more disheveled than they had been the last time I saw him, but he still looked better than the mental image I had just been channeling. Jack glanced down at the board, crossed his arms, and shook his head.

"Who killed you?" I asked, not wasting any time on niceties.

He continued to stare at me. The planchette did not move.

I tried again, tapping on it to get his attention. "Who killed you, Jack?"

This time, Jack lunged for the board, sweeping an arm across the table to try to knock it to the floor. Everything remained where it was; he didn't have the substance to do any damage. He did, however, make his frustration quite clear.

"Look, I'm trying to help you," I told him. "But you have to do your part." I picked up the planchette and waved it at him before setting it back on the board. "Since you can't talk, this is our best bet."

I crouched on the floor next to the coffee table, looked at the board, then back up at him. He made no move toward the board, which also meant he made no effort to spell out his murderer's name. So much for my aptitude for communicating with the dead. I racked my brain for something to say that would get him to cooperate.

"I don't know." His voice was faint, rough.

At the unexpected sound, I rocked back on my heels and snapped my head up. "You can speak?"

"Obviously," he said, waving his hand impatiently.

I stood, facing him. "You don't know who killed you?"

"No." His voice grew steadier, stronger with each word.

"You must have seen something."

He shook his head. "Whoever it was came up behind me."

"Well, did you hear anything? Did the killer say something?"

"It happened so quickly." Jack moved his hand to his neck, stroking the unblemished skin there.

It was always this way, at least for the ones who found me.

People thought ghosts retained the evidence of their death: that a drowned girl's lips would remain blue and that a Vietnam vet who had placed a revolver in his mouth would return with a ravaged face. That's not how it worked, though.

Maybe it was because ghosts returned to their appearances from happier days, the way aging women seem to carry a mental image of themselves from their youth. Maybe it was because the thing that held them tethered to this world wasn't rooted in the event itself but what came before. Whatever the reason, the ghosts I had encountered appeared whole, untouched by the tragedies that birthed them.

As I watched Jack run his fingers across his throat, I was grateful for that. Seeing where my attention was focused, Jack dropped his hand.

"It's all right," I assured him. "We're going to find whoever did this to you."

Jack didn't look convinced. "Listen, I was working on something. I was on the verge of breaking a big story."

I wasn't sure if he was trying to distract himself from his murder or if he really was that concerned about finishing a story he'd started. I was certain that whatever entertainment exposé he had in the works wasn't exactly the priority here.

"Okay," I acknowledged. "But is there anything you can tell me that might help find who killed you?"

He dug in his heels. "Yeah. This story."

"What kind of story?"

"The kind that a lot of people would kill for to prevent going public," Jack said.

I leaned forward. Now we were getting somewhere. The type of news articles that got people killed usually involved politics, big money, or corruption. Often, all three. Suddenly, that organized crime angle didn't seem so far-fetched.

"What was the story about?"

Jack started pacing, pausing to look at me as if gauging my trustworthiness. What exactly did he think I was going to do? He was already dead.

"You wouldn't believe me if I told you," he finally said.

"Try me."

Jack sighed. "First, I need you to chase down some leads."

"I'm not a reporter, Jack. I just want to help find whoever killed you so that you can rest in peace." *And I can get back to my life.*

"Things are not what they seem."

"Cryptic much?"

Jack kept right on talking as if I hadn't said a word. "I was supposed to meet a source, but..." He ran his fingers over his throat again.

"Is that why you were at Howl? Were you meeting the source at the haunted house?"

Jack didn't answer, but he kept pacing the floor, deep in thought. I guess there was a certain appeal to meeting in a crowded place where everyone would be focused on the show.

"What kind of evidence?" I prompted, trying to drag his attention back to our conversation.

Jack scowled. "It was supposed to be an anonymous drop that would give me proof."

I wasn't sure I believed the anonymous part. Jack was being pretty dodgy with his details. "Proof of what?"

Jack started pacing again. "Doesn't matter because I don't have it."

"Whatever." I bit the inside of my cheek because it was impossible to strangle a ghost. "Back to the killer." I held my hand up when he started to object. "I've got a couple leads."

Jack sat on the couch with an exaggerated sigh. "Fine. What do you got?"

I started with my stalker, describing what he looked like and where I'd seen him. "Do you know him?"

"No. I don't know anyone who fits that description."

Damn it. "Could he be your source?"

He thought about it for a second. "Maybe."

"Could it have been a setup? What if whoever you were meeting wasn't actually a source but someone who wanted to squash the story? That could be our killer."

Jack scoffed. "You watch too much TV."

This was getting me nowhere. "Is there anyone you can think of who would want to see you dead?"

Jack barked out a laugh. "I'm a reporter. That's a long list."

I was beginning to understand why someone killed him. "You've got to give me something here, Jack."

"I need you to do something for me, first."

I stared at him. "What?"

"I need you to track down the owner of Howl."

"You're a journalist. Why didn't you find the owner?"

"It didn't matter before, but I heard something the night I was killed that makes it matter now." He waved me off before I could object. "Don't worry about what I heard. Just get me a name."

"Do you think this mysterious owner is your killer?"

89

He shrugged. "No idea. But whoever it is, I need that piece of the puzzle."

"Fine."

Satisfied, Jack left without another word while I was left wondering how I'd just got roped into being a dead man's girl Friday.

CHAPTER 9

J wasn't sure why Jack needed to know who owned Howl, but the only way I'd find out was by getting him the name he'd demanded. Thanks to Craig, at least I had a first name. I grabbed my laptop and typed in "Max," "Howl," and "Kansas City." After wading through three pages of search results, I had nothing useful. Max wasn't mentioned in any of them. I took a break to make hot cocoa, adding a shot of Baileys Irish Cream to the steaming mug.

I set my cup down on the coffee table and eyed the stack of old mail next to it. It was all junk mail, except for the annual business registration renewal for my shop. The return address for the Missouri Secretary of State gave me an idea. Every corporation in the state had to file an annual report, which was just the kind of breadcrumb that could lead me to the owner.

I pulled up the Missouri Secretary of State website and typed Howl in the search bar. A dozen results came back. I selected Howl Haunted House, LLC from the list. Under the profile, I noted the matching address. The business was listed as a DBA/fictitious name. The listed owner was yet another LLC with a mailing address in Kansas.

Twenty minutes, three states, four shell corporations, and another generous shot of Baileys later, I found what I was looking for: Volkov Industries, Inc. It sounded more like a vodka distillery than a company that operated a haunted house. I downloaded the biennial registration report, which listed one Maxim Volkov as President and CEO along with a corporate business address.

Although I had made up the possible ties to the mob when I talked to Craig, the more I dug into this guy, the more I wondered. While it might be normal for a large corporation to set up a DBA for each venture, hiding behind a maze of states and fictitious names didn't exactly fit with an above-the-board enterprise. If I had any sense, I'd leave this alone.

Instead, I dug in deeper, jotting down the business address before doing a general internet search for Maxim Volkov. This time, the search results were more productive, turning up two pages, including a Volkov Industries website listing. While Maxim Volkov was identified as CEO, I couldn't find an accompanying headshot or bio typical of corporate websites.

My search did yield a few local charities that listed him on the board of directors, including the county library association and the local humane society. I wavered. How could someone who safeguarded libraries and abandoned pets be the bad guy? Then again, people were complicated.

I kept digging. Even after wading through multiple pages of marginally related results, there wasn't a single picture of Max Volkov to be found, which, given his community connections, was odd. Most wealthy CEOs were photographed like celebrities, their pictures splashed across newspaper articles. Every article I pulled up, from annual fundraiser events to newspaper articles on a recent warehouse renovation funded by Volkov Industries, his photograph was noticeably absent. The man was either a recluse or was homely enough that he avoided cameras. Since men rarely gave much thought to how they looked, the former was more likely. I imagined that CEOs of criminal organizations needed to keep a low profile.

Now that I had a name, I had a choice to make. I could wait for Jack to show up again and give him the name. However, as cagey as he was being, I wasn't convinced Jack would be forthcoming about why it mattered. The other option was to investigate the man myself so that the next time I talked to Jack, I knew what questions to ask.

I tore off the corner of the envelope where I'd written the business address. Tomorrow, I was going fishing.

My first foray to Volkov Industries, I didn't make it past Mr. Volkov's formidable receptionist. Based on the industries part of the business name, I had expected a sprawling manufacturing plant. What I found were corporate offices located on the fourth floor of a brick building just off I-435. Even in the early fall, the grounds were lovely, with a still-lush lawn and a flowerbed full of mums blooming next to the building. The interior was stock office space, nearly identical to dentist and lawyer offices throughout the KC metro area: off-white walls, tiled floor, coordinating artwork.

I stepped into the building and paused by the elevator sign, looking at the tenant names and offices arranged in tidy white letters. Unlike the more personalized Dr. Bruner M.D. and C.

Harrison, CPA, Volkov Industries, Inc. was listed under the business name rather than by individual offices. I headed up to the 401-408 office block, taking the stairs in hopes it would burn off some of my nervous energy. I found room 401, the main office, easily enough. Inside was a standard-issue waiting room, complete with flat-screen TV tuned to a morning talk show, neat rows of magazines arranged on end tables, and padded chairs lined up against the far wall.

The woman at the receptionist desk glanced up from her keyboard without missing a key in her furious typing. "May I help you?"

The woman was young, probably mid-twenties, and looked more like a lawyer than a receptionist. Her dark hair was smooth, and she wore it in a neat bob that grazed the top of her expensive navy jacket. The white blouse she wore underneath the jacket was unbuttoned to her collarbone, showing off a slim gold chain. Everything about the woman was polished.

"I'm here to see Mr. Volkov," I said, smiling at her.

She continued typing. "Do you have an appointment?"

"Um, no, but this is somewhat urgent."

Her fingers paused briefly, her eyes meeting mine. "Mmm hmmm. I'm certain it is. However, Mr. Volkov is a very busy man. You'll need an appointment."

I looked around pointedly at the empty waiting room. "I only need a few minutes of his time."

She shifted her attention back to her keyboard. "You will need an appointment."

I sighed. "Okay, then I'd like to make an appointment with Mr. Volkov. Does he have time available tomorrow?"

She laughed. "I'm afraid not."

"All right. Then I'll take his next available appointment."

"What is this in regard to?"

Because he'd gone to great lengths to shield Howl behind several layers of businesses, I figured my chances of scoring an appointment would be higher if I didn't mention stumbling over a dead body.

"It's personal."

She gave me the once over, clearly finding me lacking. "Personal? As in, you and Mr. Volkov..." she trailed off.

"Eww, no, not like that. I just mean that the topic is one I'd prefer to discuss directly with Mr. Volkov."

"Fine. Let me check his calendar." She paused her typing to click through his calendar, taking her time tapping through several dates. "He has a 2:00 open on November 12."

"November 12? That's over a month away!"

"As I said, Ms.?"

"James. Kali James."

She smiled at me, the smile never quite reaching her frosty blue eyes. "As I said, Ms. James, Mr. Volkov is a very busy man. Would you like me to hold this appointment time?"

I doubted I'd still need an appointment a month from now. At least, I hoped the police would make an arrest long before November 12. I decided to take the slot, just in case.

"If that's all you have open, pencil me in."

"Great," she said brightly. "November 12 at 2:00 p.m. Please be prompt, Ms. James."

The sound of her typing followed me into the hallway as the door latched behind me. That went well.

When it came to digging up information, Claire had once accused me of being like a dog hunting for a buried bone.

Once I had a lead—even when I knew I should leave it alone—it was nearly impossible for me to walk away from. Max Volkov wasn't going to be the exception.

If Volkov was half as reclusive as he seemed to be, there was one surefire way to get him to agree to see me sooner than November 12, and that was to shake up his tidy, private little world.

I dug around in my purse until I found the crumpled sticky note with Craig's number scrawled on it. He picked up on the second ring.

"Hey Craig, this is Kali. I was thinking about what you said the other night about the owner of Howl not having any mafia connections." I paused, as if gathering my courage. Craig didn't interrupt. "It's not that I doubt you, but I was just thinking that I should tell Detective Woodson about something Riley said. I mean, I wouldn't want to hold anything back that could be helpful in the investigation."

Craig cleared his throat. "Riley?"

Crap. I hadn't meant to let her name slip. *Forgive me, Riley.* "Yeah, one of my customers. She mentioned the rumors about Mr. Volkov's supposed ties to criminal elements."

The pause was long enough I wondered if Craig had hung up on me. When he answered, his voice had lost any hint of friendliness. "I didn't tell you Max's last name," he said, the gravel in his voice a warning.

I swallowed. This was not going well. "No, you didn't, and neither did Riley." I didn't want to get her in hot water with Craig. Even though she didn't work for him, the staff who worked the haunted houses were a close-knit community. Everyone seemed to know everyone. "Google did."

"Google?" He sounded skeptical, probably because he knew as well as I did that Max Volkov went to a lot of trouble to distance his name from Howl. And I was going to find out why.

"Uh-huh. It took a little digging, but I found him." I failed to keep the smugness out of my voice. "Like pulling a thread on a sweater."

"Why were you looking?" That note of warning hadn't left his voice.

I told him the truth. A version of it, at least. "I can't get the picture of Jack Gates out of my head. No one deserves what happened to him. I don't want his murderer to get away with it."

"I'm not sure how sharing a rumor would help the police."

"You're probably right. But I've been thinking. Why would a reporter be asking a lot of questions about Howl's owner? I mean, Gates had already written his article about the haunted house. It was published a week before. But if he was snooping around asking questions, it must have been about something else, maybe a bigger story. And if Gates thought Volkov had ties to crime..." I let the thought trail off.

Craig took several seconds before he answered. "How do you know he was asking questions?"

"That's what my customers told me the next day." This time, I tried to leave Riley's name out of it, but Craig didn't.

"Let me guess. Riley?"

"And others."

"If you are determined to go to the police with this information, why are you calling me?" The gravel was back in his voice.

"I thought you could help me get an appointment to see Mr. Volkov. I tried to make an appointment myself, hoping he could clear this up, but he wouldn't see me."

On the other end of the line, I could hear what sounded

suspiciously like choking. "You wanted to make an appointment so you can ask Max Volkov if he is in the mob?"

"I wasn't going to ask him directly," I countered. "I just thought if I could meet him, I could see what kind of man he is for myself."

"That's a bad idea."

"So, you think I should call Detective Woodson, then?"

"I didn't say that." Craig took a deep breath. "Trust me when I tell you Max didn't kill Jack Gates."

"Sometimes we don't know people as well as we think we do," I said.

"I'll tell you what. Why don't you sleep on it? A day or two isn't going to make a difference. I can't get away tonight, but I can meet you tomorrow to talk it through. If you still want to go to the police, I'll take you myself. Deal?"

"Alright."

"Great. What time do you close the shop?" The relief in Craig's voice was blatant.

"6:00."

"We can talk over dinner," Craig said.

I had expected him to suggest meeting at his office or grabbing a quick cup of coffee. Dinner was moving toward date territory. I knew I should say no, but men like Craig were my kryptonite. I bit my lip and waited for my good sense to kick in.

Craig didn't wait for a response. "I'll pick you up at 7:00." And if the memory of him in a t-shirt didn't make me say yes, the command in his voice certainly sealed the deal.

"7:00 it is."

"Everything is going to be all right," he assured me before hanging up.

I didn't have to wait long for my cell phone to light up

with a phone number I recognized. When I answered, the receptionist's voice on the other end was positively frigid.

"Ms. James, you're in luck. It seems that Mr. Volkov has had an unexpected opening in his calendar. He'll see you Tuesday morning at 9:00 a.m."

I decided to push my luck. "Any chance I could see him tomorrow or Monday?"

"No." Her voice was curt. "Mr. Volkov is out of town."

"Business or pleasure?" I had to try, even though I doubted she'd give me an answer. After several seconds of pointed silence, which confirmed my hunch, she said, "Tuesday at 9:00, Ms. James." It wasn't a request.

"Lovely," I said in my sunniest voice. I didn't have a chance to thank her before she hung up.

I had no doubt that my little chat with Craig was what opened up Volkov's calendar. Now that I had an appointment scheduled, there was no need to meet with Craig. But instead of calling him back to cancel, I left the ball in his court. I ignored my phone for the rest of the day, feeling a little thrill when I finally glanced at it after work. No messages cancelling our dinner. Now for the hard decision—what to wear.

CHAPTER 10

*I*f the way Craig looked in a dark blue Henley wasn't enough to assure me I'd made the right decision, the maple bacon Brussels sprouts he ordered as an appetizer did the trick. I wasn't sure how he managed it, but the man made holding a menu look sexy. Craig ordered the surf and turf special, and I ignored first-dinner-with-a-hot-guy etiquette and went for the spaghetti. If he couldn't handle a little mess, there was no future for us anyway.

Although Jack's murder hung in the air between us, neither of us mentioned it. Instead, we talked about our career choices and bonded over pop culture, discussing the last great movie we'd each seen and whether we were in the Marvel or DC camp. Craig and I had that in common, rebels who claimed affinity for both. I let myself relax into the conversation, enjoying the company of an attractive man.

Craig caught me staring.

"How's your food?" I asked, dropping my gaze to his plate, as if that was what I was coveting.

"Delicious." He offered me a bite of lobster, and I took it, trying not to drool on his fork.

He recovered first. "So, you said you were from Chicago. What brought you to Kansas City?"

"Believe it or not, someone else's mail."

He raised an eyebrow.

I smiled. "I'd been saving up to open my own costume business for a couple years after I finished my business degree. One day, out of the blue, I got a Kansas City magazine in the mail. There was no name, just my address on it. The cover article was about the haunted houses here. Between that and the features on the Kansas City Renaissance Festival and the local theater scene, I was sold."

"Just like that?"

"Just like that," I said. "Within a month, I had leased my space and moved here."

He set his fork down and leaned back in his chair. "How did your family take the move?"

I laughed. "Not well, but they got over it. I've always been something of a black sheep in my family."

"You come from a big family then, I take it?"

My smile hollowed as the pang in my chest whenever I thought of Claire came back. "In the end, it was just my dad, my brother Drew, and me." I sipped my wine until the lump in my throat disappeared. "What about you? Oldest?" I guessed.

He grinned. "Only child." Although he was less forthcoming about his background than I was, I chalked it up to the reserve typical of men with military backgrounds.

When the check came, I offered to split it, but Craig insisted on paying. I'd dated my share of attractive men, but Craig's air of quiet confidence put him in a category all his own. He was a man used to getting what he wanted, and the way he looked at me left no doubt that this was a date. As we waited for the valet to bring his car, Craig kept his hand on the small of my back, positioning his body between me and the road.

It wasn't until the drive home that he brought up Volkov. "I spoke to Max, and he insisted on meeting with you." There was a tic in his cheek as he said it.

"Thank you," I said. "His receptionist called to make an appointment."

Craig kept his focus on the road, merging in and out of traffic with the ease of someone used to driving in cities. "Take my advice. Tread lightly with Max Volkov. He's not a man used to being questioned."

Volkov sounded like a real peach, but I appreciated the warning. "Noted."

The easy banter at the restaurant disappeared on the drive home, the mention of Volkov spoiling the illusion of this being an ordinary date. When we reached my building, Craig parked in the alley. He shut off his truck and walked around to the passenger side to open my door for me.

I stepped out and turned to face him. "Thank you for dinner."

"My pleasure," he said. "Let me walk you up."

He let me lead the way up the stairs to my apartment, his presence at my back reassuring in the gloominess that surrounded the area this time of night. I paused on the landing, my key in hand.

I reminded myself of all the reasons I should definitely not invite him inside. I barely knew the man, other than superficial chit chat. Then there was the fact that we met on the scene of a murder. He worked for a dangerous man who might have been involved in Jack's death. Most importantly, I lived alone, and no one had any idea I'd went out with him.

I turned around to tell him goodnight. "Would you like to come in for a drink?" I asked instead.

Craig hesitated before answering, and I wondered if I'd read the situation wrong. Maybe this wasn't supposed to be a date after all.

"I wish I could." He didn't elaborate on the why.

"Of course." I hid my disappointment at having misread his intentions.

Before I could turn back to unlock the door, he dropped his hand to my waist and bent down. For such a hard man, his kiss was soft, as if he were testing the waters. I leaned into him. By the time he broke the kiss, my libido was in high gear. I was relieved to see he appeared as affected as I was.

"Until there is an arrest in Gates' murder, things are complicated," Craig said.

My head still buzzed from the unexpected kiss, so the oddity of his statement didn't hit me in time to question it.

"When this is all over, I'd like to see you again." He didn't wait for an answer. "Goodnight, Kali."

He spun around and descended the stairs to his truck. I was still standing there, trying to figure out what just happened, when his taillights turned the corner and disappeared down the street.

Ironing dozens of pattern pieces before stitching them together might have been tedious work, but it also provided an ideal time to plot a murder investigation. I was ten pieces in before I came to terms with the fact that, like it or not, my next stop needed to be Howl.

So far, I had three suspects: my newfound stalker, the elusive Maxim Volkov who may or may not have criminal ties, and the ex-con Leon Matthews. Four if I dwelled on Craig's parting shot about things being complicated until there was an arrest. For both our sakes, I hoped there was an explanation other than the one that incriminated him.

I'd called Jack back using my Ouija board, but he'd been tight-lipped about why he was interested in Volkov. He'd been even less forthcoming about any details that might hint at his killer.

I was in a holding pattern until my meeting with Volkov, and patience had never been my strong suit. Oh, I knew going back to Howl was a bad idea, but in my book, a bad idea was better than doing nothing. If I could get in and out without being spotted, I could get my hands on Howl's security footage.

The only people who showed up on a visitor log were those who purchased tickets, which meant that anyone who worked at Howl or owned the place wouldn't be on that list. The security footage would show everyone who went in and out the night of Jack's murder. I was hoping it captured Max Volkov on camera. Although Craig had handed over the footage from that night to police, I was betting he hadn't included the full day's footage. If there was something incriminating on that footage, I wanted a front-row seat.

From my workstation in the back of the shop, I heard someone banging on the front door. It was still over an hour before opening, so I was alone. Because most of my morning customers tended to be walk-ins looking for Halloween costumes, I ignored it, assuming whoever it was would read the store hours posted on the window and come back later. By the third round of knocking, I gave up on my project and peeked out to see who it was.

Recognizing the familiar shock of bubble-gum pink hair, I unplugged the iron and headed for the front door. Riley was a lot of things, but an early riser wasn't one of them. I was surprised to see her at 9:30 a.m. Unlike Bennie, Riley wasn't a fan of standing appointments. She wandered in whenever she felt like it. However, this was the first time she'd shown up so early.

In contrast to the business casual dress of my usual morning customers, Riley sported head-to-toe funeral black, from her seasonally inappropriate halter top right down to her scuffed combat boots. On anyone else, the outfit would look depressing. But what Riley lacked in clothing color, she more than made up for with her physical appearance. On Riley, the black served as a backdrop, showcasing her bright hair, vibrant blue eyes, and colorful tattoos snaking up her arm and weaving down her back.

Today, she was empty-handed, making it unlikely she was stopping in for a costume repair. Curious, I unlocked the front door. "Good morning, sunshine. What brings you here bright and early?"

Riley smiled. "Can't a girl check in to see how you're doing?"

"At 10:00 in the morning? Color me skeptical."

"Got me," she said, locking the door behind her.

I raised an eyebrow. "Should I guard the till?"

Unfazed, she laughed. When Riley laughed, she did it with her whole body, the kind of belly laugh most of us left behind in our childhoods. Even if she was here to rob me, the laughter was contagious, and I felt my mood instantly lighten.

Wiping her eyes, she leaned in. "Okay, okay. I come bearing gossip, and this is some Grade A, juicy stuff."

"In that case, do you want a cup of coffee? I was just getting ready to make a pot."

"Any chance it's decaf?" I must have looked appalled because she shrugged and added, "Caffeine and I don't mix."

"Sorry. No decaf here. I think I have a bottle of water in the fridge, though, if you want it."

She waved me off. "I'm good." She plopped down in one of the chairs next to the fitting room and gestured for me to do the same. "You'll definitely want to be sitting for this."

Forgetting about the coffee, I sat down.

Riley rubbed her hands together, her eyes lighting up. "I learned two things. Both of which are interesting. Do you want the lowdown on Howl's owner first, or the reporter's dirty little secret?"

Although I already knew Volkov owned Howl, I didn't have the heart to steal Riley's thunder. "Let's go with the Howl owner first."

"Well," she said, steepling her fingers and drawing it out. "It seems that he paid a visit to Howl the day Jack Gates was killed." She didn't use the owner's name, and since I already had it, I let it slide.

"Are you sure?"

"A thousand percent sure. Rumor has it, he was pissed when he arrived and even hotter when he left."

Another reason to get my hands on that security footage. "About what?"

"No one seems to know. But I heard that he showed up around 3:00 in the afternoon in a mood so dark, all the staff except Craig hightailed it out of there to avoid landing in his war path."

"The staff are scared of him?"

"On a good day, let's just say everyone has a healthy dose of respect for his power." She arched an eyebrow. "And this was not a good day."

"Was Gates there?"

"The reporter? Not that I've heard. It was just Craig, Ruby, some staff, and the owner." Riley was careful not to use Volkov's name, and I wondered if that was out of fear, or if she really didn't know it.

"Max Volkov?" I prompted.

It wasn't often that I managed to surprise Riley, but this was one of those times. Her eyes were shrewd as she assessed me. "You know who owns Howl?"

I shrugged. "It took me a bit of digging, but I found him." Riley was uncharacteristically quiet, so I continued. "In fact, I have a meeting with him on Tuesday."

"You do?" Riley's eyes widened, and for a second, I could have sworn they shifted, her pupils elongating within those stark blue irises. When she blinked, her eyes were back to normal. I chalked it up to too little sleep and a hyperactive imagination.

"I thought you didn't know who owned Howl?"

She sobered. "I lied."

"I know. But why?"

"There are some men you don't want to tangle with, Kali, and Maxim Volkov is top of the list."

That seemed to be the consensus. "Because of his mob ties?"

For a second, Riley looked confused, as if she hadn't been the one who had planted that seed, but she caught herself quickly enough. "Something like that. He is a dangerous man, surrounded by dangerous friends."

"Dangerous how?"

Riley wouldn't meet my gaze, toying with a loose thread on the hem of her shirt. "Just dangerous." It was clear I wasn't going to get more specifics no matter how hard I pushed. "Why do you need to go see him anyway?"

"I can't let Gates' death go. He needs justice, and I think Volkov might know something that could help."

"And you think you're the one who has to get justice for Gates?"

"I do."

Riley ran her fingers through her pink locks and shook her head. "Why you?"

For one insane minute, I considered telling Riley that Jack Gates was my new shadow. Years of practice safeguarding my freakishness kicked in, and I went with a half-truth.

"The police aren't making headway." Although I'd been hopeful the police sketch would be the lead they needed, the crickets I'd heard since then had dashed my hopes of quick justice. I looked at Riley. "Someone has to step up."

Riley took a deep breath and held it for several seconds before letting it out in a whoosh. She squared her shoulders and nodded. "Okay. Then I'll help you."

"What? No." The last thing I expected was for Riley to throw her hat in the ring, but maybe I should have. Riley was the most balls-to-the-wall person I'd ever met. "It's too dangerous."

Riley rolled her eyes. "If it's too dangerous for me, it is absolutely too dangerous for you."

"What is that supposed to mean?"

"Let's just say I've got skills," she said, tapping her chest with her knuckles.

Attitude she had in spades. However, combat boots aside,

there was little about Riley that hinted at an inner badass. She was five-eight and had a runner's body. If it wasn't for her unconventional hair and body art, she could've walked a runway somewhere. I was smart enough not to say that out loud, though.

"Thanks. Really, I appreciate it, but I don't want to get you involved."

"Too late. I'm in."

I knew Riley well enough to know I wasn't going to change her mind, so I did what I had done on every dreaded group project since elementary school. I tried to manage the damage she could do.

"Okay," I said, trying to force enthusiasm into my voice. "You can be my woman on the inside. Gather intelligence."

"Gossip?" She grimaced. "You want me to bring you gossip?"

"Isn't that what you are doing right now?"

"Exactly. That's not the kind of help I'm talking about. I'm talking some Bonnie and Clyde action."

"Clyde was a man," I reminded her.

"Did you really just go there?"

"Okay, you're right. Clyde's gender hardly matters, but for the record, both Bonnie and Clyde went down in a barrage of bullets. Plus, they were most certainly the killers, not the good guys."

"Right, bad analogy," she agreed, tapping her chin. "*Charlies Angels* then."

"The classic or the remake?" I asked, getting distracted.

Riley smiled. "The original. No one does ass-kicking, super-sleuthing women like the 1970s. Amiright?"

I got up, stalling. "I'm going to go grab that cup of coffee. I think I'm going to need it."

Instead of giving me space, she jumped up and followed me to the back. I cleaned out yesterday's coffee filter and put a fresh pot on to brew while Riley bounced on her heels like a boxer.

I turned back to her. "Fine."

"I can help?"

It was obvious she wasn't about to leave this alone. Discreet didn't seem to be in Riley's wheelhouse. I figured she'd be safer working with me than poking around on her own.

"You can help."

I'd have to figure out how exactly she could help without A) putting her on the killer's radar, and B) telling her my prime source of intel was coming from none other than a dead Jack Gates himself.

She clapped, actually clapped, before jogging back to the front of the shop. She rummaged around under the counter until she came up with a pad of paper and a pen.

"Let's lay out what we've got so far." She looked at me expectantly.

I should've known she wouldn't waste any time now that I'd caved. I kept it vague. "Not much, I'm afraid."

She handed me the pad, "Write down everything you know. What you know about Gates, what you saw that night, and anyone you suspect."

Teamwork was not something I'd had a lot of experience with. Not since Claire died, anyway. As I watched Riley's eager face, I couldn't help but think how nice it would be to have someone in my corner again. What was the harm in having a person to bounce ideas off of? As long as I was careful about oversharing, this could work. I started writing down the details I'd gathered about Jack's death and handed it back to Riley.

She barely glanced at it before tossing it back to me. "Stop holding out on me. Suspects?"

I gave her my anemic list: Max Volkov, who she already knew about, Leon Matthews, and Stalker X. I couldn't bring myself to list Craig's name there.

She pointed to the last name on the list. "Who the hell is Stalker X?"

By now, I had described the guy so many times that I had it down to an art. I was hoping that Riley could put a name to a face, but she came up blank.

"And who is Leon Matthews?" Riley asked.

"Ex-con. He was there the night Gates was killed. I thought it was worth checking out."

"Do you know him?"

"Gates?"

"No, not Gates." She sounded exasperated. "Matthews."

"Oh, no, I don't know him."

"Then how did you know he was there that night?"

She caught me there. I debated making up a story, but as she looked at me expectantly, I came up blank. I went with the truth. "I got my hands on the visitor log for Howl the night of the murder and recognized his name. After I found Gates, I did a quick Google search and ran across an old article on Howl. Leon Matthews was mentioned in it."

"How did you get the visitor log? Craig?"

Riley clearly wasn't going to leave it alone. I had two options, here. I could lie and say Craig gave it to me, but that could easily be disproven if she asked him. Plus, I didn't want to tip him off about how much I was digging around. The other option was to trust Riley to have my back enough that she didn't run straight to the cops and report me. Everything about Riley screamed screw-the-establishment, so I rolled the dice.

"The police."

"Wait, what?" She lifted one perfectly arched eyebrow. "The police just gave you a list of visitors?"

"Not exactly."

Riley sucked in a breath. "You stole it?" She grabbed me by the shoulders and gave me a little shake. "Oh my God, you stole the list from the police, didn't you?"

I swallowed. "Maybe."

She planted a kiss right in the middle of my forehead. "You and me, girlie. Soul sisters," she squealed.

I laughed. "So, what was the gossip about Gates?" At her blank look, I reminded her. "You said you knew his dirty little secret."

"Oh yeah." She waved her hand as if it were of little importance. "Apparently, Gates got fired from his last job. He was some bigshot reporter in DC. Covered real news out there."

From my Google search, I already knew Gates had worked in DC before coming to Kansas City. The fact that he had been fired was new information, though. I had no idea whether the reason he was fired was relevant to his death or not, but I made a mental note of it.

"Any idea why he got fired?"

"Nope." She was just about to grab the pen and paper again when someone tapped on the shop door. Seeing Bennie there, she changed gears. "I'll pop by tonight. I'll bring sticky notes and thumbtacks."

"Huh?"

"For our murder board. You know, the one the cops make by taping up clues and photos of all the suspects on the wall."

Before I could object, Riley headed for the door. She flipped the sign to open and unlocked the door on her way out, nodding to Bennie as she passed. I was going to have to confiscate the thumb tacks when she got to my place, or I'd be kissing my security deposit goodbye.

CHAPTER 11

*B*ennie was more predictable than Riley, so that made his early morning visit even more suspicious. Unlike Riley, Bennie had a nine-to-five, and the police department wasn't exactly known for flexible hours. I wasn't sure if he was here as a concerned friend or as a peacekeeper/snoop for Craig, or even Volkov himself. I waited until he made it into the store before questioning him.

"Are you here to check on me?" I wanted to give him the benefit of the doubt.

"Hello to you, too," he said, his voice light. Today, Bennie was dressed in khakis and a black button-down. Work clothes.

"Playing hooky?"

He laughed. "I wish. I had an early appointment and thought I'd drop by to check on you before heading in to work."

"Craig didn't send you?" I thought it best to leave Volkov's name out of it.

He frowned. "Why would Craig send me?"

He genuinely seemed confused, so I played it safe. "He seems like the overprotective type, that's all."

"You got that right. You hanging in there?"

"Yeah. Just trying to stay busy." I didn't mention that my choice of activities for staying busy lately consisted of stealing police evidence and plotting break-ins. I offered Bennie a cup of coffee.

"No thanks," he said. "I've got to head in to work soon. I wanted to see if you had some time tonight."

"Sure. What do you need?"

"Time to change it up. I'm thinking a cross between the Grim Reaper and a glow-in-the-dark skeleton."

Normally, I'd be all over a costume change. Creating new character costumes was hands-down my favorite part of my job. With Jack's ghost breathing down my neck, I was off my game. Business was business, though, and this could be the perfect distraction.

"I can do that. Any idea when Howl will be able to open again?"

The last time I had been at Howl, there'd been still police tape strung across the stairway, blocking access to all but the staff offices. Timing was everything in costume design. Give me an hour and a makeup palette, and I could make that off-the-shelf costume look legit scary. Give me a week, and the sky was the limit.

"You didn't hear? We got the green light to reopen tonight."

"Wow."

Reopening was great for Howl and for the Leon Matthews' of the world. Not so great for me. The chances of me getting in and out of Howl without being detected would have been much better before the show was up and running again. A visit during business hours was not an option. Normal people did not come back for an encore after discovering a dead body. The last thing I needed was another check in the murder suspect column.

I forced a smile. "That's good news."

"Yeah. Closing the production for a week is costly. At least it isn't late October." Bennie ran his hand through his hair as if catching himself. "Well shit. That was insensitive, considering a man was murdered."

I waved him off. "I know you didn't mean it like that."

Bennie sighed. "It's been a long week."

"Preaching to the choir." I rummaged through the bins beneath the counter where I stashed makeup supplies until I came up with a tube of glow-in-the-dark face paint.

"Bingo." I held it up. "I should have everything I need for Grim-o-ter."

"Grim-o-ter? Really?" Bennie's eyes crinkled with laughter. "That's what we're going with?"

I shrugged. "Skeletor is already taken."

"Skele-reaper," he tried.

I stuck my index finger in my mouth and gagged like I was eight.

Bennie threw his hands up in mock defeat. "Fine. Grim-o-ter." He gave me a quick hug. "I've got to get to work, but I'll see you tonight."

After he left, it was almost an hour before another customer came in. I busied myself gathering the supplies I needed to create Bennie's costume, grabbing an off-the-shelf reaper cloak with a deep hood, a wicked-looking scythe, and the glow-in-the dark makeup to create a pile under the counter. Because I wanted the overall effect to be terrifying rather than comic book, I rooted around in the back until I found a skull face mask that I could cover with the glow-in-the-dark paint.

It was a good start, but it still needed something to elevate it from ordinary to scream-worthy. Snapping my fingers, I headed for my stash of blood-red contacts. Knowing Bennie would be game, I grabbed them and added them to the growing pile. Satisfied, I sent him a quick text telling him to bring his steel-toed black boots.

With nothing else to do until my next customer arrived, I settled myself behind the counter and tried to ignore the little voice in my head that questioned if crafting a harbinger of death was tempting fate.

I was just closing the shop when Bennie returned. He had traded his work clothes for black jeans, t-shirt, and boots. Although the all-black ensemble would work fine under the reaper cloak, I needed to get him into the changing room. I'd had plenty of time this afternoon to come up with a plan that would get me into Howl. I just needed an excuse to put Bennie's keys and wallet under the counter where I could lift Howl's key without him noticing.

I held up a black unitard and waggled my brows.

He laughed. "You've got to be kidding me."

"Come on," I cajoled. "It's for the greater good."

He grumbled but reached for the unitard. Bennie was nothing if not a good sport. I held out my hand, and he handed over his keys and wallet for safekeeping before heading back to the changing room.

I ignored the flash of guilt and avoided his eyes as I accepted them. "How is everyone feeling about going back to the haunted house after the murder?" I asked, my nerves making my voice a little higher than usual.

I waited until he was inside the dressing room before examining his key chain. There were a half a dozen keys, everything from a small key that must be to a fire safe or file cabinet to an assortment of door keys. Fortunately, Howl's key was easy to spot. One was specially made, cast in black metal. Even without the name or address stamped on it, I was sure it had to be the key to Howl. I almost fumbled them when Bennie poked his head out of the dressing room.

"I haven't talked to anyone other than Craig and Ruby," he said. "But I'm sure it'll be tense for a while."

He ducked back in the room, and I worked the key off as quickly as I could. Once it was free, I pressed it firmly into the blob of silly putty I'd put under the counter. The alternative would be to swipe the key and hope Bennie didn't notice before I could put it back. There was zero chance I could convince him that it had somehow fallen off the key ring on its own. If he discovered it missing, he would know it was stolen and sound the alarm immediately. I checked the impression to make sure it was complete before weaving the key back on the ring.

Most men in a form-fitting black unitard would feel self-conscious. If Bennie's smirk was any indication, he was not among them. Although he wasn't overly muscular, he could have been a model for a sketch class. His body was proportionate, with the kind of lithe muscles that soccer players possessed. The tight fit of the unitard also left very little to the imagination. When I finally made eye contact, he had tears in his eyes from laughing.

"Somehow, I doubt this is quite the look you were going for."

"Ummm, no. I guess I didn't think that one through. On the bright side, the cloak has pockets. You know, for all the college girls to slip you their phone numbers." I whistled. "Along with some 20s."

Now, we were both laughing.

"Maybe you should go back to the jeans and t-shirt."

"You think?" He pivoted back to the dressing room.

Unlike some of Bennie's costumes, this one was a quick creation. Twenty minutes later, Bennie was ready to head out. He didn't even glance at the keys I handed back to him. I watched him walk out, the small bell on the front door chiming as he left.

I didn't think I had it in me to play detective with Riley and break into Howl on the same night, so I texted Riley. *Rain check*, I begged, unsurprised when her immediate response was a series of angry faces followed by several heartbreak emoji. I tried again. *Tomorrow? Got a headache tonight.* It took her a couple minutes, but she finally agreed.

Relieved, I headed to the hardware store to make a key from my impression. Although I planned to get in and out of Howl tonight before anyone was the wiser, there was a reason people muttered about the best laid plans and all. A key of my own would give me options in case things didn't go well. As I walked to the hardware store, I tried not to think about how easy it was becoming for me to justify criminal behavior.

After being turned down at the local hardware store, I made four phone calls to locksmiths. None of them were willing to make a key from a silly putty impression, and two of them threatened to call the police to report me. I was left with few options.

I could wait until Bennie came back and steal the key itself, but the odds of discovery seemed stacked against me. I could break a window to gain entry, but that was a straight path to a criminal record, particularly since it was the scene of a recent murder. Or I could call my clingy ex and ask him for a favor. It took the better part of an hour and a date with a shot glass before I settled on option C.

There were many reasons why our relationship fizzled, but Gavin's looks were not one of them. He had long, black hair that parted in a widow's peak and a year-round tan from all the time he spent outdoors. His body was corded with muscle, a result of hours in the saddle wielding a shield and lance.

From late summer through early fall, Gavin was a jouster at the Kansas City Renaissance Festival, which is where I'd met him. The nature of my job meant I mingled mostly with actors and performers this time of year, which translated into dating a lot of eccentric men. Not that I particularly minded. I'd much rather date jousters and monster men than accountants and lawyers.

During jousting season, Gavin took his job seriously—very, very seriously. The rest of the year, he parked cars for one of the restaurants in the Plaza, Kansas City's shopping and fine dining destination spot, and plotted his rise to stardom as a professional jouster. One too many of our dates were spent listening to Gavin wax poetic about the masculine tradition of jousting. As far as I was concerned, jousting with blunted ends while medical staff stood ready with an assortment of Band-Aids and ice packs took the machismo straight out of the sport.

Because of his jousting gig, Gavin was chummy with a modern-day blacksmith who dabbled in jewelry making. And that guy had the tools and expertise to make a key from a mold.

Although I crossed my fingers and hoped for voicemail, Gavin picked up on the second ring. "Kali?"

I shut down the urge to mumble, "wrong number," and hang up. Instead, I leaned on standard Midwestern niceties. "Hi Gavin. How are you?" After a few minutes of inane small talk, I broached the real reason I was calling. "I need a favor."

"Of course," he agreed too quickly. I could be calling for bail money or for help digging a shallow grave to bury a body for all he knew, but there was no hesitation in his voice.

"I need a key made."

"Okay." He chuckled.

Before he convinced himself that my call was a lame excuse to talk to him, I continued. "All I have is an impression, and no one will make a key for me." The line was silent for a minute. I prepared to explain why exactly I needed a key made from a silly putty imprint, but he never asked.

"I can make it tonight," he said.

"I get off work at eight," he said, his voice dropping low. "Do you want me to pick it up? I can come by your apartment."

I pinched the bridge of my nose. "That would be great." I hung up and went upstairs to find the least flattering outfit in my wardrobe, hoping it would counter any talk of getting back together.

CHAPTER 12

The hours after midnight provided an ideal window for breaking and entering. Although several local businesses had banded together to invest in private security and a PR firm that touted the area's new image as a revitalized urban mecca of art and bargains, there were still plenty of things that went bump in the night around here. People venturing out after the crowds went home seemed to sense it, and they hustled on their way.

When I'd first moved here, it had been easy to get lulled into believing in the welcome mat reception rolled out during First Weekends or the boisterous camaraderie of the haunted house production hours. The key to getting along here outside those hours, I had soon found, was to keep your head down and your pace steady. Venturing illegally into a shuttered haunted house was clearly breaking with that wisdom. I hoped I wouldn't regret it.

By 2:00 a.m., I was up and dressed. I didn't have a lot in my wardrobe suitable for late-night trespassing. I settled for a little black number I'd been working on for a cosplay outfit.

The foundation piece was form-fitting black pants with a corset-style waist decorated with hammered metal studs and rings. Beneath it, I wore a soft button-down black tank top. A matching set of custom buckles wound around each thigh. I even donned the fitted arm guards—because why the hell not. This outfit was ninety percent badass, ten percent accessories.

I rounded it out with a more practical hooded sweatshirt, flat-heeled boots, and a ski mask I'd impulsively bought a month ago. Sometimes, you find the accessory. Other times, the accessory finds you. In this case, I'd spotted the black ski mask among a sea of cotton candy beanies at a clothing stall at an outdoor craft fair. At the time, I imagined that I'd use it for the bitter cold spell *Farmer's Almanac* was predicting. Had I known then I'd be using it to disguise myself while I broke into a neighboring place of business, I probably would've kept my money for the inevitable bail.

I tucked the ski mask and a heavy-duty flashlight in my sling bag and headed out the door. Without the mask, I could always pretend I had insomnia and circle back home if I ran into someone. With the mask on, I was a guaranteed 911 call.

I palmed my key I'd copied from Bennie's. If there was a metaphorical line in our friendship, I was sure that I'd already stepped both feet over it. Hopefully, I'd be in and out with no one the wiser. I'd save my guilt until after Jack's killer was caught.

Luck was with me because I made it to Howl without seeing so much as an alley cat. I wasn't certain which door the key opened, but I was hopeful that it was the service entrance around the side of the building and not the main door with a camera aimed down on it. When the police had asked Craig for security footage, he said the only camera was the one out front.

I put my mask on before I reached the building. Just in case. At this point, if someone saw me, it would be better to be identified as a burglar than the Costume Shoppe owner. I'd probably wind up with a record either way, but at least with the mask on, I'd have a chance to make a run for it. Hopefully, a long summer of snow cones and marathon costume construction sessions in lieu of actual physical exercise wouldn't hamper my escape too much. I vowed to get my out-of-shape backside into a gym, or at least invest in a pair of sneakers. I could take up jogging. *Who am I kidding?* I was so not a jogger.

Reaching the door, I scanned both directions like a kid waiting to cross the street. When I didn't spot any moving shadows, I fumbled for the key, my heartbeat kicking into high gear. Once I turned that key, there was no backing out. Before I had time to change my mind, I slid the key in the latch. It fit perfectly.

Inside, I quickly closed the door behind me. I pulled the ski mask to the top of my head. Although flicking on the flashlight was tempting, I needed to wait until I was deeper in the house. The windows had been lined with black tar paper to block light from the street, but I wasn't willing to risk light on the main level shining through the cracks around that paper.

My first stop was Craig's office. Normally, I wasn't the kind of girl who went through a guy's things after a first date. But in this case, my need to find Jack's killer outweighed my sense of decorum.

Craig's office was windowless, which meant I could turn the light on without risking anyone seeing it. He had your standard office furniture: desk, chairs, and file cabinet. Beyond that though, it was largely empty. No pen cup next to the computer, no pile of paper clips out of place, and certainly no wall art to detract from those no-frills beige walls. I turned the photo on his desk around. Despite being here for Jack, I was relieved to see it was a solo rock-climbing photo rather than him posing with a girlfriend, or even worse, a wife.

I turned my attention to the reason I was here, checking Craig's computer first by tapping a key to see if the machine was on. The computer was old, like the dinosaurs we'd used in elementary school old, which meant no password prompt as the screen lit up. Sometimes things did actually go my way. Not that I was going to get cocky about it, hanging out as I was in someone else's office. Although I'd toyed with the notion of being a spy when I was seven, my sweaty palms and thumping heart confirmed that particular career choice would have been disastrous.

Craig, it seemed, was a stickler for organization. There were folders, labeled by month. Inside, each night's security footage was in date order. I pulled up the footage for the night of the murder and waited for what seemed like an eternity for it to load. The time stamp at the beginning was 6:00, a full hour before opening time. Despite knowing Volkov had shown up earlier in the day, I scanned through the first hour, just in case. I didn't see anyone come in the front door that I didn't recognize.

I did see a familiar face approach the front door thirty minutes before opening, though. Jack stopped and had a short conversation with Ruby before leaving the way he came. *Weird. He must have left and came back again later.* There was no sound on the security footage, so I couldn't make out what they said. From their body language, neither of them seemed upset.

I forwarded the footage to 7:45 and slowly clicked

through in five-minute increments until I saw Jack again. Ruby let him in early, while the rest of us waited in line. When I spotted myself, Emma, and Riley, I backed it up fifteen minutes. The killer had to have entered the haunted house shortly before or after us. I paused when a man who could have been Leon Matthews went inside as soon as it hit 8:00. It was hard to ID someone you'd only seen in a grainy newspaper photo, so I couldn't be positive it was Matthews.

Although I didn't see anything else notable, I recorded the footage on my cell phone to reference later. I only captured the first twenty-three minutes before my battery died. In my prep, I'd neglected to charge my stupid phone. I'd take what I could get.

I watched the next couple minutes to make sure I hadn't missed anyone armed with a knife. The remaining footage seemed benign; throngs of customers moving like cattle, costumed actors milling among them. The most suspicious-looking person was a man in a biker jacket and full beard who appeared at the beginning of the footage. Considering the trio of fourteen- or fifteen-year-old girls he seemed to be escorting, he was an unlikely suspect.

I checked my watch: 3:37. Since I'd already broken into his office, I figured I might as well snoop around. I was surprised to find every desk drawer unlocked, including the one that had a fully loaded handgun. He was security, I reasoned. *It could be worse. I could've found a bloody knife.* Just to be sure, I searched the entire office, even crawling under his desk and looking around. Nothing.

As I scrambled out from under the desk, I noticed I had company. Jack was sitting in Craig's office chair, one ankle casually crossed over the other, watching me.

I jumped, knocking my head against the underside of the desk and sending my sling bag crashing to the floor.

"Damn it, Jack! What are you doing here?" I kept my eyes on him as I stuffed everything that had fallen out back into my bag.

"Supervising."

"Ugh. I'm done. There's nothing useful on the security tape, and as you can see," I gestured around the room, "nothing incriminating here either." I stood up and tossed my dead phone in the bag before heading for the exit.

Jack jumped in front of me and braced his arms across the opening. "Not so fast. I want to check out the room where I was killed."

"Fine. Check it out. I'm going home."

Jack didn't budge. "I can't go anywhere without you."

"Really?" I didn't know that. I'd never given much thought to what ghosts did when they weren't attached to my hip.

He scowled. "Yes. Let's go." Jack headed for the stairs, looking over his shoulder to make sure I was following.

I stayed where I was. "Why do you want to see the room where you died? I'm sure the police removed everything that could be evidence."

"I'm not looking for the murder weapon."

"Then what are you looking for?"

"I'll know when I find it." You'd think a reporter would be a bit more forthcoming, but Jack was a pro at evasive answers. He waited on the bottom stair until I turned my flashlight off and reluctantly followed him.

When I reached the upstairs landing, I turned my flashlight back on. Without the actors, the place was eerily quiet. The only sound was my own steady footsteps echoing through empty rooms. Although the actors did a fine job of crafting terror, there was something infinitely more frightening about being in a vacant haunted house with no one except a dead man for company.

Even with the flashlight, it took me awhile to make it to the room where Jack had been killed. The body, of course, was long gone, but the house staff had capitalized on Jack's death, taping an outline of a body in glow-in-the-dark tape on the hardwood floor. The blood-stained wood was almost covered by the tape, but some of it still bloomed, dark despite whatever industrial cleaning solution the crime scene cleanup crew had used.

Even though the outline was staged—it was closer to the size of a preteen than a grown man, and its location was slightly off—I still felt a chill looking at it. *Bastards.* Some things should be off limits, and monetizing a dead man's crime scene for cheap screams ought to be among them.

Judging from the fury on Jack's face, he agreed. While Jack examined the props, I made my way around the room. With the flashlight in hand, I double-checked entrances and exits in the room. One way in, the way I came, and one way out, into the room with the slide. That meant I had been on the heels of the murderer all the way through the house.

In that case, it should have been easy enough for the police to pull the front door camera footage and question the half a dozen or so people who had come through before me. Of course, Emma and I stumbled around the identical rooms for quite some time before finding our way out. The police would also need to look at people who entered Howl after us. Still, it seemed like an obvious pool of suspects, unless the killer was an employee or Volkov himself. There would be no video evidence of anyone who came in through the side entrance or through the gift shop accessible through the next room.

Now that I thought about it, my stalker hadn't been on the security footage either. I hadn't seen him waiting in line, but he had definitely been in the house that night. That meant my stalker probably hadn't come in through the front door. While his washed-out skin and bleached hair had seemed authentic, I wondered again if he was one of the dozens of actors who worked here. It would certainly explain his penchant for antiquated clothing, pale complexion, and unnatural movement.

If my stalker was an actor here, he would have come in the side entrance just as I had earlier. But if that were the case, why wouldn't Bennie have told me? And why would Craig have lied when I asked him? If he wasn't an actor, it seemed unlikely he could've snuck in the staff entrance without getting caught. But if he worked directly for Volkov, he might have access. None of that explained how he could get out of Howl without being seen. There were only two ways in and out of this room.

"I don't understand why the police haven't been able to make an arrest." I joined Jack as he peered down at the grotesque outline on the floor. "There are only two entry points. The front door and through the gift shop. One has a camera, and one was through a locked door. Even if the killer went out through the gift shop, surely someone on the street would have noticed a person covered in blood coming down the stairs. It doesn't make sense."

Jack sucked in a breath. "Not necessarily. There is one other way they could get out. Check the wall over here." Jack pointed at black drapes that were hanging flush against the wall.

I crossed the room. "What am I looking for?"

"A hidden exit," Jack said.

If Jack was right, Craig had lied. I walked the perimeter of the room, one hand steadying my flashlight, the other feeling behind the curtain for hidden doorways. If I hadn't been feeling my way along the wall, I never would have found it.

Despite it being indistinguishable to the naked eye, my fingertips tingled as I ran them up a seam. The door itself had been painted to match the walls and the curtains. There were no visible knobs or hinges. In fact, there was no sign at all that a door was there. Without Jack pointing it out, I would have never looked for it.

"How did you know this was here?" I asked Jack.

He gave me the side-eye. "Doesn't matter. What matters is that it is there."

My fingers caught on the shallow notch that opened the door. I felt a zap like static electricity and then the outline of the door appeared. *That was weird.* Without a knob, the door swung open silently with no telltale slide and click of metal against metal.

"I wonder who else knows about this door?"

"Only the people who work here," Jack said.

"But you knew," I countered. "And you don't work here."

"I saw an employee open it." His guarded expression told me there was more to that story, but he didn't seem inclined to share.

I opened the door and peered down the steep passageway. The stairs were serviceable wood, but barely. They were pitched steeply, like steps in a hundred-year-old farmhouse, and descended to a landing for another flight of stairs.

Clearly, this was another way out of this room. What were the chances that the guy in charge of security wouldn't be aware of a hidden door? Zilch, which meant Craig had lied to the police. While there were a few logical explanations for lying to the police, none of them were good.

"Find anything interesting?" A man's voice snaked through the room, making me fumble my flashlight. That wasn't Jack.

I turned around, holding the light in front of me like a shield. Jack was nowhere to be seen. A warning would have been nice before he ditched me.

My stalker stood just inside the door, arms crossed, one shoulder braced against the frame as if he were trying to appear casual. He was sporting the same dark fedora that he had the night of the murder, its brim shading the top half of his face even in the beam of my flashlight.

I took a step backward toward the next room and closer to the other door.

He pushed himself off the doorframe. "Uh-uh. No need to run out."

My heartbeat kicked up a notch despite my best efforts to remain calm. "Do you work here?"

The man smirked. "Hardly."

"Then why are you here?"

He brushed imaginary lint from his shoulder. "I followed you, of course."

The fact that he'd been watching me, perhaps this whole time, was frightening enough. The fact that I hadn't so much as had a hair-prickle awareness of his presence was far, far worse.

"Why?" I demanded.

He shrugged. "Curiosity." He tipped his hat up higher on his forehead and scanned me from head to toe. "Nice getup." He smirked. "Playing dress-up, are we?"

I hated everything about him. His pallor, the way his expensive clothes hung off him like he was some gaunt mobster, his smug demeanor. I chose not to respond, going on the offensive instead.

"Did you kill Jack Gates?" It wasn't the smart play, confronting a potential killer, but I did it anyway.

He unfurled his long body from the doorway, but when I took a step backward, he stopped and held up his hands as if he meant no harm. Not that I was buying it.

"No," he said. "Did you?"

I snorted. "Do I look like a murderer?"

"More than you look like a ninja," he said with a straight face.

"I'm not supposed to be a ninja," I snapped.

He pulled a metal cigarette case out of his jacket pocket, the gleaming silver catching and reflecting the light. He shook out a slim cigarette, lifted it to his lips, and lit it. Taking a long drag, he held the smoke in before blowing it out in a series of rings.

"You shouldn't have come here."

The smell of fire and ash filled the room. I inhaled without flinching. "Spoken like someone who killed him."

His expression didn't change. "I already told you I didn't." He looked at bloodstain on the floor where Jack had been. "Such waste," he tsked.

"If you didn't kill him, why were you here that night?"

"Same reason I'm here tonight."

"You followed me?"

He nodded.

"What. The. Hell." I raised the flashlight higher, shining the beam directly in his eyes. He didn't blink, and his pupils looked ringed in red. Although I told myself it was either a trick of the light or a product of an overactive imagination, it was unsettling.

"You're interesting to me." He reached inside his jacket pocket and pulled out a folded sheet of paper. I knew what it was before he unfolded it, revealing the charcoal drawing from the police sketch artist. "Fairly good likeness," he boasted, holding it up next to his face.

The sinking feeling in my gut intensified. "How did you get that?"

"It was a gift." He held it out like an offering.

No way was I moving close enough to accept it. I wasn't sure what kind of game he was playing, but right now, him clutching the original police rendering of himself as he stalked me back to the murder site didn't exactly herald his innocence.

"Who are you?" I demanded, keeping the flashlight trained on him while I scanned the room for objects large enough to do some real damage. The room was still outfitted as a dungeon. Unfortunately, he was just as close as I was to any implements of torture that would make good weapons. If I couldn't get to them faster than he could, drawing his attention to them probably was a bad idea.

He laughed. Coming from him, the sound was unsettling. It hummed along my skin. "They call me Twitch," he said. "But you're asking the wrong question."

Suddenly, he stilled. When I opened my mouth to speak, he held a finger up to his lips and canted his head toward the door behind him.

"They're coming."

"Who?"

He didn't answer. Instead, he thrust the drawing at me until I took it, then pointed to the next room. "Take the back exit before they get inside. Their hearing is exceptional," he said, emphasizing the last word.

The sound of the front door opening echoed up the stairs. He pointed again to the room with the slide. When I heard boots hitting the stairs, I bolted for the next room. I looked over my shoulder, but Twitch was already gone. I opened the latch and slid the board blocking the exit out of the way as quickly and quietly as I could.

I killed the flashlight, jumped in feet first, and pushed off from the top of the slide, praying for a quick descent. When I reached the ground, I didn't look back. Pulling the ski mask over my face, I hit the alley at a dead run and didn't stop until I was panting and wheezing inside the safety of my own apartment.

CHAPTER 13

*I*mage was a powerful thing. It wasn't who you were that determined success, but who people perceived you to be. When I arrived at Volkov Industries for my Tuesday morning meeting, I was a film noir kind of woman. I had modeled myself after those cigarette-smoking dames in old detective movies, all attitude with a touch of glamour. I'd worn high-waisted black dress pants with straight legs that fell to the top of my favorite leopard-print flats. I'd tucked in a long-sleeved silk shirt that was the color of fresh cream and wound a string of pearls around my neck. Soft curls and matte red lipstick cemented my femme fatal status.

This time, I spent far less time in the waiting room. Within minutes of my arrival, the Ice Queen receptionist ushered me into a smaller, more private waiting area outside Volkov's office. Unlike the main sitting area, this room was elegant, with sage walls and floor-to-ceiling bookcases filled with hard-bound books that had been artfully arranged, a few scattered collectibles nestled in between. On the far side of the room were two faded brown leather chairs. There were no fluorescent lights to be found here, only a matched pair of floor lamps that bathed the room in soft light. This was the kind of room one invested a whole afternoon in, lost in the worlds found in the leather-bound volumes lining the shelves.

I wandered over to the ordered bookshelves and ran my fingertip along the spines. I wasn't sure what kind of books I'd expect a man like Volkov to read, but what I found on the first shelf was an assortment of classics, my favorite—*Doctor Zhivago*—among them. One shelf was filled with design and Gothic architecture books. Higher still was a collection of mythology. I had just reached for a well-worn copy of *Mythical Creatures: A Sixteenth-Century Bestiary* when a man's deep voice broke the silence.

"Ms. James."

When I'd imagined the elusive Max Volkov, I'd envisioned someone older, with a receding hairline. I'd thought he would be moderately fit, in that way middle-aged men who loved to golf were kind of fit. He'd have an affable charm that hid the shark underneath. His office would be filled with diplomas and a certificate heralding his membership in the Rotary Club, or some other organization of respectable men.

The real-life Maxim Volkov was anything but middle aged or charming. If I'd had to guess, I'd put the man standing in front of me in his late thirties, surprisingly young for a reclusive businessman. The man was well over six foot and built like an NFL linebacker. Maybe he played for the Kansas City Chiefs, poor soul, before the golden age of Patrick Mahomes.

I made a mental note to Google "Max Volkov" and "Kansas City Chiefs" when I got home. Perhaps he'd started Volkov Industries after sustaining a career-ending injury, probably in his late twenties. Smart man. The haunted house investment was still a head scratcher.

Unlike my imaginary Max Volkov, this man looked out of place in the tailored business suit he wore. He hadn't bothered with a tie, and his dress shirt was unbuttoned a couple of buttons as if the mere thought of a closed collar was suffocating.

"Please, call me Kali." I introduced myself with a soft smile meant to break the ice. "Thank you for seeing me."

He ignored my outstretched hand. "You're here, Ms. James, because you ask a lot of questions."

I dropped my hand and followed him into his office, settling into one of the leather chairs in front of his sleek mahogany desk. "It's not every day I stumble over a dead body. I'd say that warrants a few questions."

He remained standing. "It's generally better to leave the questions for the police. It is unfortunate enough that you had to witness such…unpleasantness."

"Far more unfortunate for Jack Gates," I said, raising an eyebrow.

"Indeed."

I tapped the gold-lettered nameplate on his desk. I considered going straight for the jugular, even though I had assured Craig I wouldn't confront Volkov about his alleged criminal ties. He was already scowling, so I attempted a softer opening.

"About Gates."

"What about him?"

So much for a soft opening. "You know, for most businesses, a dead body would be a serious crowd killer, but for your haunted house," I looked him in the eye, "dead men just seem to add to the theater, now don't they?"

Volkov studied me the way my dermatologist studied a new mole. "What precisely are you implying?"

If the rigid set of his shoulders was any indication, this line of questioning wasn't going to get me far. "I'm not implying anything. It's just been a hard few days. Please," I said, indicating his own chair. "You're giving me a crick in my neck."

He glided past me and settled his big body in the tall-backed chair behind his desk.

"What do you know about the man who was murdered at your place of business?"

He took his time answering. "Probably about as much as you know, Ms. James. He was a reporter with *The Kansas City Star*, thirty-seven, unmarried, no kids. Craig tells me he wrote a review for Howl several weeks before his death." He paused. "Glowing, apparently."

"You didn't read it?"

"No, I did not."

Weird. "And Gates didn't contact you for a quote for the review?"

"All PR for Howl is handled by Ruby. I do not have the time nor the temperament to be a spokesperson, Ms. James."

He had that right. From what I'd seen of Ruby, I was skeptical that her temperament was any better suited to public relations than his, but I kept that observation to myself.

"Have you talked to the police since his death?"

"Of course."

"And?" I prompted.

"And, as I'm sure they have told you, they are working on any leads they may have."

"Do they have any leads?" Even if he had been privy to such information, he wasn't likely to share it with me, but I still asked. It was always best to cover the bases. Occasionally, I got lucky.

"If by lead, you mean me, you'll be sadly disappointed." He crossed his arms and leaned back in his chair, emphasizing the breadth of his shoulders under his expensive suit jacket—on purpose, no doubt. "I'm a simple businessman, regardless of what silly rumors the actors from competing houses have dreamed up."

I let that go, not willing to put Riley any more in the crosshairs of a man like Volkov than she already was. "Of course."

"But," he said, standing up and moving to my side of the desk, his body now crowding into my personal space. "I'm concerned that your continued fascination with this case will lead you into trouble." The underlying edge in his voice was a warning.

I'd known plenty of men like Volkov, men who played dominance games with their body language. I narrowed my eyes and leaned into him. "I've lived there most of my life."

"Perhaps," he continued as if he hadn't heard me, "you would be better off leaving the detective work to the actual police before you get in over your pretty head."

"I appreciate your concern. Really. Thank you. But I'm having a hard time letting go of the image of Jack Gates lying in a pool of his own blood in your haunted house. I would think the fact that he was found on your property, in your place of business, would make you anxious to find the murderer. And frankly, I find your lack of interest in the matter more than a little odd."

"Oh sweetheart," he said, the flash of his teeth saying he knew damn well he was pushing my buttons. "Rest assured that this case has my undivided attention."

Jack strolled through the door as if he were invited to this appointment. *Speak of the devil.* He stopped directly behind Volkov so that he was staring at me from over Volkov's shoulder. "Ask him what kind of people he hires off the books."

"What?" I hissed.

Volkov frowned and repeated my question. "What?"

I cleared my throat and looked toward the door, hoping Jack would take the hint. "What...are you going to do about it?"

"Nothing. I trust the police to do their job. Perhaps you should get out of their way and let the professionals take care of this. This is not something you want to be in the middle of," Volkov said.

Jack slammed his hand down on Volkov's desk, and even though there was no force behind it, I jumped a little anyway.

"Ask him."

"Scared of something?" Volkov sounded pleased, as if his intimidation routine had made me jumpy.

I glared at Jack but directed my question at Volkov. "How many people do you have working for you?"

Volkov scowled. "I'm not in the habit of talking payroll with busybodies."

I smiled as if he hadn't just insulted me. "And how many of those employees are off the books?" From the way he narrowed his eyes, I could tell I hit a nerve.

"Ask him about the guy he hired off the books the night I was killed," Jack insisted.

That was news to me. It would have been nice if Jack had been this forthcoming earlier. I wanted to grill Jack about it, but I couldn't do that without looking crazy, so I relayed the question to Volkov.

"You should watch yourself." Volkov's voice was low and dangerous.

I stood up. "Are you threatening me, Mr. Volkov?"

"I don't make threats."

As hard as I tried, I couldn't meet his eyes. That didn't stop me from pressing the issue. "You didn't answer the question. Did you hire someone to kill Jack Gates?"

"What?" Volkov and Jack asked at the same time.

Jack shook his head. "You're really jumping to conclusions there."

If I could have leapt over the desk and punched Jack, I would have. He and I were going to have a little come-to-Jesus talk when we walked out of here.

Oddly enough, Volkov seemed to relax at the accusation of murder-for-hire. Some of the tension went out of the room, and I was able to look him in the eye again.

"You have quite the imagination. I suppose that's to be expected in your line of work." He made it sound like I was working street corners.

"Look, I am going to keep digging, whether you like it or not. You can either clear up my questions, or you can stay out of my way. But make no mistake, I will find out what you are hiding."

He laughed, the sound rumbling through the room. "I'm not hiding anything."

"In my experience, only men hiding something tell people to stop asking questions." I left his office without looking back. Jack was smart enough to not follow me out.

The next day, I slept later than usual. When I woke, it was in stages, the smell of coffee hitting me first. My sleep-addled brain didn't immediately register the fact that I lived alone, so it took me a few minutes to panic.

Once I was fully awake, I didn't waste time getting dressed. I hastily tied my ratty terrycloth robe over my nightgown. After grabbing the taser I kept in my nightstand, I paused at the door to listen for intruders. I wasn't sure what kind of person broke into someone's house to make coffee, but I wasn't taking any chances.

I opened the bedroom door and cautiously made my way to the kitchen. My stomach growled as soon as the smell of bacon registered. Riley was perched on one of my kitchen chairs, guzzling a glass of orange juice.

"Damn it, Riley!"

She eyed the taser still clutched in my hand. "Wow, girl. You don't mess around." She gave me a thumbs up and went back to her orange juice.

"Good morning, beautiful," Gavin said as I rounded the corner into the kitchen. His back was to me as he flipped a perfectly cooked omelet on my stove.

I dropped the taser into my robe pocket before he noticed it. "Gavin, how did you get in here?"

Before I could register what he was doing, Gavin leaned down and planted a kiss on top of my head. It was way too early for this.

He pointed to Riley with his spatula. "Your roommate let me in."

"Riley and I are not roommates." I ducked a hug from Gavin and turned to Riley. "And how exactly did you get in here?"

Riley shrugged. "Maybe you left your door unlocked."

"I didn't."

Riley grinned at me over the top of her glass. "A man who can cook and rock a pair of leather pants. I can see why Kali kept you to herself."

I looked at Gavin. Sure enough, he was wearing leather pants and a loosely fitted button-down shirt. His long black hair was tied back at his nape. He looked like a freaking pirate. All he needed was the eye patch.

"Did your key work?" he asked, still waving the spatula in the air.

Riley perked up. "Key?"

"Yup! Worked great." I changed the subject before she could pepper me with more questions I didn't want to answer. "Why are you here, Gavin?"

"Just wanted to stop by and see my girl," he said.

I groaned. Before I could correct him, Gavin handed me a plate piled high with thick-sliced bacon and a cheese omelet filled with sauteed onions and mushrooms. He gestured for me to take a seat and put a steaming cup of coffee in front of me. Then, he set a second plate in front of Riley. It really was too bad that he was so clingy. The man could cook a mean omelet. My eyes practically rolled back in my head at the first bite.

"Riley told me all about what you've been going through. Breakfast is the least I can do."

I raised an eyebrow and looked at Riley.

"Jack Gates," she said around a mouthful of eggs.

Someone knocked on the door, saving me from a long, drawn-out conversation about Jack. After yesterday's debacle in Volkov's office, the last person I wanted to talk about was Jack.

I opened the door expecting Emma, since she was the only person who normally dropped by my apartment this early. But when I opened the door, I came face-to-face with Craig. The way he'd left things, I hadn't expected to hear from him again until after Jack's killer was in police custody. I was surprised to see him on my doorstep.

Craig cleared his throat, and I looked down. My robe had

come untied, exposing the thin, red satin chemise I was wearing beneath it. I quickly retied my robe and invited him in, only remembering Gavin after Craig took a step in the door.

This morning couldn't get any worse. I understood what it looked like, me standing here fresh from bed while a man cooked me breakfast. "This isn't what it looks like," I said quietly.

Gavin didn't waste any time, stepping up behind me and trying to put an arm around my waist. I quickly stepped away from him.

Gavin wasn't easily deterred. "Who do we have here, honey?"

I stand corrected. Definitely worse.

Craig took one look at Gavin, pirate outfit and all, and his mouth quirked up. I closed my eyes and prayed for the floor to swallow me.

"Craig Ward." He reached out to shake Gavin's hand.

Riley turned around and waved at Craig before getting up for seconds.

"Are you hungry?" Gavin asked, playing host. "I made plenty."

"No, thank you. Don't let me interrupt your breakfast." He was looking at me when he answered. "I just need to speak to Kali for a moment." Craig was all business now, any hint of a smile gone.

I wanted to talk to him in private, to explain Gavin's status as my ex. The only two options for that were to invite him into my bedroom—awkward—or to step outside. I slid my feet into the slip-on shoes I kept near the door and motioned for Craig to join me outside.

"Hold up." Riley intercepted us before we could leave. She

nudged me out of the way and held her phone up to take a quick picture of Craig. "All good," she said when she was done.

Craig looked at me, but I had no idea why Riley did half the things she did.

"No clue what that was about," I said as I stepped outside. The chilly air hit me, and I pulled the robe tighter around me. "I should explain," I started.

Craig stopped me. "That's a good idea. Why don't you start by explaining what you were doing in my office?"

"What?" I squeaked, taken totally off guard by his question.

He reached into his jacket pocket and pulled out a dog-eared piece of paper with his phone number on it. It was the same sticky note he'd given me the day I went to Howl to see him.

I snatched it out of his hand. "Where did you find this?"

"On the floor beneath my desk." He studied me, waiting for my response.

I forced a smile. "I must have dropped it on my way out that day."

As soon as it was out of my mouth, I knew I'd picked the wrong man to lie to. He didn't contradict me. He just turned away from me and headed for the stairs.

Craig waited until he reached the bottom step for his parting shot. "You're messing with things you don't understand here, Kali. For your own good, stay out of it."

By the time I got back inside, I didn't have the energy for a soft letdown. I thanked Gavin for breakfast before chasing him out of my apartment.

Riley was harder to kick out. While I was showing Gavin the door, she was stealing the food from my plate. Riley was a bottomless pit when it came to food. I let her have it, my appetite long gone.

"What was that about?" I asked. "Taking Craig's picture," I prompted when she looked at me in confusion.

"Oh, that. He's still a suspect, isn't he?"

I didn't want Craig to be a suspect, but want and reality weren't always the same thing. "And?"

"And we need pictures for our board."

I wasn't in the mood to argue, so I let it go. When she asked what Craig wanted, I told her he was just checking on me. She raised an eyebrow but didn't push. Riley finished my breakfast and helped me with the dishes. After she left, I got to work.

Jack hadn't made an appearance since dropping his bombshell at Volkov's office, so I couldn't question him about the off-the-books hires. It had clearly struck a nerve with Volkov though, so I knew I was on to something.

If Volkov was hiring someone he didn't want on the books, there had to be a good reason for it. Criminal activity was a pretty good reason, which brought me back to the name on the visitor log that belonged to an ex-con. Who better to work off the books for you than someone with an established skill set?

I turned on my computer and skimmed the two articles I'd bookmarked about Leon Matthews, haunted house superfan. I reread the article about a local t-shirt factory that gave ex-cons a second chance.

"I made a terrible mistake when I was younger," he said in the article, "but now I'm rebuilding my life." I read the whole article, but there was no mention of what he had been convicted of.

I spent the next hour searching the state offender registry

and online police reports but came up with nothing. For a man who appeared to be in his late forties, younger could be twenty-five years ago. Plus, there was no guarantee that the crime was even committed in Kansas City. There were hundreds of little towns across Kansas and Missouri, many of them without independent police offices much less online records. And that was if he had even been in Kansas or Missouri when he committed the crime. There were forty-eight other states he could have been a resident of at the time.

Online research was only going to get me so far. The fastest route to information was to go directly to the source. I shifted gears and searched for a home address. No luck. I did, however, find an address for the factory where Matthews worked. It was a start.

CHAPTER 14

*B*lending in wasn't really my thing, which meant I had to search for clothing appropriate for a stake-out. If this was going to become a regular occurrence, I would need to stock up on jeans and sweatshirts. I worked with what I had, pulling on faded boot-cut jeans from the back of my closet. To fight off the early morning chill, I wore a dark merino wool sweater I'd scored for under ten bucks at my favorite thrift store and a black windbreaker Emma had left at the shop.

Although the t-shirt factory was a short drive from my apartment, I chose the thirty-minute bus ride, leaving my too-distinctive car at home. I didn't know whether t-shirt manu-facturing had enough demand to warrant multiple shifts, but since Leon Matthews kept popping up at the haunted house, I was confident that he didn't work nights. To be safe, I took an early morning route that got me there before 7:00 a.m.

I stepped off the bus, taking in the surroundings. Online, the warehouse looked run-down; in person, it looked worse. From the bus stop, I had a view of the building's nondescript walls of concrete, broken only by a row of dirty windows. I settled onto the park bench, angling my body to see both the parking lot and the building.

I waited a good forty minutes before anyone showed up. I stood to stretch my legs as the first car pulled into the lot, and a woman dressed in head-to-toe denim climbed out. It wasn't long before a stream of employees began arriving. I hoped Matthews would show. The newspaper article about ex-cons had been published over a year ago. It was possible he no longer worked here.

I spotted him a few minutes before 8:00, walking in with two other men. Matthews looked rougher in person than he had in the articles. Despite walking in with coworkers, he didn't share their morning banter. Instead, he walked stiffly beside them, his pinched features not inviting conversation. He was a big man, average height but stocky. Dressed in jeans and coat, it was hard to say whether his bulk was muscle, but he made the two men walking next to him look skinny by comparison. None of them so much as glanced at me. Once they were inside, I checked my watch. Fifteen minutes later, I was back on a bus bound for home.

Now that I had found him, I needed to figure out what I wanted to do about it. I'd like to strong-arm Jack into coming back with me, so I could give him my version of a police lineup to see if he recognized Matthews. Unfortunately, sitting in a lemon-yellow Volkswagen Beetle while talking to a dead man was guaranteed to get me noticed.

Plan B was to tail Matthews home.

That was as far as I got with Plan B, following an ex-felon to his house and lurking about. It wasn't like I could just outright ask him if Max Volkov hired him to kill Gates. I could do what the police would do: ask his neighbors if they noticed anything weird, but that would tip Matthews off. It also wasn't likely to get me anywhere.

No one thought they lived next door to a killer. Even the BTK killer's neighbors thought he was a real standup guy, never guessing that the man they waved to while mowing their lawns and grabbing the mail was a serial killer. The guy spent two decades murdering people, mostly women, and sending taunting letters to police, all while installing security systems and working as a city compliance officer. Even his wife and kids had no idea who they'd lived with.

No, it had to be Matthews himself that I questioned. Usually, I asked myself what Dad would do, but playing cop wasn't going to cut it. Without a badge, it complicated things. I closed my eyes and leaned my head against the bus window, racking my brain for a way I could grill Matthews without ending up dead and buried in his back yard.

What would Jack do? And then I had it. Leon Matthews didn't shy away from the spotlight; the frequent newspaper quotes and photos demonstrated that much. If I posed as a reporter writing an article about the haunted house murder, I was betting he'd be more than happy to talk to me. I'd throw in some questions about Jack and about Volkov and see how Matthews reacted.

First, I needed his phone number. I'd already searched online with no luck. While rooting around in someone's trash looking for a cell phone bill wasn't my first choice, I wasn't above it either. I could call his employer, but the chances of them handing out his number were slim to none. If I left a message, I risked him not calling me back or worse, calling the paper to ask if I worked there. A neighbor might have his number though, which brought me right back to following him after work tonight to find where he lived.

Tailing him at 5:00 meant I'd either have to close the shop early or ask Emma to stay late to cover for me. I picked up my phone and dialed Emma, who answered after the first ring.

"Hey Em. I hate to ask this, but I need a favor."

She didn't hesitate. "Of course. What do you need?"

"I know this is short notice, but could you work this afternoon?"

"Sure," she agreed. "What's up?"

I hated lying to her, but I wasn't about to tell her I was planning on following an ex-felon to his house. I didn't want her involved in this, not the talking to the dead and certainly not the hunt for Jack's killer. And it wasn't just because I was afraid she wouldn't believe me. I was more afraid that she would, that I'd drag her down into the darkness that was lurking around the edges of my life. Emma was like my sister Claire had been, soft and kind-hearted. I wanted her to stay that way.

"My tooth is killing me," I lied. "My dentist can get me in at 4:30, but I'd need to leave by 4:00 to make the appointment. If you've got plans, I can close up early, but…"

She cut me off. "It's not a problem. I can stay and close up."

"I owe you one." I could see my bus stop ahead, so I cut the call short.

Before heading down to the shop, I swapped my sweater out for a long-sleeved black and nude lace shirt. Even with the dressier shirt, Emma raised her eyebrows.

"Jeans?" she teased. "You must be feeling bad."

"I've felt better." That much was true; it just had nothing to do with my tooth. Emma gave me a quick sympathy hug, and

I handed her the key. "I'm not sure how long this will take. Can you lock up at 6:00?"

She nodded. "Go," she said, shooing me out the door.

When I got to my car, I put on the windbreaker I'd left on the seat and a dark baseball hat from my costume props. I wasn't planning on getting out of my car, so I hoped it would be enough to disguise my face. My car was another story. In hindsight, I wished I hadn't sprung for the wash and wax last week. A little dirt would have at least knocked down the shine.

I parked in front of the pawn shop down the street rather than in the factory parking lot, hoping the distance would be enough to keep me off Matthews' radar. I still had a clear view of the door, allowing me to watch for Matthews leaving work. I also had a view of the parking lot to see which car he got into.

It was fifteen minutes before the door opened, and a group walked out, Matthews among them. I held my phone up to my ear, talking to myself, just in case he looked my way. He didn't. While his coworkers chatted and joked, he headed straight to an old blue and white Chevy pickup. Thankfully, he didn't drive a white Corolla. His truck would at least stand out in traffic.

I waited until a couple other cars pulled out before following him. I hung back until he hit I-70. Not wanting to miss him exiting, I passed a semi that was between us before dropping back again and following him onto I-35. He took the Broadway exit and drove several blocks before parking in front of a small, one-story white house. I drove past, giving him a good five minutes before circling back to the convenience store on the corner.

I pulled up the maps app on my phone to drop a pin on his

location, so I could come back tomorrow morning while he was at work. I looked at the houses around his. It was a block of modest homes and cracked sidewalks, not exactly the kind of neighborhood where people chatted while walking their dogs.

Several of the houses had porches, but most were empty, without so much as a plastic chair. The exception was a house three doors down from his. Its porch was better kept than the others, with fresh paint, a pair of wicker chairs, and an assortment of potted plants. If I had to put money on it, I'd guess that it was owned by an older woman or a retired couple. That house would be my first stop tomorrow. If I was lucky, I'd catch her outside drinking her morning coffee. I hoped she was as friendly as her porch looked.

My stomach growled, reminding me that I'd skipped lunch. I grabbed my purse and went inside to get a candy bar and a cup of bad coffee, needing a quick shot of energy. One sip of the coffee was all it took to dump it on the curb. Even as bone tired as I was, I wasn't desperate enough to drink convenience store coffee. I started my car.

Before I could pull out, Matthews came out of his house. He had traded his work clothes for nicer blue jeans and a dark button-down shirt. He got in his truck and headed north. I considered following him, but I didn't want to push my luck. Because he'd changed his clothes, I was guessing Matthews was headed somewhere that would take longer than a simple errand.

I took off my baseball cap and laid it on the seat next to me, fluffed my hair, and swiped on some dusky pink lipstick. Since I was already here, I might as well get a closer look at his house. If I happened upon a neighbor and could save myself a trip tomorrow, all the better.

I headed up the sidewalk to Matthews' house first, intending to act like I was looking for him, in case any neighbors were snooping out their windows.

As I climbed the steps to his front porch, a man parked in front of the next house over. I made a show of knocking loudly on the front door. When the man made it to his porch, I looked up. "Excuse me," I said, waving to get his attention.

I didn't hear the door open.

"Yeah?" The woman standing in Matthews' doorway was dressed in a Judas Priest t-shirt and ripped blue jeans. She appeared to be in her mid-60s. Too old to be a girlfriend, I assumed she must be Matthews' mother.

I stood up a little taller and improvised. "Hello. I'm looking for Leon Matthews."

She didn't smile back. "He's not here. What do you want?"

"I'm Karen Jones." I sucked at coming up with fake names. "I'm a reporter for *The Kansas City Star*." I gave her my best impression of a news anchor smile.

Her face brightened, and she swung the screen door open. Apparently, my hunch about Matthews being a media hog was a good one.

"Oh, you just missed him." She gestured inside. "Come in."

I followed her into a room that looked more like a bachelor pad than the home of a man who lived with his mother. There was a pile of shoes next to the door, and empty food wrappers and newspapers littered the coffee table. The couch was bare, but the chair next to it held a pile of unfolded laundry. She grabbed the remote to mute the TV and sat down on the couch, offering me the seat next to her.

"I don't want to take up a lot of your time, Ms.?" I paused to let her fill in the blank.

"Matthews, but you can call me Patty. I'm Leon's mom."

"Patty," I said, wishing I had a notebook so I would at least look the part. "I'm writing a story about the haunted houses and was hoping Leon would be willing to give me a quote."

She frowned. "But Leon just did an interview for an article on a haunted house." She rummaged around the stack of newspapers until she came up with the clipped article about Howl and handed it to me.

Crap. "Of course," I hedged. "That's why I'm reaching out to him. I'd like to do a follow-up story now that there's been a murder in one of the houses."

"You're writing about that murder?"

"No, no," I said. The last thing I wanted was for Matthews to think I was poking around looking for the killer. "I'm writing an article for the business section about the impact of escalating crime rates on tourism." I silently congratulated myself for coming up with that one on the fly.

"That was a bad deal."

"A real tragedy," I agreed.

"Leon loves those haunted houses. He goes nearly every weekend they are open. He's been glued to the news since it happened. He wanted to go back the next night, even called the haunted house to see when they'd be open again. Can you believe that?" She shook her head. "I told him he was crazy. Whoever killed that reporter was psycho, doing it like that in a crowd full of people."

I nodded my agreement. "It's just terrible. I can understand why you'd be worried about Leon going back there, but I'm sure the police will catch whoever did it soon," I assured her. "I would love to talk to a few regulars, like your son, to get their thoughts on the murder and whether it will change how often they are willing to go. It sounds like Leon would be the perfect person to talk to." I smiled apologetically. "I'm sorry to just drop in like this. I would have called first, but his phone number wasn't listed."

She stood up and headed for the kitchen. "Let me grab a pen and paper, and I'll give you his number," she called over her shoulder.

She came back waving a small piece of paper. Before she could hand it to me, the front door swung open, and Leon Matthews walked inside.

CHAPTER 15

*P*atty looked almost as surprised as I did to see her son.

"Forgot my wallet." His voice was rough, like a lifelong smoker, and his eyes never left my face. "Who's this?"

I stood up, stepping around the coffee table and moving closer to Leon, which also happened to be closer to the door, should I need it.

"Hi Leon. My name is Karen Jones, and I'm with *The Kansas City Star*. I'm writing a story about the haunted houses and was hoping you'd have some time to talk to me."

He didn't move from where he stood blocking the exit.

I cleared my throat and continued. "I'm writing about the impact of the recent murder on peoples' willingness to venture back to the haunted houses, particularly Howl." I watched his face closely for any reaction, but his expression gave nothing away. He did, however, take a step into the room, clearing a pathway to the front door. "It looks like you are busy, though. I'm happy to catch you another time. Your mom gave me your number. I'll be in touch." I tried to edge my way past him.

Before I could reach for the handle, he braced his arm across the door. "I can make time now."

"I'll make some coffee," Patty chirped before scuttling out of the room.

For a minute, we both stood there awkwardly until he pointed at the couch I'd just left.

"Sit."

"Okay." I turned my back to him despite the little voice in my head that was screaming *get out now while you still can*. I could feel him at my back as I made my way across the room.

Leon didn't join me on the couch. Instead, he scooped up the pile of clothes from the chair and deposited them on the floor before sitting down. I could hear coffee brewing from the other room, but Patty stayed in the kitchen. Without a buffer, I chose to launch right in. The sooner I got him talking, the sooner I could get out of here.

"Your mother tells me that you are Howl's number one fan."

He grunted and nodded, giving me precious little to go on.

"I'm assuming you heard about the murder."

Again, he nodded. "You knew him, right?" he asked, his face neutral. At first, I wasn't sure who he was referring to. "The dead guy. Gates," he prompted. When I didn't respond immediately, he continued. "You worked together. You must have known him."

Of course. "A little," I said. "Jack Gates was the kind of guy who kept to himself." If only that were true, I'd be neck deep in a bubble bath right now instead of sitting in a stranger's home interrogating a potential murderer.

His face was shrewd. "It must have been a shock to have someone you worked with turn up dead."

I shifted uncomfortably. "It was. But you probably knew him about as well as I did, having met with him for the Howl interview."

Leon didn't so much as blink. "Not really. He just showed up on opening night and started asking everyone in line questions."

"Mmmm. That makes sense." I smiled at Leon, trying to break the ice, but he didn't smile back. "I am here because I wanted to do a follow-up with some regulars. Your mother mentioned that you were anxious to go back once Howl opened again. Were you nervous at all, after the murder?"

"Nervous?" He furrowed his brow. "Not really."

"You didn't worry that there was a murderer on the loose?"

"Nah. I'm a big guy. People don't usually mess with me."

"No, I suppose they don't."

Leon leaned forward in his chair, his knees bumping the coffee table between us. "Is that why you came here?"

"What?" I calculated the distance between me and the door. "I don't know what you mean."

He smirked at me. "Were you nervous to go to Howl to interview regulars? Is that why you came here?"

"I guess I was," I said, forcing a lightness I didn't feel into my voice. "Much better to sit down over a friendly cup of coffee, right?"

He nodded. "What do you want to know?"

I wanted to know if he had cut Jack Gates' throat and left his dead body for me to stumble over. But what I asked was whether he had ever seen anything odd or threatening while at Howl.

"A lot of things are odd at a haunted house, Karen."

"Yes. I imagine they are. But since you go there frequently…"

He cut me off. "Every week."

Interesting. Almost like he worked there off the books. "Since you go there every week, you would notice if anything seemed off lately, right?" I tried flattery. "Clearly, you are the kind of man who pays attention to what's going on."

"I do." This time, his smile held a hint of friendliness, which, strangely enough, did nothing to settle my nerves. "The only odd thing I saw was a dog on opening night."

"A dog?" I had no idea why a dog would be noteworthy. "What kind of dog?"

"A mean one. I could hear it snarling and growling."

"You couldn't see it clearly?"

"Not really. I just caught a glimpse of it through an open door. From what I could see, it was a big dog. Almost looked like a wolf."

Few of the rooms in the haunted house had doors to get in the way of traffic flow through the house.

"Where was this door?"

"First floor, down the hall. I think it was the security office."

"I guess security could have had a dog on-site," I said, even though having a guard dog in a house full of drunk revelers seemed more like a lawsuit-in-waiting than a valid security plan. Plus, I'd been in Craig's office twice now, and there had been no sign of a dog.

"Well, Craig seemed surprised. Craig is head of security at Howl," he explained, demonstrating that he was on a first-name basis with staff.

"And was he surprised to see the dog?"

"Oh yeah. Rushed right in the room and shut the door

behind him. When Craig came back out, everything seemed fine."

"Hmmm. Was there anyone else there that you saw? Someone who brought the dog?" I decided this was as good of an opening as any to see just how familiar Leon was with Howl's owner. "Like Mr. Volkov?"

"Who?" His confusion seemed genuine.

"Howl's owner." When that still didn't spark a response from Leon, I changed the subject. "Were you there the night of the murder?"

Even though I knew very well he had been, since his name on the visitor list was the whole reason I was here, I wanted to see if he'd own it.

He leaned forward. "Oh yeah. I was there."

I kept my expression carefully neutral. "Did you see Jack Gates?"

"No." Leon looked disappointed. "But I talked to the police after."

"They took you to the police station?"

"Nah. They just asked everyone in line a few questions. Then I came home."

The fact that the police questioned him and let him walk away so easily surprised me. Perhaps they hadn't run a criminal check during on-site questioning. Or maybe they were in Volkov's pocket. Men with enough money tended to operate by a different set of rules, even with law enforcement.

"Did you see anything that stood out that night?"

He shook his head. "Other than the cops? No."

"The police believe that the only way the killer could have left was through the back alley. It makes sense you wouldn't have seen him." I left out the bit about me knowing this because I was in said room when the police arrived.

"Maybe," Leon said, a glint in his eye that looked suspiciously like excitement. "Or he could have gone out through the staff exit in the next room. It leads down to the gift shop, you know."

Patty interrupted before he could say more. "How do you take your coffee? Creamer?"

"Just black is fine with me. Thank you."

She nodded and headed back into the kitchen.

Why did Leon know so much about escape routes from the murder site? Even though she wasn't in the room with us anymore, I was banking on the fact that Leon wouldn't kill me in front of his mother when I asked my next question. If I was sitting across from Gates' killer, I figured the damage was already done. I might as well barrel forward.

"How do you know which room Gates was found in?"

Leon didn't look me in the eyes. "I asked."

Patty came back in the room holding two cups of steaming coffee. She handed the first to me and sat the second on the coffee table in front of Leon. "Do you need help?" she asked him.

He glared at her. "I can do it."

I had flashbacks to every hillbilly slasher movie I'd ever watched and kicked myself for assuming Leon's mom would be harmless. "Oh no, look at the time. I should get going," I said, standing abruptly. "Thanks for your time, Leon."

Leon looked confused. Patty looked offended.

"Don't be silly," she said. "You haven't even touched your coffee."

Nope. And I wasn't about to drink coffee after that conversation. Bitter grocery store coffee seemed tailor made to hide a smidge of arsenic. I wasn't taking any chances.

"I'm sorry. I forgot that I was supposed to meet Detective

Woodson for an interview this evening." I hoped name-dropping a police officer might give me an opening to get out of here, or at least make them think twice about sawing my body into teeny tiny pieces. Assuming, of course, that Woodson wasn't on Volkov's payroll.

Patty was standing between me and the door.

"Okay," Leon said, his full concentration on the coffee cup he was lifting to his lips. His hands shook, coffee sloshing over the sides of the cup and onto the carpet.

Patty moved toward him. "Why can't you ever accept my help?"

Leon brushed her away. "I'm not an invalid."

It became clear the help she was offering had nothing to do with disposing of my body. Curious, I stayed where I was, staring at his still trembling hand.

Leon looked up at me as his shoulders drooped. "I hate this damn shaking."

I didn't know what to say to that, so I waited.

"Parkinson's," Patty said.

"Stage 2," Leon elaborated. "It comes and goes."

"I'm sorry," I said. "That must be difficult."

For the first time since I met him, Leon looked small.

"I still have some good days, but they are less frequent. I hate feeling useless. I'm a grown man who has to have his mom cut up his steak for him like a damn toddler. Do you have any idea what that's like?"

"No, I don't." I should have left, but instead, I sat back down on the couch and lifted the coffee cup to my lips. "Detective Woodson can wait. You seem to have the insider scoop. Can you tell me more about Howl, Leon?"

I let him talk for the next half an hour, prodding him for information about the staff, the house layout, and the history.

By the time I left, I had a wealth of information but no idea how any of it was useful. One thing I could do was rule out Matthews as a suspect. Barring a knife-wielding accomplice, it was obvious that Leon Matthews had nothing to do with Jack's death.

Investigation or not, some things couldn't wait. The trash piling up in my apartment was one of them. I had punched down the collection of empty takeout containers and junk mail as many times as I could before my cheap plastic trash can was so bloated, I couldn't even stack things on top anymore. I wrestled the bag out, pausing long enough to stuff the overflow into a shopping bag before heading down the stairs to the dumpster in the back alley. Although it was barely after 7:00, it was already dusk, with just enough fading sunlight to cast shadows that spanned the alleyway.

I had just pitched the bag into the dumpster when I felt someone's presence behind me. For a second, I froze. A younger version of me would have chalked it up to an active imagination, but I'd seen too many dead bodies to still be that girl.

I slid my left hand into the pocket of my pajamas, securing the taser I had started carrying after my last encounter with Twitch. I spun around as quickly as my drugstore flip-flops would let me, aiming the taser in front of me as I turned.

"Woah," Jack said, holding his hands up as if he were still corporeal enough to be threatened by electrocution.

I dropped the taser back into my pocket.

"Could you not creep up on me in dark alleys?" I was still irritated with him for withholding information.

"I don't creep. You're just jumpy."

"Wonder why," I muttered.

Jack was agitated, shifting his gaze between me and the end of the alley.

"What do you want?"

"You need to go to my apartment." When I didn't immediately move, he reached out as if to grab my arm.

I stepped back. "I'm not dressed for field trips." I may have been willing to risk someone spotting me outside my apartment in pajama pants and pink flip-flops, but I wasn't about to go out in public looking like this. "What's at your apartment anyway?"

He looked up and down the alley as if he expected someone to be lurking around us. Satisfied we were alone, he turned back to me. "My work."

"You mean the story you were writing?"

He nodded.

I narrowed my eyes. "Why didn't you tell me where it was to begin with?"

Jack ran his hand through his hair and looked over his shoulder again. "I needed you to tie up some loose ends first."

"Like Volkov?" I didn't even try to keep my annoyance out of my voice. I was tired of his half-truths and manipulations. I was doing him a favor by hunting down his killer; the least he could do was cooperate.

"Yes," he said, acknowledging he set me up in Volkov's office.

"Not cool, Jack."

He didn't even have the decency to fake remorse. "I needed to see how he'd react."

"How did you even know he hires people off the books?"

"I overheard a conversation."

165

I frowned. "You heard Volkov talking about hiring people off the books?"

Jack fidgeted but didn't answer right away.

I had been around him enough to pick up on his tells. "Don't even think about lying to me. Who was Volkov talking to?"

"My source."

I let out a frustrated breath. Protecting a source was all well and good, but surely that responsibility didn't extend postmortem. "You know, this would be a lot easier if you'd just tell me who your source was."

"Forget about the source. We need to go get my story before someone else finds it," he insisted.

"Why are you suddenly so worried about someone finding it?"

Jack didn't answer.

"Is the story about Max Volkov?" I asked. "Were you investigating possible criminal ties?"

Jack gave me a funny look, his eyes darting to the end of the alley as if to ensure we were still alone. "It's not that simple."

"Explain it to me, then."

"No. You need to read it for yourself." Jack leaned in, his voice becoming more urgent and his movements more aggressive. "Otherwise, you won't believe me."

"I will," I assured him.

"You won't." He lunged for my hand again, but I jerked it back. Jack threw his hands up in frustration. "Look, it's important. You're the only one who can break the story now that..." He paused, lifting his fingers to his neck. "Now that I'm dead."

It would be a lot quicker if Jack would drop the cloak and

dagger routine and tell me what he'd been working on. Even if it was an investigative piece on Volkov's shady business dealings, I didn't know why he thought I wouldn't believe him. Unless it was bigger than that. Perhaps Max Volkov was just the tip of the proverbial iceberg.

I bit my lip. "It's at your apartment?"

Jack's shoulders loosened, and he nodded. "I'll take you."

I glanced down at my pajamas. "I'm not going like this."

"Who cares what you're wearing?"

"Have you met me?" I asked. "How far away is your apartment, anyway?"

"A mile, give or take," he said.

"I'm not about to walk a mile, half dressed, through the sketchy part of Kansas City in the middle of the night for a story. No story is worth that risk."

He looked as outraged as any investigative reporter worth his salt would have been. "This one is."

I didn't budge. "It's going to have to wait until tomorrow."

Jack opened his mouth to argue, but I cut him off. "No. I'm tired, I've had a craptastic week, and I have a date with a pint of double chocolate chunk ice cream. Meet me at my car at 8:00 a.m. tomorrow, and we'll go get your story."

He ground his teeth, but after a minute, he conceded. "Fine. Tomorrow." He walked past the overflowing dumpster before disappearing.

And if that wasn't a metaphor for my life these days, I didn't know what was.

CHAPTER 16

I was rooting around in my purse for my keys, concentrating on balancing a strawberry cream cheese bagel and a thermos of extra strong coffee, which is why I didn't see Riley until I was almost to my car. She was perched dead center on the roof of the Volkswagen, her legs crossed underneath her. As soon as she saw me, she blew a bubble with her chewing gum and waved.

"Finally," she said. "You're here."

"What are you doing on top of my car?"

"Waiting for you." She rolled her eyes. "Obviously."

"But why are you waiting for me?" I set my bagel next to her, so I could open the door and put my coffee inside. She grabbed it and took a bite.

"Really?"

"We can share." She slid the other half of the bagel toward me.

"How did you even know I'd come to my car this morning?" It wasn't like I was a big driver. Most of my life revolved around a six-block radius of my shop. More often than not, my car stayed parked.

She unfolded her legs and scooted to the passenger side before hopping to the ground. "I didn't. I was waiting for you to come down to open the shop."

"On top of my car?"

She grinned. "I like climbing." She said it as if that was a normal thing for a twenty-something-year-old woman to do.

"Um, okay. Sorry, but I'm running late this morning. What do you need?"

"Where you going?"

"I need to pick up something for a friend," I said, trying to keep it vague.

"What friend?" Riley wasn't your typical wave-as-you-drive-by kind of neighbor. I should have known she wouldn't let up that easily.

I debated using Em for cover, but knowing Riley, she'd just ask Emma later what she needed me to pick up. Instead, I tried to shift the subject. "I really am running late. Let's catch up tonight. We can even start your murder board," I said, trying to placate her.

She scrunched up her nose. "Murder board? That's just creepy, Kali."

"Your words." I should have brought ibuprofen.

Riley looked at me over the car, all wide-eyed innocence, before pulling the door open and sliding into the passenger seat. "I'll come with you."

I had no idea how to dislodge her from my car. I took a long drink of my still scalding hot coffee while praying for patience.

"Riley."

"Kali."

"You can't come with me."

"Why not?" She tapped her fingers on the dash. "Unless you're sneaking off to tail a suspect?"

"Tail a suspect? This isn't a TV show, and we are not cops."

"You are! You were going to leave me behind." She pouted. "And here I thought we were partners."

"Riley," I started again, turning in the seat so that I could look her in the eyes.

"Don't Riley me. I'm coming."

"You don't even know where I'm going."

She dropped the visor to block the morning sun, crossed her arms, and leaned her seat back.

"Fine, but you're staying in the car."

She didn't argue, but she didn't agree, either. I pulled the address Jack had given me up on my maps app and hit navigate. Jack still hadn't made an appearance, but I wasn't in the mood for stalling with small talk. I put the car in reverse and checked the rearview mirror for traffic. Although the street was empty, my backseat was not.

Jack glared at the back of Riley's head from his vantage point. "Who is she?"

Since answering him with Riley playing tag-along was guaranteed to open a can of worms I wasn't ready to deal with, I kept my mouth shut. Every time I glanced in the mirror on the drive to his apartment, Jack was glaring at me, but he didn't ask again.

Jack's building was a nondescript multiplex with your standard hard-to-kill evergreen shrubs dotting the landscape. I parked the car and looked at Riley. "Stay here. I won't be long."

She shrugged and closed her eyes. I crossed my fingers,

hoping she'd fall asleep, because I had no idea how long this would take.

Jack trailed me up the walk. Inside the building, there were four ground-floor apartments and a stairway to the second floor. When Jack didn't volunteer his apartment number, I prodded him.

"Well, which one?"

He brushed past me without saying a word and climbed the stairs, stopping in front of apartment 7. Once there, he walked through the solid wood door and disappeared inside. I rattled the doorknob, but of course, it was locked. I looked under the doormat and felt along the top of the doorframe for a spare key but came up empty-handed.

"That's just great." I knocked on the door in the hopes that Jack would reappear and tell me where to find his key. Several seconds later, I was still looking stupidly at the locked door, with no Jack in sight.

"I could pick that lock for you."

I jumped. I hadn't heard the door open or Riley come upstairs, but she was close enough that I felt her breath on my ear when she spoke. So much for napping in the car. I started to argue with her but then thought better of it. The sooner I got into Jack's apartment, the sooner I could get this story he desperately wanted me to read, a story I hoped would lead me to his killer.

"Can you do that?"

"Pick a lock?" Riley asked. "Easy peasy."

I wasn't sure what I was expecting, but it wasn't the lock-picking kit she pulled out of her back pocket. She winked at me. "I like to be prepared."

Riley obviously had some practice because we were inside the apartment a minute later. It wasn't until we were standing on the threshold that she asked, "Ok, whose house did we just break into?"

At this point, there was little incentive to lie. "Jack Gates."

"No shit?" When I didn't answer right away, she shrugged. "Alrighty. I'll take the kitchen." She headed for the refrigerator, opening the door and leaning inside.

"What are you doing?"

She poked her head around the door and waved a yogurt at me. "Looking for clues."

"In the refrigerator?"

She ducked back inside, only her body visible. Her voice, when it came, was muffled by the door. "It's where I'd hide things."

At least it was something to keep her busy. I looked around for Jack but didn't see him. His apartment was a cross between industrial and modern, with exposed bricks on one wall of the living room and abstract paintings in plain black frames on another. The furniture, while sparse, was midcentury modern and stylish. Unlike my thrift store decorating style, Jack's apartment looked like it belonged in a magazine spread. Everything was in its place.

Jack darted back into the room, visibly upset as he looked under the couch and the coffee table. Not finding what he was looking for, he rocked back on his heels before standing up. "It's gone." His voice was strained.

"What's gone?"

Riley popped her head out of the kitchen where she had been snooping, an unopened yogurt container and spoon in hand. "Huh?"

"Just talking to myself."

Seemingly satisfied, she went back to her snooping.

I looked at Jack, this time whispering. "What's missing?"

"My laptop." He looked around wildly, as if a laptop could be hiding in a room this organized. "Someone took it."

"The story?"

"On it."

I looked around. Everything was neat and orderly. "Anything else missing?"

He shook his head no.

"Are you sure?" The large flat-screen TV and stereo were the only valuables in sight, and both were still here. Perhaps he had a fire safe in a closet.

"I'm sure."

"Then whoever took it came looking for it. Why?"

The look Jack gave me was condescending. "Why do you think?" His voice rose with each word. "They wanted to make sure my story was buried where no one would find it."

As much as I wanted to chalk this up to petty theft, it was hard to argue his point. "Now what?" I knew he wasn't going to let it go. "Can't you just give me the highlight reel?"

"No. You need to read it for yourself."

"Come on, Jack. You're being ridiculous."

Riley rounded the corner. "Jack?" When I opened my mouth to deny it, she held a finger up. "As in, dead reporter Jack?"

"Just thinking out loud."

"And do you usually think out loud with a ghost?"

I didn't say anything, fearing I was just going to dig myself in deeper.

Riley cocked her head to the side and studied me. "Why didn't you just say you were a necromancer?"

I reared back as if she had slapped me. "How do you know about necromancers?"

"Who doesn't?" She peeled the top off her pilfered yogurt

and ate a spoonful, as if we were having a normal conversation.

"It's not something I tell people."

Riley looked hurt. "I'm not just people."

"I didn't mean it like that."

Before I could say more, someone pounded on the front door. "Who's in there?" a woman's voice called out.

I looked at Jack and mouthed, "Do you know who that is?"

"Neighbor."

"Will she leave?" I didn't bother lowering my voice now that Riley knew I was the resident ghost whisperer.

"If you don't come out right now, I'm calling the police," the woman shouted.

Jack sighed. "Not bloody likely."

Riley crossed the room, but I intercepted her before she could reach for the doorknob. "Are you crazy? We can't be seen here."

"Why not? It's his house, right?"

"Dead men don't get to have house guests." I pulled her with me as I headed down the hallway to the bedroom, Jack trailing along behind us.

"Where are we going?" Riley asked.

"Your bedroom is located toward the back of the building, right?" I waited for Jack to confirm it before turning to Riley. "How do you feel about climbing out windows?"

"Yes!" she whooped, beating me into the room. "Looks like someone beat us to it."

Sure enough, the window was wide open, and the screen was popped out. I stuck my head out but didn't see a way down. "Jack must have left the window open. No way someone jumped down two stories without breaking a leg."

"I didn't leave it open," Jack insisted. "And most humans couldn't jump that far…"

"We don't have time for this," I told Jack. "I don't suppose you have an emergency fire ladder in here?"

"Don't be absurd," he said.

Jack watched as I yanked the sheet off his bed and tied one end around the heavy iron bedpost. "I guess we're going to see if this really works."

The sheet barely reached out the window. Not helpful. I opened his closet to look for extra sheets, noting the neatly hung clothes that were all color-coordinated and facing the same direction. Unfortunately, there were no spare sheets to be found. The closet was completely organized, making the gold hoop earring on the floor seem starkly out of place. Since I couldn't imagine Jack allowing such disorder to remain for long, it was probably a recent addition. I picked it up.

"Whose earring?" I asked.

Jack flushed. "It's not important." Before I could question him, he stalked out the door and down the hall.

I looked back at the window. "I guess we're going to have to jump."

"Amateur." Riley looked at me, disgusted. "Hold up," she said over her shoulder as she headed back down the hall. A few minutes later, she was back with a long extension cord, which she quickly looped and secured to the bedpost.

Jack's bedroom faced a side street, which fortunately was dead this time of day. The street in front of the apartment, however, was teeming with cars. I crossed my fingers and hoped the drivers were too preoccupied to notice two women climbing out a second-story window.

I eyed the extension cord apprehensively. "Do you think this is actually going to work?"

"It'll work. Watch and learn." Riley glided down the cord and dropped to the ground in a crouch. She made it look easy.

It took me a lot longer than Riley to get up the courage to climb out the window, much less slide down. I wiggled out backward until I was balanced on my stomach, clutching the extension cord in a death grip. *This was a bad, bad idea.* Figuring it was now or never, I lifted my torso and slid down the cord.

Unlike Riley, there was nothing graceful about my descent. My shirt snagged on a protruding nail on the outside of the sill and ripped, leaving half my bra showing. When I finally got moving, all I could do was keep my hands wrapped around the cord as I slid down. Reaching the plug, my hands caught briefly before I fell the remaining few feet to the ground, landing unceremoniously on my ass on the sidewalk —right in front of a group of teenagers who gaped at me from the sidewalk before bursting into laughter. *That went well.*

I held my shirt together with as much dignity as I could muster and headed to the car, Riley close on my heels. Although Riley didn't say a word on the way to the car, I dreaded the twenty-minute drive home that would no doubt be filled with the kinds of questions I'd spent most of my life avoiding.

I couldn't shake the feeling that someone was watching us, but when I looked around, not even the teenagers were anywhere in sight. When we got to the car, Jack was already sitting in the back seat.

"He's here, isn't he?" Riley peered in the windows.

I nodded. "Yup."

She opened the passenger door. "I'm not going to sit on him, am I?"

Jack huffed. "Idiot."

"Be nice."

"She can't hear me."

Riley climbed in and spun around, staring at the back seat where Jack was sitting.

I started the car. "Well, that was a bust. Who do you think took your laptop?"

He waved his hand dismissively. "It doesn't matter. It's gone. But there is another option." Jack hesitated long enough that I was sure I didn't want to hear whatever he was going to say next. "But you're not going to like it. It'll be harder."

"Harder than scrambling out a two-story window before your neighbor calls the police?"

"Yes because breaking in won't be an option." He looked pointedly at Riley.

"Why not?" I asked.

Riley was practically vibrating in her seat. "Why not what? What is your ghost saying?"

"He's not my ghost." I held up my hand to Riley before turning back to Jack. "Well?"

"I have a copy of the story." Of course, he did; he was a reporter.

"That's great," I started before realizing that Jack didn't have a car that he could've left it in. And if it wasn't in a car and wasn't in his apartment, I had a bad feeling about where it would be. "Where is it?"

"On a flash drive at work."

I groaned. "As in, the freaking newspaper?"

Jack nodded.

I relayed the conversation to Riley, mostly because I needed time to come up with a plan.

"What time does the paper close?" Maybe I could find a way in at 3:00 a.m. I tried not to think about how all my ideas seemed to come with mandatory sentencing guidelines. Oh, the slippery slope of criminal behavior.

Jack laughed. "Newspapers don't close."

Riley clapped her hands together. "We can go in 007 style."

Watching her fidgeting in the seat, I couldn't imagine Riley going into stealth mode. "We are talking about criminal records here. And," I told her, "you are not coming."

"If your ghost can come, so can I."

"He's not my ghost. Plus, he can't be caught."

"Well, buckle up, buttercup, because I'm coming along for the ride."

"Enough," Jack shouted from the back seat, as if Riley could hear him. "Breaking in won't work."

"Then what exactly do you suggest?" I asked.

"You walk in the front door." He didn't elaborate, disappearing before I could question him. It was becoming a real annoying habit of his.

Surprisingly, Riley took the whole necromancer thing in stride. "How long have you been summoning the dead?"

I pulled over into a strip mall and parked at the far end, away from the other cars. "I didn't summon him. He just showed up."

"Uh-huh." Riley unbuckled and twisted in the seat. "Except that isn't how it works."

"How do you know?"

She sighed. "Everyone knows that."

I wanted to argue, but I didn't actually know how it worked.

"You expect me to believe that Jack is the first ghost you've seen?" she scoffed.

"No, of course not."

"That's what I thought." Her stark blue eyes were intense in the small confines of my car.

"The first was my twin sister, Claire." I couldn't keep the sorrow out of my voice.

She didn't pry. "I'm sorry."

"Yeah, me too." I blinked the tears away. "There were others before Jack, mostly when I was a teenager. But I left that all behind me."

"You stopped calling them?"

"I never called them." At her skeptical look, I gritted my teeth. "Never. I didn't ask for this."

"No one gets to choose who they are." She looked away, but not before I saw the flash of pain. "Didn't your mother teach you how to use your power?" she asked.

"My power?" She made it sound like some kind of super-hero gig. "More like a curse. And no, she didn't. She took off. And besides, my mother wasn't exactly tuned into my life before she left."

Riley touched my shoulder, sympathy radiating off her. "She left when you were young?"

"Not exactly young. I was fifteen. She took off after Claire died." I shifted in my seat until Riley pulled her hand back to her lap. "Even if she had stuck around, what could she have taught me? She didn't see ghosts."

"Maybe not," Riley said. "But necromancers inherit their ability. I don't know much about how it works, but I do know that. I also know that ghosts can't just appear. They have to be called."

"But I didn't," I started to object but stopped myself as I thought about Jack's penny that had clearly been the tether that bound him to me in those first days after his murder. These days, he didn't seem to need an invitation to pop in and disrupt my life. "I didn't mean to call him. And now that he's here…"

"He's not leaving until you find out who killed him," she finished for me.

I dropped my head to the steering wheel and groaned.

$\mathcal{A}$s I stood in front of the doors to *The Kansas City Star*, I wondered how many times I'd have to pose as a reporter before I felt like one. The early morning sun heated my face as I stalled, checking my reflection one more time in the office window. It was one thing to pose as a reporter interviewing people for a story. It took a lot more moxie to walk into a newspaper pretending to be one, which is why I opted for the easier route of going in as an applicant for the paper's internship program.

I'd managed to land the interview after Jack dictated my faux resume and writing samples. I used a fake name, Victoria Bennet this time, also courtesy of Jack. I was fairly certain the paper wouldn't waste HR time vetting a part-time intern, but just in case, I'd listed Riley as a reference and coached her on my cover story.

Jack had spent the better part of last night drilling me on the office layout and our plan. Fortunately, his desk was located between the conference room where interviews were conducted and the bathrooms. The location should theoretically give me an opportunity to grab Jack's flash drive. Although it had been weeks since his death, we were counting on the fact that hiring was notoriously slow, staff were overworked, and desk space at the paper was plentiful.

Because Jack never got past his Washington-level paranoia about people stealing his stories, he kept his flash drive in a manilla envelope he had duct-taped under his desk. The man was driving me nuts, and the thought of him becoming a regular fixture in my life due to my failure to get his damn story was unthinkable. It had to be there.

I hadn't been sure how to dress for a fake interview, so I'd played it safe with black dress pants, a long-sleeved striped button-down, and ankle boots. I'd skipped the makeup and pulled my hair into a high ponytail, aiming for fresh-faced college girl.

The receptionist greeted me and led me to a standard conference room, complete with an oversized whiteboard and uncomfortable plastic chairs. I didn't have to wait long.

The interview itself was over almost as soon as it started. Apparently, the editor mostly wanted to make sure I was a reasonably normal person capable of working with others. Despite the praise for the writing samples I'd submitted—thank you Jack—my guess was that interns didn't do much actual writing. The bulk of the interview was spent verifying my willingness and ability to run standard office equipment.

The editor who interviewed me was a harried man in his mid fifties who carried himself like he had better things to do. After a few minutes, he looked at his watch and stood. "There are three things you need to know about working here."

I waited.

"First, don't be late. Second, no one is going to hold your hand."

"And third?" I asked after an uncomfortable pause.

"We're in the business of news. If you're looking for a place to pat you on the back for stringing together pretty sentences, this isn't it."

Even though I had no intention of working here, I liked his no bullshit approach. "Of course."

I waited for the "we'll be in touch" spiel. He shook my hand firmly and asked me if I could start Monday. I sputtered for a few seconds before assuring him that Monday would be great. I guessed I would be leaving a thanks-but-no-thanks voice mail after I left.

On the way out the door, I asked for directions to the bathroom, despite knowing exactly where to find it, thanks to Jack's coaching. The editor gestured down the hallway before bustling off in the opposite direction.

Fortunately for me, everyone in the office seemed glued to their computer monitors. When I reached Jack's desk, I dropped a pen and paused to pick it up. Glancing around, I made sure no one was paying attention before fumbling around under Jack's desk until I felt the envelope. I reached inside and pulled the flash drive out. Once it was safely tucked in my pocket, I relaxed and headed home.

As soon as I was inside my apartment, Jack appeared. "You got it?"

I held up the flash drive. "The story and the job."

Jack puffed up at that, clearly claiming credit for my landing a job I didn't want. I booted up my computer and plugged his flash drive in. Jack's files were as orderly as his apartment, with stories nested in folders and categorized by title, publication, and date. I clicked on the *KC Star* folder, but Jack interrupted me before it opened.

"Not that one."

He had buried the story in a folder labeled Misc. I'd expected an exposé on organized crime or political corruption—standard investigative reporting fare. What I found was an article that read like fan fiction.

"Werewolves?" I couldn't keep the skepticism out of my voice. "Is this why you got fired from your job in Washington?"

"What? No." He stiffened, his face turning red. "I have proof."

"This?" I asked, holding up the computer screen and pointing to the slightly out-of-focus photograph of what appeared to be a person shifting into a werewolf. The angle of the camera showed a closeup of someone's torso from behind, the spine contorted into an unnatural arch, with hair covering the person's body in patches. Although the subject's arms were muscular in that lean swimmer kind of way, they were human except for the claw-tipped hands.

"There's more," Jack said defensively.

I scrolled down and clicked on the next photo in the folder. This one showed a side profile of what appeared to be a werewolf, also partially shifted, but cropped at the neck, so there was no face visible in the photograph.

I snorted. "That's helpful."

Jack gestured for me to keep going until I opened the last photo, this one showing the profile of a fully shifted, massive werewolf. Even from the side, the beast looked deadly, its mouth partially opened in a roar. I studied it for a minute, looking for evidence of photo editing. Although I didn't see anything obvious, it wasn't hard to fake a photo these days. I'd also constructed some realistic costumes, and while this didn't have the hallmarks of a costume, I couldn't rule it out, either.

I clicked back through the first two photos, pausing on the

partially shifted side view. While the body was mostly wolf, the neck was sleek and human. The photo itself was a different size than the other two. The missing head was not the product of a bad shot, then.

"Why is the head cropped out of this photo?"

He refused to look me in the eye. "I have to protect my source."

"Your source?"

He nodded.

"If I believed you, which I'm not sure I do, your source," I said, emphasizing the word, "was the reason you were killed."

He kept his lips tightly closed.

"Jack, you're dead. You can tell me who your source is."

"I can't."

No matter how many times I tried to coerce the information out of him, he didn't budge. "Fine." I tried to tamp down the anger that was threatening to boil over. "Even with the head, this wouldn't be enough proof. Any twelve-year-old with a Snapchat filter could probably fake this."

Jack scowled at me, but he didn't argue. "There's more," he said.

"More photos?" I scoffed.

"No. More evidence."

I waited for him to elaborate.

"There are medical records."

I sucked in a breath. "You have medical evidence of werewolves?"

He shifted his weight back and forth. "Not exactly."

I slapped my hands to my forehead. "What does that even mean?"

"There is DNA evidence."

I wanted to write all this off as the mad ramblings of a

dead man. If I wasn't standing in my living room talking to that dead man, it would've been easier to dismiss as impossible. But as much as I wanted to cling to my disbelief, something about those photos struck a chord. Even if I could rationalize them away, they felt real.

If there were people like me who could raise the dead, people sprouting fur and howling at the moon didn't seem like that big of a stretch. "Where is this DNA evidence?"

"I don't have it, but I have a contact who does."

"Great." I closed the computer. "Let me guess. You can't give up your source?"

Jack looked down his nose at me. "Don't be ridiculous. He's not my source if I haven't even met with him, now is he?"

"So, you haven't met with him?" I battled to keep my voice from rising. "Wait. Is he the anonymous source you were planning to meet the night you were killed?"

"I've talked to him online," Jack said defensively, not quite answering my question.

"Oh, okay. You met the guy on the internet." I took a deep breath. If Jack wasn't already dead, I'd consider killing him myself. "If you haven't met with him, how the hell do you know he's not some internet quack trolling you?"

Jack clenched his jaw so hard, it hurt my teeth looking at him. When he spoke, his voice dripped with disdain.

"I'm a reporter. You don't think I vetted him?"

It was probably a wild goose chase, but it was all I had to go on. "Fine. What's this guy's name?"

"It's not that simple."

I let out a frustrated breath. "Of course, it isn't."

Jack grimaced. "I have a username."

I didn't bother to point out that it was difficult to vet someone through an internet persona.

"Naturally," Jack continued, "he's skittish about coming forward. We had a meetup set, but…" he trailed off.

"But you were killed." I finished.

He nodded. "I can tell you how to contact him, but you'll have to get him to trust you before he'll agree to meet with you."

"You're not going to leave until I do this, are you?"

His eyes were hard. "Not a chance."

It was a long shot, but I wrote down the man's username and Jack's log-in info for the forum where Jack had been communicating with him. At this point, even a long shot was better than the other leads I had.

The forum Jack frequented was a hotspot for a wide range of conspiracy theories, spanning everything from grainy photos of Area 51 to DIY vampire hunting kit instructions. None of which inspired confidence that this source was legit. But even if the source turned out to be the fruit loop I suspected he was, maybe debunking the story would be enough to satisfy Jack, and I could get back to figuring out who killed him.

I checked Jack's inbox first, hoping to find communications between him and the elusive Wolfsbane. However, Jack kept his inbox as tidy as his home, without even a single deleted email in the trash. I spent the next hour down a rabbit hole, surfing through endless threads devoted to all manner of supernatural creatures, wondering how many of them might not be so mythical after all.

I reigned myself in and went back to searching for Wolfsbane. Clicking on his user profile proved to be next to useless. Like many users, he opted for an avatar rather than a photo, probably so that his neighbors and coworkers couldn't easily ferret out his crazy with a quick internet search.

I stared at my cursor, unsure how to begin. I could message him through Jack's account. But I'd be messaging a man who frequented conspiracy sites; chances were that he harbored a healthy distrust of virtually everyone. If he had seen the news about Jack's death, I risked him disappearing altogether. The fact that Jack had been killed in a haunted house made the story sensational enough to hit the national news cycle. What were the chances he hadn't seen it?

Convincing Wolfsbane to talk to a stranger was going to be a challenge, though. I logged out of Jack's account and created my own. I was careful not to pick a username that could be traced back to me—no variation of my name or location. After a couple tries with more generic names, I settled on Starling_1 and entered a password easy enough that I'd remember it.

It was tempting to cut straight to the point and message Wolfsbane about Jack's death and ask him for the evidence. But I couldn't risk spooking him. I'd have to play the long game.

I combed through Wolfsbane's recent posts, looking for something that would give me a viable in. I commented on a couple threads about werewolves, dropping veiled hints that I had insider knowledge of their existence. Next, I posted on the introduction thread, fabricating a sob story about losing my mother to an unsolved murder that had been dismissed as a dog mauling and then losing my boyfriend, who was on the verge of exposing the abominations for what they were. Then I waited, hoping it was enough to lure Wolfsbane into a reply. After twenty minutes of staring at my inbox and compulsively refreshing the screen, I closed the laptop. This was worse than online dating. But like it or not, the ball was out of my court.

CHAPTER 18

hree days, twenty-two messages, fourteen likes, and an avatar that made me look like a screw-the-establishment type. That was what it took to get Wolfsbane to agree to meet with me in person. After Jack's bombshell that werewolves existed, I spent all my time either working or holed up in my apartment. That meant I had ample time to build an online relationship with a whack-a-doodle.

A few messages in, I told Wolfsbane that I was Jack's girlfriend. I knew it was risky, but my growing impatience outweighed the risk of him taking off. To convince him of my girlfriend status, I shared several details about their conversations that only Jack would know, like when Jack was planning on breaking the story. Jack had been more than happy to pop in to coach me.

Although Jack had tried to talk me into letting him tag along, I'd nixed that idea. A ghost hovering over my shoulder was distracting, and I didn't want to risk doing or saying anything that would send Wolfsbane underground. When he didn't get his way, Jack left in a huff and hadn't made an appearance since.

Wolfsbane claimed that he had indisputable DNA evidence that werewolves existed. While he hadn't committed to bringing the evidence, an in-person meeting in a crowded public place was one step closer to getting my hands on information that could potentially corroborate Jack's story.

I wasn't even sure what I would do with the story once I had all the pieces. Jack made his wishes clear; he wanted me to break the story wide open. I wasn't sure the world was ready to know what went bump in the night, but I hoped Wolfsbane could give me something to help identify Jack's killer.

We'd chosen to meet in the Power and Light district at 8:30 p.m. The area was packed with restaurants and events, which made it easy to blend into the crowd. I'd parked a few blocks away. As I walked, my pulse sped up, the feeling of being followed growing. I looked over my shoulder but didn't notice anything out of the ordinary. I scanned the crowd, wondering if Wolfsbane was already here, watching me.

Although we'd been trading messages for a couple weeks, I knew very little about the man I was meeting. Despite several attempts, he'd dodged my attempts to get a first name. No age, no description—all I had was his gender and an internet username. Even if he was right in front of me, I wouldn't be able to recognize him.

Wolfsbane had directed me to a coffee shop around the corner from the main entertainment district and instructed me to give the barista the name Betty when she took my order. When I arrived, there were already several people in line. I took the opportunity to scan the area.

The place was half full. A pair of thirty-somethings, who

were clearly on a date, laced their fingers together next to their steaming cups of coffee. A group of college students sipped overpriced cappuccinos and talked about the live music that brought them here. Beyond them, a trio of middle-aged women with tight jeans and perfect hair traded office war stories. Not one of the tables held a single occupant, though, which made me jumpy. I didn't know if Wolfsbane was lurking outside, watching through the window, or if he'd stood me up.

When I reached the counter, I told the bored-looking barista my name was Betty and ordered the agreed upon drink, a white chocolate mocha with skim milk and three pumps of vanilla. She scribbled my name on the order and took my money, quickly turning her attention to the next person in line.

I took a seat in the corner where I could watch both the door and the back of the coffee shop. No one came in while I waited. I scanned outside, but everyone milling around outside looked like they had somewhere else to be. Even though the place wasn't overly busy, the barista took her time with my drink, calling out several names before me.

"Betty." Rather than setting my drink on the counter like she had all the others, the barista waited until I came up to hand me my order.

"Thanks."

She nodded and went back to the register.

I carried the cup back to my corner table and sat it in front of me. Several minutes passed, and Wolfsbane was still a no-show. Even though I hated frou-frou coffee drinks, I lifted the cup and took a small sip, trying to look inconspicuous. As I sat it back down in front of me, my finger brushed against a small slip of paper tucked under the brown paper sleeve. *Red*

Lion Pub 9:00. Order gin & tonic. That would be two wasted drinks tonight.

I checked the time on my phone; it was 8:55. After quickly Googling the location of the bar, I crumpled the paper and stuck it in my pocket, leaving my drink on the table. Thankfully, the Red Lion Pub was less than a block away. I found myself checking over my shoulder several times before I got there. I couldn't shake the feeling that someone was watching me. Wolfsbane's paranoia was clearly rubbing off on me.

The bar was much busier than the coffee shop, and it took me awhile to get the bartender's attention. Once I ordered my gin and tonic, I didn't have to wait long for a man to slide onto the empty barstool next to mine. I glanced at him, making sure my gaze didn't linger. The man was the definition of average: neatly kept brown hair, soft jawline, slight build, friendly eyes. Only the rigid way he held himself gave him away. I would have laid money on this being my guy, but I waited for him to confirm it.

He shifted in his seat. "Gin and tonic, huh? You don't see many people drinking that these days."

"It was a recommendation from a friend." I made it a point to look up at the television over the bar before glancing back at him.

When he spoke again, his voice was barely above a whisper. "Starling?"

"That's me."

The bartender laid down a coaster and set my drink in front of me. I handed him a ten and told him to keep the change. Wolfsbane waited until the bartender was occupied at the other end of the bar before responding.

"I'm sorry about what happened to Jack," he said.

Because I was supposed to be Jack's girlfriend, I dabbed

my eyes as if I were fighting back tears and then nodded. "Me, too."

We were both quiet for a minute, pretending to watch the Chiefs game. It was a close one, and the bar crowd was fired up, adding plenty of background noise to blanket our conversation.

"Do you think his story is what got him killed?" he asked.

"Probably." I turned to face him so I could gauge his reaction. "If you had met with Jack that night... well, I'm just glad you weren't there when it happened." I could read the relief on his face. "Did you see something that spooked you?"

"You mean like the news story?"

"No, I mean the night he was killed. Weren't you going to meet him that night to hand over your evidence?"

"I wasn't meeting Jack the night he was killed. We set up a meeting, just like this," he indicated the bar around us, "for the next week." He looked at me suspiciously.

I covered as best I could. "Of course. Jack didn't give me the specifics of your meeting. I think he was afraid I'd try to come. He was protective like that."

I almost choked on that last bit. Protective was the last word I'd use to describe that lying weasel. I didn't know why Jack had lied about meeting Wolfsbane that night, but I was damn well going to find out.

Wolfsbane looked around the room, checking for anyone paying too much attention to us, but everyone was still engrossed in the game or in their own conversations. "Maybe you should leave it alone." He took another drink of his beer. "A pretty young woman like you doesn't want to get caught up in something like this."

"Too late," I said, and it was true. I was already neck deep in this, whether he helped me or not. "Do you know anything about who might have killed Jack?"

He was quiet long enough that I didn't think he was going to answer. "What, not who. You saw the photos and read the story. One of those monsters must have gotten wind of it." Wolfsbane shifted uncomfortably in his seat. "I shouldn't be here." He downed his beer.

Before he could stand up, I grabbed his arm. "I need the evidence you were going to give Jack."

He flexed the muscles in his forearm but didn't pull away. "I don't have it with me."

I figured as much. "But you still have it?"

He nodded.

"Please. We need to finish what Jack started."

"There's no we," he said.

"You were willing to hand it over to Jack before he was killed. If you give it to me, I can end this." I didn't specify how I'd end it because I had no idea what I was going to do with the information yet. I just knew it was a piece of this puzzle that I needed.

I tried to come up with something that would persuade him. Before I said anything else, Wolfbane grabbed my coaster and wrote on the back. He shook off my hand and left without another word.

Tucking the coaster in my pocket, I followed him out the door, but he was long gone by the time I hit the sidewalk. I pulled out the coaster, my pulse quickening at what he had written: *5 days, bus stop at 67 and Elmwood by Swope Park, check under the bench.* Five days was four too many, but there was nothing I could do about it except wait.

As soon as I walked in my door, I snatched the penny off the coffee table where I'd left it. "Jack! Get your ass in here."

"Did you get it?" When he noticed I was empty-handed, he scanned the room to see if I'd stashed the evidence somewhere.

"No. I didn't get it."

Jack threw up his hands, but I didn't give him a chance to launch into a rant.

"There's a five-day waiting period on that evidence." I picked up the coaster and waved it in front of his face. "The drop site has been arranged."

Jack relaxed and moved to sit on my couch.

"Good. Get comfortable because you and I are going to have a chat." I sat on the coffee table so that we were face-to-face.

"Why are you all bent out of shape?"

"Oh, I don't know, Jack. Maybe because you lied to me. Why did you tell me you were meeting Wolfsbane the night you were killed?"

"I didn't lie to you. I said I was meeting a source. I never said it was Wolfsbane. You assumed." He sounded tired.

I thought about it for a second. "You were meeting whoever was in those photos."

He didn't answer.

"But you still won't tell me who your source was?"

"No." He didn't elaborate, and he didn't stick around. "I'll be back in five days."

"You need to talk to Meira about this," Riley said as she rifled through the costume props under the shop counter.

I had latched onto Riley as soon as she came in the shop, demanding she tell me everything she knew about were-wolves. She hadn't batted an eye at the mention of were-wolves, but she wasn't being forthcoming, either.

It didn't surprise me that Riley knew Meira. She seemed to know everyone who worked in West Bottoms. "I don't want to ask Meira. Why can't you just tell me?"

She shook her head. "That's not my information to share."

"Volkov's a werewolf, isn't he?" *Of course, he is.* I shook my head. "Howl? He might as well have put out a Werewolves-R-Us neon sign out front."

Riley wouldn't look at me. From the stubborn set of her jaw, I knew she wasn't going to elaborate.

"Fine." I studied her while she continued rummaging through my costume props. "Can you tell me what you are, at least?"

"Why do you think I'm anything other than human?"

"If you were human, you wouldn't have known what I was."

"Maybe," she conceded, pulling out a pair of oversized sunglasses to try on before returning them to the box where she'd found them. "Or maybe I'm some kind of occult expert."

"You're, what, twenty-five? Pretty young to earn your expert badge."

"Twenty-four." She grinned. "Maybe I'm a quick study."

I nudged her out of the way and grabbed the box of blood-red contacts I kept for costume emergencies. "Here." I handed them to her before settling into a nearby chair and watching her expectantly. "Are you a werewolf, too?"

She clutched her chest and staggered. "You think so little of me?"

"Then what? Vampire?"

"Do I look like a bottom-feeding bloodsucker to you?"

"Um, no?"

She glared at me. "No. I'm not a vampire."

"If you're not a vampire and not a werewolf, what's left? Witch?"

Riley tore the foil off the package and popped one contact in her left eye before pausing to look at me, then to the costumes hanging behind me. "I thought you had more imagination than that."

"Okay, then. Some kind of cat shifter." I studied her before guessing. "Tiger? Leopard? Ooooh, I know—mountain lion."

"Nope." Riley smirked. "I'll give you a hint." She pointed to her mismatched eyes, one red from the contact she'd just popped in and one her natural vibrant blue. She winked at me, and when she opened her eye again, the pupil in her contact-free eye had narrowed to a slit. As far as clues went, it was lit.

I moved closer to her to examine her eye. "That's wild." The elongated pupil looked familiar, even if, in Riley's case, it was ringed with startling blue. I racked my brain to remember where I'd seen eyes like that before. "It kind of looks like a goat's eye."

Riley shifted her eye back to normal as I watched. "B-I-N-G-O."

"Wait, what?" I screeched. "You're a weregoat? Is that even a thing?"

"Weregoat." She laughed and shook her head.

"Yeah, okay, I guess the world isn't ready for weregoats. Then, what are you?"

"Well, ready or not, here I am." At my look of confusion, she said, "Oh, I'm a goat shifter all right. But weregoat? Now that's just funny."

I rushed across the shop and flipped the closed sign before dragging her with me into the back storage room. "Show me?" I begged.

"Only because I like you." Riley took the contact back out and put it in the plastic case. She shed her clothes without a hint of modesty, glanced at the door, and then promptly shifted into an honest-to-God goat. She was larger than your standard barnyard goat, her head reaching chin level. Her sable coat was marbled with streaks of lighter brown, and the blue of her eyes was her only recognizable feature. She nuzzled my hand before headbutting me, careful to avoid hitting me with her horns.

"Hey." I laughed, watching as she quickly shifted back into a woman. I waited until she was dressed again before harassing her with questions.

"You really need to talk to Meira about this." She dropped into the office chair behind the counter.

"Why Meira?"

"Because she's a necromancer, like you."

"So?" I countered. I knew I sounded childish, but the last person I wanted to talk to was Meira. Hanging out with a goat shifter, oh yeah. Spending time with someone else who spent her days talking to dead people? That would be a hard pass.

"So, you're completely clueless about our world, and you need someone to teach you."

"Why can't you teach me?"

"If you needed to know how to buck authority or escape a jail cell, I'd be your girl. But this? I don't know crap about calling the dead." Before I could object, she held up her hand. "You can't keep avoiding who you are. Meira can help you. Besides, it doesn't hurt to have a Tribunal member on your side."

"Tribunal? What is this, the Middle Ages?"

Riley looked at me. "You really don't know anything about this world, do you?"

The Tribunal, it turned out, was the ruling body responsible for policing supernaturals. It was made up of representatives from each major faction: shifters, vampires, necromancers, and witches. Unlike a city council, the Tribunal's reach extended over an entire territory, in our case, the Interior Territory. The territory I found myself in was the largest in the country, stretching from North Dakota to Oklahoma and as far east as Ohio. Without knowing it, I'd spent my entire life living within its borders. I wondered if this Tribunal would investigate Jack's death if they suspected it involved one of their own.

"Who else is on this Tribunal?" When she didn't answer, I threw out the first name that popped into my head. "Volkov?"

She didn't answer.

"Wait here." I darted in the back room to grab the police sketch of Twitch from where I'd left it. "What about this guy? Is he on this Tribunal?"

Riley picked up the paper and whistled. "I didn't know you could draw."

"I didn't draw it. A police sketch artist did."

She sobered. "You went to the police with a description of a vampire?"

"That's what he is?"

"Yup. One hundred percent bloodsucker. He's an odd one, too." Riley tossed the paper back to me. "Did you swipe this from the police like the visitor log?"

"What? No." I pointed to his face. "Somehow he got it from the police and gave it back to me. Do you think he could have killed Jack Gates?"

"Could have? Absolutely. Did? Not a chance."

"How can you be so sure?"

Riley gave me a pitying look. "He wouldn't walk away from an all-you-can-drink smorgasbord any more than you or I could throw away a full carton of triple fudge ice cream." Riley's face turned serious, all trace of the fun-loving girl gone. "You can't be running to the police with this stuff. Ask Meira for help before you get in over your head."

"I'm already in over my head," I muttered. "And I don't need Meira's help. All I want is to find Jack's killer. Then I can go back to my life."

"You act like you can keep your life separate from who you are."

"Maybe I can," I said, sharper than I'd intended.

"There's no partway in this world. You're either all in or..." Riley left it hanging.

"Or?" I prompted.

"Or you're a danger to be eliminated." Her voice softened, begging me to understand.

I took a step back, shaking my head. The more I learned, the less I wanted to wade into this world.

Riley threw up her hands. "Hey, I don't make the rules."

"But you don't disagree with them, either."

She shrugged.

I sat down again in the chair next to her. "What are the rules?"

Riley rolled her eyes. "There are a shit ton of rules, most of them stupid attempts to micromanage us." That sounded more like the Riley I knew. She sighed as I waited. Clearly, the idea of reciting a litany of rules was tedious to Riley. "I'm sure Meira will be thrilled to run down the dos and don'ts in excruciating detail. But." She looked at me. "There is really only one rule you need to worry about."

"What's that?"

"Never, and I do mean never, reveal yourself or the others to outsiders." She kept her eyes locked on mine until I nodded.

"Got it." I thought of Jack. "What happens to people who break that rule?"

"Use your imagination."

And that sounded a lot like motive to me. Jack had been on the cusp of breaking the biggest story on the planet. If anyone had gotten wind of it, he would have had a giant bullseye on his back. What I couldn't figure out, though, was how the story had stayed under wraps for this long.

"How does the world not know about us?" My voice caught on the us; it felt strange to lump myself in with creatures that until recently I thought only lived in the pages of novels and in the collective imagination.

"Think of it like supernatural PR. Information leaks are inevitable. People have been telling stories about vampires and werewolves for centuries. It's all about the spin." Riley leaned back in the desk chair, her head tilted to look at the ceiling as she spun it around like a Tilt-A-Whirl. "That guy giving an interview for a gossip rag? Conspiracy theorist. That woman who had a close call with a bloodsucker—just a chick with a vampire fetish. We've had a lot of practice packaging the truth into small, less threatening narratives."

"And you're telling me no one before Jack got ahold of evidence?"

"Oh, there's been plenty of evidence," Riley admitted. "But we have people who specialize in neutralizing those sorts of things."

"Neutralize how?"

She waved me off as if it was of no consequence. "Memory wipes, mind control, destroying evidence. You know, the usual."

Riley and I had vastly different definitions of usual.

My phone buzzed, and I was grateful for the distraction. It was a text from Emma: *Turn on the news.* I pulled the local channel up on my phone, since I didn't have a TV in the shop. I cranked it up to full volume and turned the screen, so both Riley and I could see it, and hit play on the breaking news.

An arrest has been made in the haunted house murder case. The headlines scrolled across the bottom of the screen while the footage showed officers putting a handcuffed man in the back of a squad car. *Leon Matthews was arrested this afternoon in connection with the death of Star reporter Jack Gates.* I sat there shell-shocked while the rest of the clip played.

"Well, it looks like you'll get your wish." There was a sad edge to Riley's voice. "Now that they've caught Jack's killer, you can get back to that life you wanted."

CHAPTER 19

I'd made my choice the minute I decided to come looking for her. Regardless of what the police believed, I knew that whoever killed Jack was still out there. I may not have gotten justice for Claire, but I wasn't a fifteen-year-old girl anymore. This time, I wasn't going to back down until the person who actually killed Jack was held accountable for his death.

From my vantage point, I had a clear view of Meira as she headed my way. Some women wore gray hair like an overcast day, a kind of dreary inevitability stamped across their features. Meira was not one of those women. She wore the silver strands like a crown. Even from my hiding place skulking behind a delivery truck outside her store, I could appreciate the sun lighting up her hair like fine jewelry.

Everything about Meira was regal, from the way she carried herself to the clothes she wore. Today, she was wearing a wide-legged pantsuit the color of churned butter. The material draped her body in soft lines, swaying in the light breeze as she crossed the street. It was the kind of outfit women only braved on the pages of a magazine, recognizing the absolute impracticality of it for actual living. On Meira, I would have put money on it looking as pristine at the end of the day as it did at the start. More than anything else, that convinced me she must wield magic.

I scooted around the end of the delivery truck to stay out of sight as she crossed the street, poking my head out to watch her unlock the door.

"Kali," she called out without turning around. "You look ridiculous. Come inside."

Reluctantly, I straightened and followed her with as much dignity as I could muster, avoiding meeting her eyes. Inside, she bustled around the shop, preparing for the day, as she waited for me to get to the point of my visit.

I started with the question she was more likely to answer. "Is there a way I can control when a ghost comes or goes?"

She frowned. "Of course. You're the one holding the leash."

"How?"

She reached for a book next to me and dusted off the shelf below it before returning it to its place. "For most necromancers," she looked pointedly at me before continuing, "they use a ritual to call ghosts and to banish them using an object, preferably something metal, from the deceased."

I'd already figured out that Jack's penny was the conduit, but the ritual was news to me. "Why metal?"

"Magic is a lot like electricity. Metal provides a strong conduit. Of course, some metals work better than others. Stainless steel, for example, is practically useless. But they make electrical wire out of a copper for a reason. Silver is also an excellent choice, and gold will work in a pinch." She glanced at me. "Are you experimenting?"

"Thinking about it," I said. "Is it possible to call ghosts without a ritual?"

She abandoned the cloth she was haphazardly dusting with to give me her full attention. "For most necromancers, no. For you, maybe."

"Why would I be different?"

"Just like metals, some necromancers are stronger conduits than others." She smiled. "And you, my dear, are off the charts. You have no idea how much power you could tap into."Power wasn't something I had any interest in chasing. All I wanted was to know how to make stop Jack from disappearing anytime he didn't want to answer one of my questions.

"You said I hold the leash. How does that work without a ritual?"

"You've probably noticed that ghosts have signatures, like an aura that surrounds them." Meira looked to me for confirmation.

I nodded.

She looked pleased. "That is the soul you're seeing. Not all necromancers can even see souls, and few can touch them. But for those of us who are strong enough, we can manipulate those souls."

Great. But what I needed was a paint-by-numbers explanation, so I could prevent Jack's disappearing acts, not vague platitudes about what a special snowflake I was.

"How?"

"That's a lesson for another day."

"But…"

"Another day," she repeated before turning her back to me and tidying up another shelf.

I looked out the window to make sure no customers were

headed for the store before addressing what brought me here. "I need to know everything you can tell me about the werewolves."

"Keep your voice down." Meira's earlier friendliness was gone. She marched to the door to flip the sign back to closed, gesturing me toward the back of the store.

"Well?" I prompted.

"I'm afraid you're going to have to be more specific, my dear."

I crossed my arms. "All right, I need to know whether the werewolves are capable of murdering a reporter."

"Obviously, they are capable," she said dismissively. When I met her gaze, it was assessing. "I presume we are talking about Jack Gates?"

"We are."

She looked at me from the corner of her eye. "Perhaps you didn't see the news. They arrested his killer yesterday."

"Leon Matthews did not kill Jack Gates."

She didn't ask me how I knew that. "And you think a werewolf did it?"

"I do."

She took her time responding. "If a werewolf is responsible for Jack Gates' death, I can assure you that it was not a sanctioned kill."

I watched her, finding no comfort in the calm way she spoke of a man's death. "One," I ticked off with a raised finger, working to keep the disgust out of my tone, "what exactly is a sanctioned kill? And two, how can you be sure?"

"Sanctioned, as in ordered by the powers that be. Think of it like a court-sanctioned death penalty." She grimaced as if talking about it was distasteful. "And as one of those powers that be, I am absolutely certain that it was not a kill we ordered."

"We?"

"It's not a monarchy, child."

"Who else is among the powers that be?" When she remained quiet, I ventured a guess. "Volkov."

She studied me intently before changing the subject "Why do you think a werewolf killed Jack Gates? Did he tell you a werewolf killed him?"

I was long past pretending not to see dead people. "He didn't see who did it."

"Then why on earth would you think a werewolf killed him?"

While I may have grudgingly accepted that I needed her for information, I wasn't a woman who trusted easily. If it weren't for Riley's nudging, I wouldn't have even been here. However, as much as I'd prefer going it on my own, there were too many roadblocks. I wasn't going to get far without help, so I put my cards on the table. Most of them, anyway.

"He was writing a story that would have outed the werewolves."

Meira dropped the polite mask she wore like her favorite accessory, her eyes narrowing. "Where is the story?"

I didn't like the intent way she was watching me, as if I posed a danger that needed to be handled. I recognized that the Meira I was facing wasn't the eccentric shop owner or even a fellow necromancer willing to take me under her wing. This was a woman with the power to sanction kills to maintain the status quo.

"No idea," I lied. "He just told me he had been working on it." I didn't mention the alleged proof I was waiting on.

Meira continued watching me for a while, no doubt

weighing the truth of my words. Finally, she nodded. "We'll handle it."

For a second, I thought she was offering to search for Jack's killer, but the look in her eyes hinted otherwise. "Handle what, exactly?"

"Killing the story."

"What about Jack's killer?"

She sighed. "Just because the man was writing a tabloid story doesn't mean that's why he was killed. From what I hear, he wasn't a very likeable guy. Even if this Matthews is not the killer, I'm sure the police will get to the bottom of it."

"And if he was killed for the story?"

"If one of ours killed him, then we will handle that, as well." Meira straightened a row of candles on a nearby shelf before turning back to me. "Enough about that. Now that you are here, we should talk about your training."

"Training?"

"Of course. You have to learn some control."

"I'm not interested in training. I want to know about the wolves and about Volkov."

Meira wasn't a woman who gave up easily. Seeing her opening, she pounced. "If you want information, it comes at a cost."

I was certain she wasn't talking about money.

"I'll tell you everything you want to know about the supernatural world, but you'll have to submit to my authority first."

I scowled. "What does that even mean?"

"It means that you agree to be accountable to me and that you will begin regular training so that you can control the considerable power you shall wield."

No thanks. Collecting the dead wasn't a superpower I wanted.

She waited patiently, a satisfied smile curving her lips. If I agreed to her conditions, I'd get quick answers. I could hand over the reins of this investigation, leave the hunt for Jack's killer to the powers that be. But I'd done that once, and Claire's killer was still at large. I wasn't going to make the same mistake again. I didn't respond, watching her smile falter and her eyes sharpen as the silence stretched between us.

I was almost to the door when she called out her warning. "Stay away from Volkov, Kali."

The more people who warned me away from Volkov, the more convinced I was that he was involved. The way I saw it, there wasn't a world of difference between covering up organized crime and ensuring that werewolves weren't outed to the world. Both were secrets people would kill to protect. But coverups were notoriously messy—just ask Nixon. All I had to do was find something that linked Volkov to Jack. To do that, though, I needed to get inside his house.

Even though I'd successfully tailed Matthews in my own car without getting caught, I had to be more cautious with Volkov. I needed a car that no one would tie to me. That eliminated borrowing one from most of my friends. Everyone knew Emma's car and Bennie's car because they worked in West Bottoms. Riley didn't drive.

Although I would pay for the mixed signals I was sending, I swallowed my good sense and asked Gavin if I could borrow his car for the afternoon while mine was at the shop. He readily agreed on the condition I pick him up for dinner.

Tailing Volkov home from work proved even easier than

Leon; it wasn't hard to blend in while driving Gavin's nondescript sedan. Volkov pulled into a long driveway off a secluded road outside the city limits. I noted the address as I drove past, so I could come back in the morning after he left for the office. Hopefully, by this time tomorrow, I would have evidence of Volkov's involvement.

Since I didn't need to pick Gavin up for our obligatory dinner date for a while, I made a pit stop at a big box outdoor store. The guy at the firearms counter enthusiastically helped me select a handgun. He offered to run the background check right away if I didn't mind browsing the store until it came back. Thirty minutes later, I had a handgun in my purse and a bottle of one hundred percent pure doe urine guaranteed to mask my scent. Apparently, there wasn't a market for werewolf scent-masking spray, so I had to settle for smelling like the wildlife.

I was a city girl at heart. I considered it an accomplishment that I'd made it to my mid-twenties without spending a single night in a tent, so traipsing around the woods behind Max Volkov's house was outside my comfort zone. My original plan had been to park my car across from his house detective-style and have myself a good old-fashioned stakeout, watching until I was sure no one was home.

One slight problem. His house wasn't visible from the street. From the satellite photos I'd studied online, I knew his house was a sprawling two-story set a quarter mile off the road and backed by woods. Behind a gate. The gate was more testament to his pretentiousness than security, since there was no actual fence to go with it. It was one of those black monstrosities anchored by twin brick columns, the kind of gate you see in the country next to the first house built in a brand-spanking-new subdivision. Everyone, it seemed, wanted their acreage and the idyllic dreams of country life that came with a fat bank account and years spent in a cubicle. From the look of it, Volkov had bought a lot more than an acre.

It was almost a half-mile walk from the nearest parking spot, a decrepit church that looked like it belonged on the set of a horror movie. Good thing I wore my walking shoes. I parked my car behind the church to make sure passing cars didn't have a clear look at my vehicle before making my way toward Volkov's house. Unlike Gavin's car that I used to trail Volkov, there would be no mistaking my car if anyone spotted it.

I had dressed for a Hollywood safari: tan button-down shirt, borrowed khakis, sun hat, and oversized sunglasses. I was going for incognito, which would have worked had Kansas City been in the desert. Here among the trees, the outfit didn't exactly blend in, so I ditched the sunglasses and took my time, careful to stay out of sight, should anyone be home to look out one of the half a dozen windows on the back of Volkov's house.

Without the cyber know-how to set up an elaborate surveillance scheme, I was forced to edge along the tree line, jockeying for position before lurking behind bushes like a peeping Tom. Creeping around in woods was slow going. By the time I made my way around the perimeter to find a prime crouching spot, my once white shoes were covered in mud and nettles. At least the mud helped conceal them. I stopped far enough away that no one was likely to detect movement but close enough I could make out the house and surrounding landscape.

With its dark wood siding and light stone accents, Volkov's house fit the surrounding landscape. The house had abundant windows that offered an expansive view of the woods I was currently hiding in. Off to one side of the bank of windows was a sliding glass door that led to the patio. The stone patio matched the house and surrounded a large firepit and outdoor seating. The man clearly had money because houses that looked this good from the back were not cheap.

I patted my crossbody purse, the outline of my new gun reassuring. Although I couldn't buy silver bullets—I asked—I was confident plain old lead would slow down a werewolf long enough for me to get away. Hopefully, I wouldn't be close enough to a werewolf to test my theory. My plan was to wait long enough to ensure Volkov wasn't home before sneaking inside to hunt for evidence of his involvement. I'd borrowed Riley's lock-picking kit when she wasn't looking and watched enough how-to videos that I was confident I could get in.

There hadn't been any cars in front of the house, and there was no movement that I could see. It was tempting to make an immediate run for the back patio door. But it was 9:00 in the morning. I had time to be patient and make certain no one was home before making my move. I settled myself behind a patch of brush, pushing sticks and rocks out of the way so I had enough room to sit, then set a timer on my phone for thirty minutes. I dug the mini binoculars out and trained them on the patio door.

When my alarm went off, I shoved the binoculars back in my bag and stood to stretch my stiff muscles. Before I could head to the house, the sliding glass door opened. I crouched back down behind the bushes and watched Volkov step outside.

He wasn't alone. Two people I recognized followed him out the door: Craig and Ruby. I hadn't seen Craig since he'd warned me to stay out of it, advice I clearly ignored, but I didn't like seeing him here. Sure, it was possible Craig and Ruby were here for a staff meeting, but it seemed more likely they were here for pack business.

Volkov stopped abruptly, Ruby bumping into his back. He stared directly at the spot where I was sitting. Even though he didn't say anything, Craig and Ruby followed his gaze. I took a deep breath and tried not to panic. I was hidden well behind the brush, the morning sun not reaching beyond the tree line. I assured myself that there was no way they could see me.

I sniffed myself, hoping that the product I'd bought to mask my scent worked as promised. I had no idea how good werewolves' sense of smell was, but I knew wild wolves could scent an animal up to a mile away.

When Volkov took a step in my direction, I bolted. I scrambled to my feet and backtracked through the woods, sacrificing quiet for speed. As I ran, I waited for someone to grab me, but I made it back to my car in one piece. I threw my hat in the backseat and bent over the steering wheel to catch my breath, willing my erratic heartbeat to calm down.

My head was still down when someone pounded on the window, making me jump in my seat.

"Get out."

I didn't have to look up to recognize Volkov. I fumbled for my keys, but before I could get them in the ignition, Volkov opened my door and loomed inside.

"Now!"

The way I saw it, I had two choices. I could confront him

about being a werewolf and hope he didn't kill me on the spot, or I could bluff my way out. One look at the fury in his eyes, and I went for the bluff.

"Thank God," I said. "Car trouble."

I watched the tic that formed in his cheek for a second before digging myself in deeper. "I love this old car, but she's just not as reliable as a new one. You know?"

I tried to peer over his shoulder to see if Craig or Ruby had followed him, hoping he'd be less likely to throttle me if we had an audience. It was impossible to see around his bulk though, so I beamed at him.

"Do you think you could give me a jump?"

"Get out of the car, or I will help you out of it, Ms. James."

His body hadn't loosened at all. Still, I forced myself to remain calm, as if I didn't feel the anger choking the air around me. "Of course. Let me just grab my purse. Are you parked close by?"

I put one foot out of the door. He obligingly took a step back, but he never let go of the car door, clearly not trusting me to stay put. I leaned the rest of my body across the car to reach the floorboards in front of the passenger seat where I'd tossed my bag.

Without looking over my shoulder, I reached inside my bag and pulled out the gun, swinging it in his direction. When I looked at Volkov, I expected to see surprise or even rage at the fact I held a gun on him. Instead, he smiled at me, the kind of smile that showed all his teeth. Before I could even register what he was doing, he'd wrapped his hand around mine and yanked the gun out of my grip.

"I'll give you five seconds to get out of the car on your own before I jerk you out."

The adrenaline spike got me out in two. He didn't give me

a chance to run, crowding me against the side of my car. I kicked myself for parking here. There was no one except the two of us here, the shell of the old church blocking us from the road.

I watched the hand that held my gun. It wasn't pointed at me, and the safety was still on, but that was little reassurance when he held it loaded in his hand. My heart was hammering loudly enough that I was sure he could hear it in the quiet of the country. Seeing where my gaze was directed, he ejected the bullets before tossing the empty gun into my car and shutting the door.

I didn't get a chance to relax because he grabbed my upper arm and started propelling me back toward his house. "Let's go have a little chat, Ms. James."

"We can talk here."

He paused, and for a second, I thought he conceded. I flinched when he dropped his head to my neck and sniffed. "What did you do?" He cut me off before I could answer, "Never mind." He grimaced and started to propel me forward.

I dropped my weight and dug my heels in, but Volkov kept pulling me along as if I weighed nothing. Even though I didn't see anyone around, I knew there were houses down the road. I opened my mouth to scream, but Volkov must have sensed it because the next thing I knew, he'd maneuvered my body in front of his and clamped a big palm over my mouth. He didn't break stride. Volkov might not have kept my gun, but the wall of muscle behind my back didn't bode well for my survival odds if he decided to kill me.

Within minutes, we were inside Volkov's house. He let go of me and shut the door behind us. At the sound of the door, Ruby and Craig stepped out of an adjoining room, staring open-mouthed at the two of us.

Craig spoke first. "Kali? What are you doing here?"

Volkov practically growled behind me. "That's what we're about to find out." He nudged me into the room they'd just come out of and pointed to an expensive-looking leather couch. "Sit."

I didn't argue.

Craig and Ruby followed us into the room, taking seats on the matching couch across from me. Volkov stood, apparently preferring to loom over me.

"There's been a misunderstanding." I looked at Craig as I said it, hoping for an ally.

However, his face was unreadable. For her part, Ruby looked as hostile as she had every other time we'd crossed paths. My mind raced trying to come up with a plausible reason to be here, but I came up blank.

"Give me one good reason why I shouldn't call the police and have you arrested for trespassing," Volkov said.

"At an old church?" I forced a laugh, but it sputtered out when I caught the amber flashing in Volkov's eyes. I had no doubt I was looking at the wolf who lived inside his skin.

He leaned closer until we were eye-to-eye. "Try again."

Fear made most people cautious. Me? The more my fear ramped up, the more reckless I became. I'd been like this since I was a child. In the close proximity to an angry Volkov as I now found myself, my fear was a solid ten. Naturally, I went on the offensive.

"Because it would be hard to explain wolfing out to human police?"

Volkov had his fingers wrapped around my throat before I finished my sentence. He kept the pressure firm, but thankfully he didn't squeeze. I swallowed, aware of my pulse thudding against the fingers splayed across my throat. Despite my earlier bravado, tears filled my eyes.

"What did you say?"

I was singularly focused on the man who held my life in his hand; I didn't hear Craig cross the room. He put his hand on Volkov's shoulder and said something to him in what sounded like Russian. Slowly, Volkov released my throat. His anger, however, didn't fade.

I sank into the couch cushions, massaging my neck. When I answered, my voice was hoarse from unshed tears. "I know you are a werewolf."

Volkov exchanged a look with Craig, but it was Ruby who spoke. "Do you want me to call a vamp to wipe her memory? Or should I just kill her?" Her eyes glowed as brightly as Volkov's.

"No one is going to kill her." Craig's voice didn't invite argument. Relief flooded me, and I looked to Craig for a lifeline. He wouldn't make eye contact.

Ruby looked disappointed. "She's a threat, Alpha."

I wasn't sure which of them she was talking to until Volkov spoke. "Is that right? Are you a threat, Ms. James?"

I knew what I must look like, eyes wide with terror, fighting back tears. "Do I look like a threat?"

"No," Volkov said. "You look like a girl who doesn't know when to stop." He ran his fingers through his hair and looked at Craig. Whatever they were silently communicating, I couldn't decipher it. "Call in a favor, Ruby. Tell the vamps to send someone discreet." Ruby nodded, and Volkov turned his attention back to me. "While we wait, you can tell me how you know about us, Ms. James."

At this point, I figured I might as well be frank. "Jack Gates told me."

Ruby's fingers stopped mid-dial, and she looked at me in shock. "The dead reporter?"

Craig narrowed his eyes. "You said you didn't know him."

"I didn't. Not when he was alive, anyway." Now that killing me seemed to be off the table, I was coming down from my adrenaline high, but my hands were still shaking.

This time, it was Volkov's turn to look shocked. "You're a fucking necromancer?" He said the last word with unconcealed disgust. His hands balled into fists, and a vein started throbbing in his forehead.

In the face of his anger, I didn't trust myself to speak. I nodded instead.

Volkov stalked across the room and grabbed the phone out of Ruby's hand. He punched the keypad and waited for whoever he called to pick up. "I have something of yours. Come deal with Ms. James, or I'll do it for you." He tossed the phone back to Ruby and stalked out of the room without a glance in my direction.

Ruby followed close on his heels, leaving me alone in the room with Craig. From the disappointed way he watched me, I would've preferred Ruby's company. I didn't know what to say, so I kept quiet until Meira got there to pick me up.

When we got outside, Meira looked over the top of her car at me. "What were you thinking, spying on Volkov?" she asked.

I ignored her question, unwilling to admit I'd been there to break into his house to look for evidence. "I can walk. I didn't park far," I said.

"I'll drive you." She raised her hand before I could argue. "We have a few things to discuss. I'll drop you at your car."

I climbed into the passenger seat. She followed me into the

car and started it. At the end of the drive, she paused, leaning over the seat to sniff at me. "What is that awful smell?"

"Deer piss."

"Excuse me?"

"It's a scent-masking spray made out of deer urine."

Meira stared at me. "You tried to hide your scent from werewolves by bathing in deer urine?"

"It was supposed to make it so they couldn't smell me. And I didn't bathe in it." I sounded defensive even to my own ears.

She didn't say another word, but she glanced at me as she pulled out of the driveway and shook her head.

Meira may not have come right out and said, "I told you so," but the subtext on the rest of the ride made the point for her.

She was less subtle about her warning to stay far away from Max Volkov.

CHAPTER 20

*T*hankfully, the next day proved to be one of my busiest of the season, keeping my mind occupied. I cycled through customers, most of whom were perfectly content with off-the-rack costumes. After a record-selling afternoon, I flipped the closed sign in time to fit in a quick shower before heading to the bar where I'd agreed to meet Riley for drinks.

Normally, I wasn't a midweek bar kind of girl, but if there was ever a week that warranted it, this was it. Besides, sitting around waiting made me antsy. Although I'd finally tracked down the elusive Wolfsbane, I was still waiting for the promised evidence. Whoever wanted to keep this information from going public already proved they were willing to kill for it.

What didn't make sense was why. If the Tribunal was willing to clean up everyone's messes, why not let them? If the Tribunal had known about the story, they would have wiped out any trace of it, erasing Jack's memory and sending him back to writing fluff pieces. Why would someone take matters into their own hands and murder Jack in the middle of a crowded haunted house? A haunted house owned by a were-wolf, no less. A risk like that meant it had to be personal. But there was a critical piece missing, and I couldn't figure out what it was no matter how hard I tried.

I may not have asked to be in this world, but here I was in the crosshairs, just the same. Until I pieced together this puzzle, my life and the lives of everyone around me would be in danger. To figure this out, I needed help.

Even if Jack wasn't MIA, I couldn't take what he said at face value. I'd already struck out with Volkov, and Meira's help came at a price I wasn't willing to pay. Riley was the one person who didn't want something from me, which meant she was the only one I trusted.

After a few drinks, I might get up the nerve to admit it.

We were meeting at Grinders, which sounded like a seedy strip club but was actually a neighborhood dive bar and coffee house. By the time I got there, Riley was waiting out front for me, tapping her foot impatiently as she slouched against the wall. She'd worn her pink hair down around her shoulders, tipping the ends with glittery turquoise. She was easy to pick out in a crowd, not that there was much of a crowd tonight. Other than a couple cars in front of Grinders, the street was deserted. Riley's face lit up when she spotted me.

I didn't see the sign until I had reached her. "Oh, hell no," I said, reading the poster taped to the door that heralded Karaoke Tuesday.

Riley wasn't easily discouraged, grabbing both my hands and bumping the door open with her hip. I tried to pull away, but she was shockingly strong for her size, and she easily pulled me inside.

The place was mostly empty. Two guys were setting up the

stage, and a man and woman sat arguing at one of the far tables. Other than that, we had the place to ourselves. Behind the bar, a giant of a man stacked shot glasses in neat rows. Since most of my visits to Grinders occurred as morning pit stops for coffee, I wasn't as familiar with the bar staff who took over midday. I'd never seen this guy before; I was certain I'd remember a guy who must have been six-five at least.

"Bear," Riley called out cheerfully.

Last month, I would have assumed Bear was a nickname. Looking at him now, I wasn't so sure.

The bartender grunted. "No trouble tonight, kid."

She held her hands up. "I'll be on my best behavior," she assured him.

He looked up long enough to scowl at her before returning to his shot glasses. Riley didn't spare him another glance, skipping to the front of the room where the stage was being assembled. Before I knew what she was doing, Riley snatched up a tablet and added our names to the karaoke list.

"No way." I tried to grab the list out of her hands, but with the extra height Riley had on me, she was able to hold it just out of my reach, laughing as I jumped for it. It gave me flashbacks to childhood battles with my brother.

I thought about tackling her for it, another skill I'd learned from my brother Drew, but after failing to pull it out of her grasp, I had my doubts I could take her down. Goats were notoriously agile, a trait I was sure came in handy for Riley. Plus, the bartender growling, "first warning," dissuaded me.

What Riley lacked in talent, she made up in enthusiasm. Although I'd refused to step foot on the stage, preferring to nurse my drink alone at a side table, Riley spent the better part of the next hour belting out one nauseating pop song after another. After a quick bathroom run, I took a seat at the bar, which was as far away from the stage as I could get without risking Riley's ire. I'd already invested an hour, what was a few more minutes? Surely the girl's lungs would give out sooner rather than later, and I'd get a chance to pump her for information. I figured she owed me after serving as her captive audience.

I was so focused on tuning Riley's voice out that I didn't notice Craig until he slipped into the seat next to me. I hadn't talked to him since the run-in at Volkov's, so I wasn't sure what to expect. I scanned his face for signs that he was still angry with me, but he was a hard man to read.

"Drinking alone?" he finally asked.

"Nah." I gestured to the stage where Riley was slaughtering an Ariana Grande song.

His lips twitched. "Did I miss your performance?"

The easygoing banter eased some of the tension knotting my shoulders. "Ha ha." I dropped my head and banged it on the bar. "Kill me now."

Craig was still watching me when I lifted my head. He looked bigger than usual, perched on the barstool next to me. He was dressed in his usual black t-shirt and jeans, and I wondered how someone could be content with a closet full of identical clothes.

"Can I buy you a drink?" He glanced at the stage and grimaced as Riley attempted an unusually high note. "A glass of wine to ease your suffering."

Clearly, he didn't know me very well.

When I was seventeen, I had my first taste of tequila. My boyfriend at the time supplied the Jose Cuervo, and I smuggled salt and lime out of our fridge. Trevor drank it like he knew what he was doing, and I had followed his lead. At that age, I hadn't been interested in good boys. I'd hung out with boys with bangs in their eyes, cigarettes dangling from their lips, and a well-rehearsed sailor vocabulary. Some things hadn't changed.

"A shot of tequila," I directed the bartender.

Craig raised an eyebrow but said, "Make that two."

Just like that first drink at seventeen, the burn settled my nerves.

The bartender held up the bottle, but I shook my head no. While I appreciated a good shot of tequila, I wasn't ready to let my guard down enough around Craig to risk two. Instead, I picked up a peanut from the small bowl on the bar, cracked the shell, and popped it into my mouth.

Craig, however, downed two more shots before turning the conversation to business. "We need to talk." He shifted his weight on the bar stool but didn't turn to look at me, keeping his attention on the empty shot glasses in front of him.

"Okay."

"Not here."

I knew better than to leave with him. While my gut may have still been telling me he wasn't Jack's killer, there were too many loose ends that pointed to his involvement. Even if he hadn't killed Jack, it was entirely possible that he had covered it up for his boss who had.

"I'm good here."

He scanned the room, but no one was paying attention to us. He must have decided that here was good enough. "Did you talk to Jack before you came looking for me at Howl?"

"Does it matter?" I already knew the answer. The when was irrelevant; all that mattered to Craig was that I had the ability to talk to Jack.

His next words proved me right. "And this?" Craig scanned me from head to toe. "Is this how you hide what you are?"

I kicked out a foot and admired my plaid Burberry ballerina flats I'd found for a steal at the thrift store. "How exactly does my choice of shoes hide who I am?"

Just because I raised the dead didn't mean I couldn't look good while I did it. These shoes were fire.

He looked down at me. "You don't look like a necromancer."

"I'm sorry. We can't all be walking billboards for the apocalypse. Sometimes you need a little pop of color." I turned the tables, giving him the once over. "And what are you?" I leaned into him and whispered in his ear. "Werewolf? Or something else?" I was close enough that I felt his body tense.

"We're not talking about me."

"Yeah, well. I guess we have that in common." I swiveled my stool to face the bar and waved to get the bartender's attention. This was going to be a two shots of tequila kind of night, after all.

"You didn't have to hide what you were." He was a man who didn't have to raise his voice to telegraph his anger. The lines of his body did that for him.

The shot of tequila and the mountain of a bartender behind the counter made me brave. "Why did you lie to me about there only being the two exits from the room where Gates was killed?"

Craig rubbed the back of his neck. He didn't ask me how I knew about the door. "I didn't want you involved."

"And the police? Why lie to the police?"

He scanned the faces of the people closest to us, making sure they were absorbed in their own conversations and drinking. He waited until Bear moved farther down the bar before answering.

"Same reason I lied to you. I didn't want them involved."

His hand on my arm stopped me when I slid off my stool to put distance between us. Although his grip was firm, it wasn't tight enough to be threatening. Craig was so close that his breath fanned across my cheek when he spoke.

"There are some things that are better handled by our own."

"Like Gates' murder," I challenged, my voice rising.

"Not here." Craig glanced around. "I'll walk you home." When I didn't move, he sighed. "You're safe with me, Kali."

I couldn't afford to believe him. But even in the face of the danger he posed, the proximity was intoxicating. He smelled like sandalwood, and I felt his body flex beside me as he waited for me to accept his offer. I jerked my arm out of his grasp and took a step back.

Maybe I couldn't help my attraction to him, but I could damn well choose what I did—or in this case, didn't do—about it. I found a lot of things attractive: my dentist, the Tuesday delivery guy. Even the bronze sculpture outside Kauffman Stadium was attractive, but you didn't see me out there dry humping it before a baseball game.

No matter how pretty the packaging, a bomb was a bomb. The last thing I needed in my life was another thing to detonate.

"Thanks for the drink." I made my way back to Riley's table and waited for her. I had to wait until a lull in the music to get her attention. "I'm sorry, Riley, but I'm beat." I forced a yawn. "I think I'm going to head home. You good?"

Riley looked past me to where Craig had been sitting at the bar next to me, but he was already gone. "It's alright. You good walking home alone? I can grab my coat."

I gestured to the sparse audience brave enough to sit close

to the stage. "And take you away from your fans?" I winked at her. "Never."

Riley laughed. "Okay. I'll catch you tomorrow." She gave me a quick hug before bounding back on stage.

I grabbed my coat and left the bar, welcoming the sharp bite of cold air as I walked back to my apartment.

I knew something was wrong before I turned the key in my lock and opened the door. But even with that tingle of unease, I wasn't prepared for the sight that greeted me. Whoever was responsible for the state of my apartment had been thorough. Everywhere I looked, the apartment was trashed. Couch cushions were slashed, tufts of stuffing bursting out of them. I spotted my collection of VHS tapes strewn across the floor, several of which had been crushed beneath a heel. I rushed inside to scoop them up before I caught myself.

A quick glance around the apartment didn't turn up anyone, but there were a lot of hiding places even in an apartment as small as mine. I kicked myself for not putting my taser or gun in my purse instead of putting them back in my nightstand. I stepped outside and closed the door behind me, waiting until I was standing on the street in front of my apartment to call the police. After reporting the break-in, I put my back to the street and kept my eyes on the door.

When they got there, the police cleared the apartment, confirming whoever did this was long gone. Then they took some photos, asked me if I noticed anything missing, and handed me a business card, so I could let them know what was stolen after inventorying my apartment.

It wasn't until I was alone again that I let the devastation fully register. I wandered from room to room, stopping the longest in the bedrooms. In my room, most of the drawers had been emptied. The bedding lay strewn across the floor, and the mattress had been slashed. Somehow the devastation had been easier to take in the public-facing rooms. Violating the privacy of my bedroom made it far more personal.

I opened the bathroom door and stepped inside. The medicine cabinet had been rifled through, and the shower curtain ripped from its rod. Unlike the bedroom, where whoever broke in was clearly searching for something, the bathroom drawers remained closed. I opened them just in case, and the room spun when I spotted my hand mirror. Someone had used my favorite red lipstick to leave me a message: *Stop Looking*. Although I'd suspected the break-in was related to Jack, that message erased any lingering doubt.

I rushed back to my bedroom with a sinking feeling in my gut. I crossed to my nightstand, pulling out the only drawer in the bedroom that remained closed. Inside, every item I kept there was untouched save three: my taser, my newly purchased and so far useless gun, and the coaster with Wolfsbane's meeting info on it were all gone. Given the state of the rest of the room, I was certain this drawer had been left intact on purpose. Whoever did this wanted me to know what was taken. I slammed it shut.

Now that the drop site was compromised, I had no choice but to contact Wolfsbane to warn him. I didn't want another death on my conscience. As skittish as he was during our first meeting, I wasn't going to hold my breath that I could convince him to arrange an alternate drop location. I grabbed my laptop on my way to the kitchen to send him a message.

In the kitchen, every cabinet door stood open, food strewn across the room. The new box of cereal I'd brought home a day ago was crumpled, its contents crunching under my feet as I surveyed the mess. The trashcan was tipped over, its contents intermingled with the food littering the floor.

I flipped one of the overturned kitchen chairs upright and dropped into it, setting my unopened laptop on the table and resting my head in my hands. I closed my eyes to the destruction. I wasn't ready to put the place back in order. I needed the reminder that somewhere outside my door, there was a person capable of destroying my place, someone determined to stoke my fear. I needed that reminder to make me doubly vigilant in and out of these four walls. I couldn't afford to let my guard down.

The creak of the floorboard next to my bed woke me, and last night came rushing back. I rolled off the bed and grabbed the only remaining weapon I had: a baseball bat I kept underneath the bed. I raised the bat above my head as I waited for the intruder.

"Good form," Riley said, eyeing my stance in approval. If she hadn't been carrying a takeout cup of coffee, I may have swung even after recognizing her.

"Damn it, Riley. You can't break into people's apartments. You're gonna get yourself killed one of these days."

"You're going to need more than a baseball bat to take me out." Riley took the bat out of my hands and traded it for the cup of coffee.

I'd texted her last night to tell her about the break-in and asked if she wanted to help me sort through evidence. The sooner I figured out who was responsible for Jack's death, the better. She'd readily agreed.

"You okay?" Riley asked.

"Not really," I admitted. Now that my fight-or-flight response had relaxed, I set the cup on my nightstand and reached for last night's clothes, dressing quickly. Riley trailed behind me into the living room, where I cleared a path through the clutter so we could both sit on the couch.

She looked around the room, taking in the damage. When she turned back to me, her eyes were hard. "Do you think this was random?"

The urge to keep the note to myself was there, but seeing the worry etched across Riley's face, it didn't feel right to hold this back from her. Whether I'd intended to or not, I trusted her. And going it alone hadn't been working out for me so far.

"No." I confessed. "The killer left me a little lipstick message warning me away."

She hissed in a breath. "As in, Jack's killer? It wasn't Matthews?"

I shook my head.

"Are you sure?"

"Positive. The message said to stop looking."

Riley was somber for a minute, watching me sip my coffee. She'd bought it with cream and some kind of sickeningly sweet syrup, but I drank it anyway, grateful for the caffeine and the company.

"It gets worse. Whoever broke in took a coaster that had the day, time, and location of the drop site where Jack's source was going to pass me evidence that proved the existence of werewolves."

For once, Riley was speechless.

I barreled on. Now that I'd opened the floodgates, I spilled it all, catching her up on the investigation details I'd left out until now. "I am afraid whoever took it was the person who killed Jack."

Riley sat up straighter and squared her shoulders. "All right. We're gonna catch this guy."

"Right." I didn't sound convinced, even to myself. I was too shaken up for optimism.

I watched Riley as she worked her way through every room, looking for a clue left behind. Even though I'd been through everything twice, I let her search. When she came up empty-handed, we agreed to meet up later tonight to come up with our next steps. In the meantime, I had an apartment to set to rights, a shop to open, and a bottle of painkillers calling my name.

After spending the next hour restoring some semblance of order to the apartment, I grabbed my laptop on my way to the shop. I had plenty of time before opening, but I couldn't bear to be in the apartment any longer. Downstairs, I perched on the stool behind the counter and opened my laptop. Thankfully, I had a waiting message from Wolfsbane. I had messaged him last night with a carefully worded warning and a suggestion for an alternate drop site.

I don't know what you're talking about.

I typed a reply. *If you're nervous about a physical drop, why not email it or put it in an online drop box?*

He must have been online because the response came through almost immediately. *Stop contacting me.*

I started to type a response, deleted it, and tried again. After several attempts, I logged off without sending a reply. Even if I could convince him to meet with me, I couldn't live with the consequences if it went wrong. Whoever took the coaster would be watching me even closer now. I couldn't risk leading them to him. One dead body was one too many.

Emma came in as I was opening the shop. I gave her the

abridged version of the break-in, so she'd be alert for anything strange.

"Speaking of strange," she said. "A woman stopped by yesterday looking for you."

"What did she want?"

"She just said she could help you. She left a business card, but all it had on it was a name and phone number. Weird, right?"

"Yeah, that's pretty weird. What was the name?" I asked.

"Merriam or something. I've got her card somewhere." She dug around in her purse until she came up with a card with Meira's name and number on it.

"Do you know her?"

"I do." I decided to give her the simple version. "She has a shop down the street. We've chatted a few times."

That seemed to satisfy Emma, and she busied herself reorganizing costume displays customers had rummaged through yesterday. The rest of the day, I distracted myself with the steady stream of shoppers and alterations.

While I was grateful to lose myself in the mundane daily grind, I couldn't help but look at every face with newfound suspicion. Was that scratch on his hand from ripping off my screen door? Did that lingering look mean that guy was checking me out or was he weighing all the ways he could silence me? By the time I closed the shop, I was more keyed up than I had been last night after discovering my ransacked apartment.

CHAPTER 21

*A*fter learning Twitch was a vampire, I'd all but forgotten about him. Chalk it up to distraction. As he moved to intercept me outside my apartment, it was clear he hadn't forgotten about me.

I weighed my options. He was between me and the staircase to my apartment. I'd just come from closing the shop, and I hadn't seen him until it was too late. I wasn't exactly dressed for running, but it wasn't like I had a better option. Without a word, I spun around to sprint for the street. I hadn't taken more than a step before I felt a cold hand on my shoulder.

I wasn't sure what surprised me more, the strength he held me pinned with using only one hand or the fact that he was speaking in my ear.

"We need to talk." His voice was deep and smooth.

"No. You need to let me go," I countered.

He dropped his hand, and I spun around and shoved him as hard as I could. I must have taken him by surprise because he stumbled backward, giving me just enough time to dart past him and run for the street. I couldn't tell whether he was following me or not. The only sound was the pounding of my own shoes as I raced down the alley. I didn't bother dodging, instead focusing on gaining as much speed as my ill-suited shoes would allow me. I was almost to the street when he called out to me.

"Stop." The command was clear in his voice.

Against my will, and most definitely against my better judgment, I stopped.

"Look at me," he said.

I turned to face him. I couldn't seem to control my body, but my voice was still my own. "Why are you still stalking me?"

"Someone would like to meet with you."

"This isn't how you invite people over for a dinner date. This is how you get arrested. You get that, right?"

He studied me as if I were an insect pinned under museum glass.

"I mean, you stalk a woman, follow her around, steal a police sketch of yourself, then show up in an alleyway and say, 'Someone would like to meet you,' and then what? You think I'm going to follow you to your death lair?"

"Death lair?" His expression didn't change. "Don't be dramatic."

I was getting tired of men telling me to quit being dramatic. Oh, hell to the no. "I'm not going anywhere with you," I yelled, this time with as much drama as I could muster. I dropped my voice and added, "I know what you are."

He sighed and gestured to a black sedan with tinted windows that was idling at the entrance of the alley. "That makes two of us. Get in the car." His voice dropped lower until it hummed along my spine.

I could feel his pull, and I took a step toward him before I could stop myself. I closed my eyes for a second and concentrated on the source of that pull. I felt something snap, and my legs were my own again.

"Are you crazy?" I stepped toward him, and surprisingly, he took a step away from me, his eyes wary. "I'm not getting in your hearse over there. I'm not going anywhere with you." I poked him in the chest with my finger for effect, becoming angrier by the second. "I've had a world-class shitty week. The last thing I'm in the mood for is crazy bloodsucking stalkers. You have until the count of three before I start screaming. Do I make myself clear?"

He shook his head as if to clear it, and then he smiled, his thin lips parting to show teeth so white and straight, they'd make an orthodontist proud. The smile was not reassuring. "I said, get in."

This time, I followed him all the way to the car. He put a hand on the back of my neck, and though he barely touched me, I shivered. No matter how hard I tried, I couldn't pull away again.

He opened the passenger side car door and told me to climb in. For a second, I braced my feet, digging my toes into my shoes in an effort to regain some control. I opened my mouth to scream, but Twitch shoved me into the car. The locks clicked behind him, and he climbed into the driver's seat.

I felt the compulsion release my body, my limbs once again my own. Fat lot of good it did, though, with me locked in the back of a car with tinted windows. I laid down on the seat, bringing my knees to my chest and kicking at the window with all my strength. The window cracked but didn't shatter. Before I could rear back for another blow, Twitch regained control of my body. I gritted my teeth, but there was no way I could break free, my body settling once again into a seated position. When I looked up, Twitch flashed me a smile in the rearview mirror, not bothering to hide his fangs.

Although I tried to reason with him, then bargain with him, Twitch remained silent for the rest of the drive. The drive lasted about twenty minutes—I was keeping track—but it was long enough for me to create a mental inventory of the ways that I would likely die. The most likely scenario was standard vampire fare—draining every last drop of my blood like a glass of cheap Merlot and leaving the shell of my body in a ditch.

Twitch, however, seemed like the kind of guy who would play with his food. I doubted it would be that uninspired. I imagined a roll of duct tape, a plastic tarp, and stakes in the trunk. Or something more original: like baling wire and vise grips. Whatever it was, he seemed the type to be methodical. No impulse kills for him.

He started humming *The Sound of Music* as he pulled the car to a stop. As soon as the doors unlatched, I dutifully climbed out after him. Every nerve screamed for me to run. Instead, I felt compelled to walk toward him. He smiled again, and I hated him more for that than for whatever was to come.

We weren't in a field, but we were close enough. We were parked behind a dilapidated farmhouse surrounded by trees. The two-story looked like it was straight out of a horror movie, with peeling paint and shuttered windows. Although there were no yard lights, there was a faint glow through a curtained window. Either Twitch had prepared for my arrival, or someone else was inside. I was on the fence about which would be worse.

Before we reached the porch, the front door opened to

frame a woman. With her silver hair and refined features, Meira was easily recognizable, even in the dim light. Whatever her intent, I didn't think she'd kill me. At least not out here in a run-down farmhouse. Meira had too much power for that. If she wanted me dead, it would be, as she called it, a sanctioned kill. But watching her greet Twitch as if he were a Saturday shopper in her store made my stomach drop.

The rage I felt looking at her, knowing I was here because of her, snapped me out of whatever control her errand boy had over me. I took full advantage, slamming my elbow into his side. When he dropped his hand, grunting in surprise, I pivoted and ran back to the car, locking the doors behind me. The keys were still in the ignition, so I started the car and threw it in drive.

Before my foot could press the gas, Twitch ripped the door clean off the car and reached around me to put the car back in park. I had assumed vampires would be strong, but being able to rip a steel door off with his bare hands strong was unexpected. He wasn't even sweating when he yanked me out and shoved me toward the house, pocketing the keys in the process.

I spun around to face him again. From the way he glared at me, I knew he'd tried and failed to compel me again.

"What's the matter? Performance issues?" I taunted.

He took a step away from me.

"That's enough." Meira's tone made it clear she was used to being obeyed.

I ignored her, but Twitch gave her his undivided attention. He moved so fast that my eyes couldn't track his movement. One second, he was by me, the next, he was on the porch crowding Meira. Despite being a tall man, he didn't have the bulk to go with it, but after his display of strength with the car, I knew what he was capable of. I shouldn't have cared what he did to her—she'd orchestrated this after all—but I couldn't bring myself to turn my back on her and run for the car.

Twitch was inches from Meira. "What is she?"

Meira didn't back away, and if she was afraid, she didn't show it. She waved her hand dismissively. "A child," she said.

Twitch grabbed her throat with one pale hand and twisted her neck to the side, but Meira didn't flinch.

"Think carefully about what you do next, vampire."

I looked around for an object to attack him with, but all I could find was a rock the size of my fist. It was better than nothing. I picked it up, pulled my arm back, and launched it at his head. The rock flew to the left and missed them both by an embarrassing margin, but it was enough to get his attention. He let Meira go.

"We're even," he told her. "Don't call me again." Then he was gone, the car speeding away, leaving me blanketed in dust.

"Come inside. We need to talk."

As she no doubt knew I would, I followed her. "Why am I here?"

She didn't answer me right away, instead leading me down a darkened hallway and into the only room with a light.

Unlike the outside of the building, the inside was well-kept, homey even. A faded area rug anchored the room, surrounded by a plush couch and side chairs. The only light in the room was from a fire crackling in the fireplace and two matching kerosene lamps on the end tables. Much like her shop, this place felt like stepping back a hundred years.

Meira settled herself on the couch and patted the cushion beside her. I took the chair across from her.

"Why am I here?" I repeated.

"I had hoped you would come to me on your own." She shook her head. "This didn't have to be unpleasant."

"Unpleasant?" My voice was shrill even to my own ears. "Kidnapping goes well past unpleasant, lady."

Meira waved me off as if it were of no consequence. "Since you refuse to leave the reporter's murder alone, there are things you need to know." Her gaze was assessing. "And there are things I need to know." This time, she left out her demand to swear fealty.

"Such as?"

"Tea?" she asked, reaching for the cup and teapot that sat on a small tray next to her. She didn't wait for my answer, instead dropping a small metal ball, presumably filled with tea leaves, into the cup. No mundane grocery store tea bags for her, of course. She poured the steaming water into the cup and studied the gold watch on her wrist to time it.

"I don't need your tea. I need answers. Stop avoiding my questions."

She leaned back against the velvet couch. "Very well. I needed to see how strong you are. That's why I sent Twitch."

"To see if I was stronger than a vampire? Are you crazy?" I had plenty of talents—my clientele could attest to that—but physical prowess was not among them.

She chuckled, like we were sharing a joke. "Perhaps, but I got my answer."

"Sorry to disappoint you." I didn't even try to keep the sarcasm out of my voice.

"On the contrary. Do you know how many necromancers can break free from a vampire's compulsion?" When I didn't guess, she continued. "Two that I know of, and we're both sitting in this room."

"How many necromancers are there?"

She picked up the teacup and offered it to me, but I made no move to take it. She might have succeeded in getting me here, but I sure as shit didn't have to play tea party.

"Not many. A hundred or so in the world. What do you know about us?"

"Other than what you've told me? Nothing."

She took a sip before setting her cup aside. "That's what I thought. I'm surprised Dottie didn't prepare you."

I felt the blood drain from my face. "You knew my grandmother?"

"Child, I just told you there are few of us in this world. Of course, I knew your grandmother." She stood up and walked to the fire that had dwindled down to glowing embers. Adding another log, she took her time returning to the conversation.

"I owed Dottie a debt I didn't have a chance to repay before her death." She turned to face me. "I will repay her the only way left to me: by training you."

"And if I don't want to be trained?"

"Then you'll die." Meira's voice was matter of fact.

Although she may have viewed her debt as extending to me, it was clear any emotional tie she'd had to my grandmother did not encompass me. This was just another transaction, a way to balance her ledger. Her lack of emotion was what convinced me she wasn't lying.

"Because I'm looking for Jack's killer?"

"Because of what you are," she countered. "Tonight, you resisted one of the oldest vampires in the city. You have no idea the power you have access to. But eventually others will take note, and when they do, they'll come for you."

"I don't want power."

"That's not the point. There are plenty who do, and to them, you will be either a weapon to wield or a danger to eliminate. Either way, you don't stand a chance in this world without my help."

"I'll consider it," I said, not that I planned to take her up on the offer. "Right now, my priority is justice for Jack Gates. If you want to help me, start by telling me about the werewolves, so we can figure out who killed him."

I should have been more specific because I spent the next two hours in Werewolf 101. I learned about their strengths, most of which lined up with Hollywood's version of them: superhuman strength, heightened sense of hearing and smell, and natural-born fighting ability. They were resistant to magic, which made them powerful allies and dangerous enemies, according to Meira.

I already knew Volkov was the alpha of the Kansas City pack, but I learned that although Volkov was a wolf, his pack was not limited to wolves. Rather, it was made up of a variety of shifters. Riley, thankfully, was not among them, operating outside the confines of any pack. As long as she stayed within Volkov's territory though, she was subject to his rule.

Meira was evasive about Craig when I asked.

It was late by the time Meira dropped me off in front of my shop. I was now armed with more knowledge than I'd asked for. Too bad none of it brought me closer to finding out who killed Jack.

Thanks to my kidnapping, I'd missed Riley. Although I texted her on the way back to assure her I was okay, she wasn't happy about it. She reluctantly agreed to wait until tomorrow night to come over.

I didn't see the bird pinned to my door until I was close enough to touch it. Held in place by two thumbtacks through the underside of each wing, the shiny silver was garish against the delicate feathers. There was no blood, but I didn't need to touch it to know it was dead. Whoever killed it had snapped its neck, the angle of the bird's head unnatural against its small body.

I had no doubt that the person who left it for me was the same person who'd broken into my apartment and stole the coaster with Wolfsbane's drop site location on it. Even pinned with its back to the door, I recognized it. This was one of the few birds that I knew on sight, one that I was fond enough of to use as a username: starling.

As a child, starlings had been the birds that returned year after year to nest beneath our eaves. My grandmother loved to tell Claire and me stories, and in them, the starling was the messenger of the spirit world, a harbinger of change. As I stared at the twisted neck of the bird pinned to my door, I couldn't help but believe her.

Death, they say, comes in threes. The starling on my door was the second tally mark in the killer's ledger. The message was clear. If I didn't want to join Jack Gates, I needed to walk away.

I didn't know how long the bird had been pinned to my door, but I scanned the area anyway. At this time of night, there was little movement in my neighborhood. Whoever sent the message was either long gone or discreet enough that I couldn't spot them.

I still looked over my shoulder as I went inside for a plastic bag. I snapped a few photographs on my phone before wrapping the small body in a paper towel and tying it in the bag. Although I had the urge to bury it, I lived in the middle of a city. It would be hard to bury a body, even one as small as a bird, along a busy street without attracting notice. Like it or not, the dumpster was my only option.

After disposing of the bird and triple-checking my dead bolt, I headed to the bathroom, intent on a scalding hot shower. My phone rang before I got there. "Hello?"

For a second, the only response was ragged breathing on the end of the line. "Kali?"

"Emma, what's wrong?" It wasn't like Emma to call this late.

"I had a late theater practice tonight," she started, her voice shaky. "And when I got out, there was something in my car."

I closed my eyes and leaned against the bathroom wall, hoping that my hunch was wrong.

"It was terrible, Kali. Someone left a dead bird on my seat." Her words sped up as she talked. "Its neck was broken."

"Oh God, Emma. I'm so sorry."

"Who would do such a thing?" she asked, her voice breaking.

"I don't know." The guilt ate at me like acid because I did know, and I had brought this to her.

"That's not all," she said. "There was also a coaster with an address written on it. It's not an address I recognized, so I looked it up, and it's a public park."

Fear for Emma clawed at me, and for a second, I couldn't find my voice.

"Kali? Are you there?"

"I'm still here." I took a deep breath. "Listen, I want you to call the police as soon as you hang up this phone. Tell them you got a threatening message."

"I already did. They took the information, but they said it was probably a stupid prank and that there wasn't much they could do about it."

The stakes were too high to keep Emma in the dark. I gave her the scrubbed-down version of my investigation, leaving out any mention of werewolves or ghosts. Then, I convinced her to take the week off and to go spend a few days at her parents' house. She only agreed after I assured her I was working with the authorities. Authority was a subjective term; I was counting Meira among them.

That gave me one week to find Jack's killer.

CHAPTER 22

$\mathcal{J}$ spent the next day on the edge of a breakdown. Jack had popped in, but as soon as he found out Wolfsbane wouldn't be handing over the DNA evidence, he left in a snit. I didn't try to stop him. Other than the people I had to interact with in the course of business, I mostly kept to myself, mentally replaying every interaction I'd had since finding Jack's body. By the time Riley shouldered her way into my apartment, I was exhausted but no closer to narrowing down my leads.

That bird had been the point of no return. For now, it served as a warning, but I wasn't naïve enough to think that the killer would stop at a warning. Whether I continued looking or not, I was too much of a threat, and eventually the killer would come for me. By default, that would put everyone around me in his path, Riley and Emma included.

But Riley was a lot harder to convince to let me go it alone than Emma had been. Riley didn't even let me finish my pitch, holding up her hand to stop me.

"I'm in this one hundred percent. Deal with it."

"And if I can't?"

Riley glared at me. "Then I'll go straight to the Tribunal." She crossed her arms. "You need my help."

Until I knew who killed Jack and why, I couldn't trust the Tribunal to do anything other than cover this up. I told myself that Riley was better equipped than Emma to navigate the dangers of this world, but I wasn't sure I believed it. Either way, I was no longer in this alone.

Riley came prepared for a long night, armed with takeout and a photo envelope. While I'd been hiding out, she'd been taking candid shots of every suspect on our list.

I looked at the array of faces she'd scattered across my coffee table. "Are you crazy? What if they spotted you?"

She laughed. "They never spot me." She said it like covert photo shoots were a common occurrence for her.

I ignored the chopsticks she offered me, grabbing a fork from the kitchen before settling on the couch next to her to consider the suspects. She had photos of everyone on my list, including those I'd already ruled out. Craig's photo was the one she'd taken inside my apartment the morning of the breakfast from hell. The photos of Leon and Volkov were clear, both outdoor pictures bathed in natural light. Twitch's photo, however, was a night photo, grainy and slightly out of focus. I didn't know how she'd managed to catch them all unaware.

Riley had also added two who weren't on my list: Bennie and Ruby.

I pointed at the two of them. "You think they are suspects. Why?"

"Both were working the night Jack was killed. And both Ruby and Bennie are wolves, not that you heard it from me," she said, shoveling another bite of lo mien in her mouth.

Ruby, I already knew was a wolf. But the news that Bennie, someone I counted a friend, was one of the shifters rocked me. I had no clue. Shifter or not, I couldn't believe he had anything to do with this. However, I knew better than to rule anyone out based purely on emotion, so I left his photo among the others.

I picked up Craig's photo and waited until she was done chewing. "And Craig? He's a werewolf?"

Riley laughed. "No."

"Human then?" Only Volkov rivaled Craig's intimidating air. It was hard to believe he wasn't something other.

Riley sat her empty food container down and reached for the photo. "Not a wolf, but not human, either." She held it up, and we both examined it.

"Then what?"

She shrugged. "Don't know. Whatever he is, he's the most dangerous of the bunch."

I eyed Volkov and Twitch. "What makes you say that?"

"He's the enforcer."

"Enforcer of what?"

Riley handed me the photo. She folded her legs underneath her and leaned back on the cushion. "Didn't you talk to Meira?"

"I talked to her, but she won't tell me anything about Craig unless I agree to abide by her authority."

Riley shook her head. "Figures." She grabbed my half-eaten container of lo mien. "You gonna eat this?"

"All yours. But back to Craig."

"He's the Tribunal's enforcer," she said around a mouth full of noodles. "He's like the supernatural's version of the law, except without the limitations."

"He's the one who investigates crimes involving supernaturals?" I asked.

"Sometimes, I guess. But mostly the factions do the investigation." At my blank look, she clarified. "You know, vamps investigate vamps, shifters look into things involving shifters."

"That seems like a pretty big conflict of interest."

"Maybe, but that's how it's done. When there is a conflict between factions or something that affects all of us, it goes before the Tribunal."

"And that's when Craig gets involved."

Riley nodded. "Yes. But more than that, Craig is the one who metes out justice."

In this world, I already knew that justice was meted out harshly and swiftly. Policing humans was one thing. The ability to keep creatures with superhuman strength and senses in line required a specialized skill set, someone capable of brutality. Someone who I'd invited into my home, someone I'd kissed. The lo mien sat like a ball of lead in my stomach.

"And Volkov? I know he's the alpha, but is he involved with the Tribunal?"

Riley didn't hesitate to answer this time. "Yes. He's on the Tribunal with Meira."

We ran through our suspects one by one, weighing their possible involvement against what we knew, while polishing off a half-full carton of ice cream. Regardless of what the police thought, Leon was an easy one to rule out. The rest were complicated.

Although both Craig and Volkov could have used the Tribunal's authority to quash Jack's story without bloodshed, it was possible one of them had a personal reason to eliminate him. However, Craig had been at Grinders when whoever broke in was trashing my apartment. I felt a rush of relief when Riley moved his photo to the unlikely pile.

Bennie and Ruby were unknowns, and Twitch was a tossup. Vampires might not normally leave a bloody mess behind, but after my last run-in with him, I refused to rule him out altogether. After an hour, we were no closer to identifying a prime suspect.

There was something that had been bothering me, though. "How did the killer manage to go down a five-story metal slide without leaving a single bloody fingerprint?"

"Gloves?" Riley offered.

"Possibly. But blood was all over that crime scene. There is no way the person who killed Jack wouldn't have at least left traces of blood at the top of that slide."

Riley stood up and paced the floor. "Maybe they used the exit through the gift shop. But how would someone manage that without being seen?"

"According to Craig, the gift shop was closed because they were short-staffed. The door was locked—I saw that for myself—but staff would have had keys." I studied the photo spread, "Even if the killer went out through the gift shop, the crowd was milling around on the street. Someone would have seen the killer come out covered in blood. Plus, there still would have been a blood trail of some kind."

"Which means whoever killed Jack didn't leave the haunted house," Riley said, finishing my thought. She looked thoughtful for a second. "But that makes no sense. Didn't you say the police didn't find the murder weapon?"

I nodded. "Yeah. All the weapons they took from the crime scene ended up being props with fake blood on them."

Riley frowned. "If the killer was still in the house, how on earth did the police miss someone covered with blood, carrying a knife?"

"The secret door," I said, forgetting I hadn't shared that detail with Riley yet.

"What secret door?" Riley asked.

I ran through my unauthorized visit to Howl, including the door Jack helped me find.

Riley tapped her chin. "And you don't know where the door leads?"

"No. I didn't have time to check it out before I ran. But I know it can't lead outside. I counted the exit doors, and there are only three: the front door, the gift shop, and the side staff entrance I went through."

"There's only one way to find out." Riley jumped up and grabbed her coat. "Time for a field trip."

I started to argue with her, but the fact was, Riley was a lot better at this breaking and entering gig than I was. Plus, she had the advantage of enhanced senses, which could serve as an early alert system, ensuring we didn't get caught. Riley pulled out her lock-picking kit and grinned.

"No need." I retrieved the Howl key I'd had made from the top of the refrigerator where I'd stashed it. I headed off Riley's next question. "I'll tell you on the way. But first, I need to change."

If Riley was nervous about breaking into Howl, she was a master at hiding it. While I was getting dressed, she'd made headlamps with duct tape and pocket-sized flashlights. They weren't the least bit comfortable, but they would keep our hands free.

When we reached Howl, Riley strolled up to the door like she owned the place. Once we were inside, she slapped a headlamp on each of us and gestured for me to lead the way. Riley's confidence was reassuring. I hustled to the room in question, eager to find out what secrets lay beyond that door.

I pulled back the heavy drapes and felt along the wall until I felt the familiar zing. "It's here," I told Riley. "Even though it's hidden, I don't know how the cops could have possibly missed this with as much time as they spent canvassing this room."

"It's spelled," Riley said.

"Huh?"

"The door—it's spelled so humans can't see it. Only other supernaturals can find the door." She ran her fingers along the seam until she found the notch that served as a door handle. "Smart," she said.

She didn't hesitate, descending the stairs in front of me. I kept my eyes trained beyond her, scanning for any sign that we weren't alone. I counted the flights of stairs as we went— six—which meant when we reached the bottom, we were underground. The room we entered was large. I fumbled on the wall until I found a light switch. Since there was zero chance anyone outside would be able to see a light on in the bowels of this building, I flipped it on.

A row of oversized industrial gray lockers lined the wall on the right. None of the lockers were locked, so we went down the row checking each one. Although none of them contained a stash of bloody clothing or a potential murder weapon, each one held several changes of clothes. None of the lockers were labelled with staff names, but it wasn't difficult to sort out whose was whose. Craig's locker was filled with identical black t-shirts and broken-in blue jeans. Ruby's locker was stocked with black ribbed tank tops and dark-washed jeans. Although Bennie's locker didn't contain a capsule wardrobe, the costume props were a dead giveaway, considering he bought them all from me.

I continued snooping through lockers until I got to one on the end that clearly didn't belong to any of the actors. Inside, crisp white dress shirts and black pants hung in a neat row, a pair of spare black dress shoes underneath.

"Check this out," Riley called from where she'd wandered into another room.

I followed her voice and found myself in a small alcove outfitted with a bathroom stall, sink, and walk-in shower. "Shit."

"I guess we know how the killer managed to get rid of the blood," she said.

I pointed to the other room. "And find a change of clothes."

"And look over here," Riley said, uncovering yet another key piece of the puzzle.

On the other side of the shower stall was a door leading to another set of stairs.

"Just a sec." I turned back to the room we'd just left. I pulled out my cell phone and took photos of every locker and every corner of the room. "Alright," I said, returning to Riley and the second exit.

Unlike the stairs we descended earlier, this one was a single flight going up. We paused at the top of the stairs, listening. When we were convinced that we were still alone in the house, Riley swung the door open. We came out on the far side of the entry way. This door, just like the one in the room where Jack had been killed, was spelled so that humans wouldn't see it. Anyone working that night could have easily come upstairs undetected.

Although we now knew how the killer could have stayed on-site without getting caught covered in blood, we weren't any closer to narrowing down our suspect pool. Any one of the staff could have easily left the crime scene to wash off Jack's blood before dressing in identical clothing and returning upstairs. If those dress clothes belonged to Volkov, as I suspected, he'd had just as much opportunity as any of the other staff. The lockers even offered a convenient place to stash a murder weapon. If there even was a weapon; I suspected a werewolf claw could slash a throat as easily as a knife. The only person our discovery seemed to rule out was Twitch.

CHAPTER 23

*R*iley and I spent another hour at my apartment poring over the evidence before calling it a night. After Riley left, I found myself on edge, unable to sleep. Rather than half-heartedly flipping through TV channels I didn't want to watch, I opened my laptop and pulled up Jack's story.

I scanned it again, then pulled up the folder that held the photos of the wolf mid-shift. I zoomed in on the werewolf's hands. Each finger was tipped with a claw that looked plenty sharp enough to slit a man's neck.

I looked for any defining characteristics, any feature that could help me match them to one of our suspect's photos. The angles and perspectives were different, making it hard to gauge the size of the person shifting. Based on the lack of Herculean muscles, it was obviously not Craig or Volkov. That left Bennie and Ruby, who had similar body types. Just because those two were at Howl the night of Jack's death didn't mean it had to be one of them. Jack's photo could just as easily have been a photo of someone else entirely.

I thought about summoning Jack and strong-arming him into naming his source, but I doubted he'd cooperate, and I still had no idea how to make him answer me. For a dead guy, he still held on to his misguided notion of reporting ethics. I needed to bypass Jack altogether and find the original unedited photos. I'd already searched his laptop, including going through his recently deleted files without luck. Based on the meticulously archived files, I was positive that he wouldn't have deleted the originals. And if they weren't saved on his hard drive or the flash drive I'd retrieved from his office, that left cloud files.

I put on a new pot of coffee to brew before opening tabs for every major photo sharing site I could think of. Opening the first site, I entered the same password Jack used for the forums. After weeks of dead ends and frustrations, the site opened on my first try.

Methodically, I went through every photo in every file. They all seemed to be personal photos, dating back to Jack's years in Washington, DC. I closed that tab and moved on to the next sites. Two of them didn't recognize the account, but the last one did. As soon as I saw the file naming convention, I knew this was it. A few clicks later, and I found a subfolder named Source Originals. My finger hovered for a second, anticipation tightening my gut. I tapped the mouse and opened the folder.

None of the photos were named, with each still labeled with the camera-generated identification. The first one I opened was instantly recognizable: the fully shifted wolf. My palms started sweating as I made my way through the remaining photos. Several were almost identical to the first one, as if Jack had snapped photos in rapid succession. When I clicked on the original mid-shift photo, I spotted a familiar face above the furred body of the beast.

Sharp cheekbones, full lips, and flaming hair. She wasn't looking directly at the camera, but there was no question it was Ruby.

"Jack!" I hadn't been able to find the penny that served as the ironclad conduit, so I focused all my energy into the command.

It didn't take him long to appear. One second, I was alone in my living room, and the next, Jack was standing before me, his hair tousled like I'd interrupted a good sleep. I didn't know if ghosts slept or not, but I wasn't in the mood to make chitchat to find out.

"Wow. Lower the volume, would you?" He scrubbed a hand over his jaw before leaning over my coffee table to examine the photos that still lay scattered across it. His gaze caught on Ruby's photo for a second before he forced himself to look away.

I clenched my jaw. "Those aren't the photos you need to be worried about," I snapped, holding up the laptop. I'd blown up his unedited photo until Ruby's face took up most of the screen. "Look familiar?"

Jack took a step toward the computer, reaching his hand out as if he could snatch it away. I jerked it behind me, and he refocused his attention on me. I was so angry that I was practically vibrating.

"Why didn't you tell me the photos were of Ruby?"

He didn't make eye contact.

Then, I remembered the gold earring in his closet. "You

were sleeping with her, weren't you?"

His shoulders slumped, and he nodded. "I didn't want to bring her into it."

"You should have thought of that when you were conducting your little boudoir shoot." I closed the computer. "Did she know?"

"Know what?"

"Did she know about the story?"

Jack had the decency to look ashamed. "She wasn't aware I took the photos, if that's what you're asking."

I tried to punch him in the arm, but my hand glided through without making contact. "And I thought I had shit taste in men." I whistled. "That's low, Jack."

"It's not like I was going to out her. I edited the photos to be anonymous." Any fleeting shame he'd shown was gone, the reporter in him crowding it out.

"Well then, that just makes it okay, doesn't it?" I couldn't even look at him. "Do you love her?" His hesitation was answer enough. I waved him off. "Never mind. Are you sure she didn't know about the photos? About your plans to release them along with a story? Because that's a pretty good reason to kill you." I glared at him. "In fact, if I were on the jury, I'd probably let her walk."

"Ruby wouldn't have killed me. She was invested in the relationship." He cleared his throat. "She wanted to move in together."

"Even more reason to kill you."

Jack opened his mouth to argue, but with one look at my expression, he wisely closed his mouth again.

"Anything else?" I asked.

Jack looked defeated. "She saw the photos on my phone," Jack admitted. "The night I was killed, she confronted me about it."

"Are you kidding me right now?" I full-on screamed. "You didn't think that was a relevant detail to share?"

"I know what you're thinking, and yes, she was upset. But I deleted them off my phone in front of her."

"But not the backups," I said, pointing to the photos on my screen.

"I needed the photos for the story," Jack said.

"Did Ruby know you were still planning on publishing the story?"

"No," Jack said. "I may have given her the impression that I would bury the story."

"You do know that this story would have been her death warrant, don't you?" I pointed at the laptop. "Those photos are proof that she exposed shifters to a human. They would have executed her, no questions asked. You get that, right?"

Jack dropped his head, all the fight going out of him. "I didn't know that. Maybe I should have. She was always scared of someone finding out about us. She thought someone she worked with was getting suspicious."

"Who?"

"She didn't say." He studied my face. "What are you going to do?"

"I don't know."

He cleared his throat. "And the story?"

"Get out!" I didn't have to tell him twice.

There were no good options. Detective Woodson hadn't been much help thus far, and if I didn't want to out the werewolves —and land myself in a psych ward—the police were out. I couldn't be sure Volkov wasn't the killer, even if he was on the Tribunal. Volkov seemed close to Ruby, so he may have been willing to circumvent Meira to protect Ruby and cover up the leak. Ruby certainly had motive to kill Jack, but if Jack were to be believed, she thought he had deleted the photos and killed the story.

I tried to come up with any other solution than the obvious one, but after an hour of fruitless brainstorming, I dialed Meira's number. Just when I thought it was going to go to voicemail, she answered.

"It's Kali. I need your help."

There was no hesitation on her end. "What do you need?"

I took a steadying breath and filled her in on everything I left out the last time I'd talked to her. I told her about each one of Jack's visits, about the story Jack was working on and the proof he had, and about Ruby's involvement in the whole thing.

"I can't prove it, but I'm afraid either Ruby or Volkov killed Jack."

"What makes you say that?"

"Ruby and Jack were having an affair." If Meira was shocked, she kept it to herself. "And Jack had photos of Ruby." I took a breath before sharing the most damning bit. "They were of Ruby changing into a wolf."

Meira hissed in a breath, pausing for a minute before responding. "Does Ruby know you suspect her?"

"I don't think so," I said. "I haven't talked to Ruby about any of this."

"Good. Do you have all the evidence that Jack had?"

"Most of it." I paused, not sure how much I wanted to divulge. In the end, I decided there wasn't much point in keeping Wolfsbane from her. She'd likely find out eventually, so I told her about the alleged DNA evidence and about him going to ground after my break-in.

As she connected the break-in with the evidence Jack was collecting, she became more insistent. "You need to bring everything you have—and I do mean everything, Kali—and come to my house. Don't talk to anyone else. Come straight here."

I weighed my options, but in the end, she was the only one I had. "Okay. What's your address?" The last time I'd been to her house had been under duress. At the time, I had been more focused on Twitch than the location. I wrote down the address she gave me and shoved it in my pocket. I wrote a quick note for the shop door saying we were closed for the day.

The drive to Meira's house was a fair distance. I'd have to stop for gas along the way. As I walked to my car, I stayed alert. I was so busy scanning the area in front of me that I never saw the person behind me until the taser took me to the ground.

CHAPTER 24

The cell phone I had been holding dropped, its screen shattering. The pain was instant and excruciating, causing every muscle in my body to seize up. Despite the pain, I willed myself to move, to open my mouth and scream for help. But no matter how much I willed it, all I could do was watch the denim-clad legs moving around my body and hands reaching for me.

It wasn't until the person hoisted me in the air that I could make out Ruby's face. As tension began to leave my muscles, it felt like a thousand fire ants swarming across my body. By the time I had regained any semblance of control, Ruby had already duct-taped my hands, legs, and mouth and shoved me in the trunk of a car. I pleaded with my eyes, trying to wiggle my lower face to dislodge the tape. She grimaced before slamming the trunk closed and leaving me helpless in the dark.

I heard a car door shut, then the spark of the engine. Instead of rushing out of the lot like I expected, Ruby took her time, allowing the car to idle. The sound of voices drifted closer, but I couldn't make out the words.

Growing up in a family of cops, I'd had countless crime statistics drilled into me since I was a child. Now they played on an endless loop in my head. My chances of surviving a gunshot wound, for example, was around seventy percent. For a stab wound, survival odds were even higher. But of all the odds, the most pertinent was that my chances of being killed skyrocketed once I was taken to a second location.

Knowing my survival could well depend on what I did now, I rolled on my back and lifted my knees to my chest, kicking the trunk as hard as I could. I paused long enough to listen, but the voices were gone. Still, I kicked and kicked until the car lurched into motion. Once we started moving, I gave up, reserving my strength for the fight ahead.

I couldn't afford to let panic take me. Odds or not, I was a damn survivor.

We drove for quite a while in start-and-stop traffic. The third time we stopped at what must have been a stoplight, I wiggled toward the interior of the car. I felt around, trying frantically to locate an emergency lever that would lower the back seat. If I could roll into the back of the car, I had a chance of attracting enough attention that someone would call the cops. Several minutes later, I gave up.

It was hard to judge time being locked in the dark, but the drive wasn't a short one. I concentrated on the route as best I could. At times, we sped up, probably on one of the freeways. Eventually, the car took a left turn and slowed to residential speeds. After several more turns, the car rolled to a stop.

I quieted my breathing and listened intently until I heard a garage door opening. On the bright side, that meant we were likely in one of the suburbs, surrounded by other houses and their inhabitants. Because it was a weekday, most people would be at work rather than at home, but it was better than winding up in an isolated area. Less encouraging was the fact that we were now in a closed garage, separated from any prying eyes that might spot me as I was hauled out of the trunk.

Gagged as I was, screaming was impossible. I wiggled my body until I'd flipped a quarter turn to ensure I could kick Ruby once she finally opened the trunk. She didn't, however, seem to be in a great hurry. My head was bent at an uncomfortable angle, and as the minutes dragged on, I fought the urge to shift positions.

I waited until I heard the click of the lock release. I braced myself. The trunk seemed to open in slow motion, and my heartbeat hammered inside my chest. Before it was fully opened, I kicked out my bound feet with as much force as I could muster, catching Ruby unprepared. The strike to the gut doubled her over, and I took the opportunity to kick my feet up, catching her beneath the chin.

She staggered backward into the closed garage door, and for a second, I thought I might have a chance at escape. Getting my footing proved more difficult than I'd imagined, though. By the time I got to my knees, Ruby had recovered, the look in her eyes promising retribution.

She grabbed a fistful of my hair, spun me around, and pulled me out of the car. The back of my legs scraped against the metal frame. Although I tried to get my legs underneath me, the long ride, coupled with the earlier shock from the taser, made my movements stiff and sluggish. Ruby did nothing to brace me as I cleared the car, letting go of my hair. My body slammed to the cement, pain ricocheting up my back where I landed. I managed to hold my head erect, so it didn't bounce off the cement. Staying conscious was the only thing currently in my favor.

"Get up." Ruby loomed over me but made no effort to help me stand.

I rolled onto my side, using my bound hands to brace myself as I pushed up onto my knees. I took my time standing, trying to get my bearings and take in as much as I could about where we were. Clearly tired of my stalling, Ruby shoved me toward the door to the house. I hated having her at my back, but I didn't have a lot of choice.

She reached around me and opened the door. A single step led into the house, but navigating even one stair was challenging because of the duct tape around my ankles. Ruby shoved me again, and my upper body flew forward while my feet remained rooted to the floor. I sprawled across the threshold, my knees taking the brunt of the abuse. I cried out, but only a muffled sound made it past the tape. This time, I made no effort to stand despite Ruby's demands.

She grabbed me around the waist and stood me up, then lifted me past the step before nudging me down the hall. The hall was a short one that passed a utility room before ending in a dated living room. Ruby flipped a switch on the wall. The two lamps that came on provided enough light to see but not enough to illuminate the space. Although there was a window on the far wall, it was covered with floor-to-ceiling black-out curtains.

Wherever we were, it wasn't a new subdivision. The walls were clad in dark wood paneling that made the room feel claustrophobic. Mismatched bookcases lined one wall, all of which were overflowing with books. Above one of the bookcases, there was a framed state of Missouri medical license for one Dr. Henry T. O'Brien. It was the name of a stranger, and I hoped, for his sake, that he was out of town on vacation.

There was no TV in the room. Instead, the adjoining wall where a TV might go served as a showcase for an impressive weapons collection. Old revolvers along with more modern guns, daggers of various sizes and shapes, and two swords were mounted there. None of them were behind glass, so I assumed they got some use. Beneath the weapons was a table pushed up against the wall, its surface cluttered with newspapers and ammunition.

This wasn't the kind of room you brought company to unless the company in question was part of a militia. None of it boded well for me walking out of here alive.

Ruby scanned the room as if she were searching for anything out of place. Seemingly satisfied, she gestured toward a worn green couch in front of the bookcases. When I didn't move, she stepped closer to me.

"Sit down, now."

Now that I was here, my best bet of staying alive was to drag out whatever this was until I had an opportunity to escape. I shuffled my way to the couch and sat, my arms still awkwardly bound in front of me.

Ruby leaned over me. "Stay here while I check the house. I promise you that if you get up from this couch, you will regret it."

While it was tempting to make a break for it the minute she turned her back and crossed the room, I knew I wouldn't get far. Even if I weren't bound, she was faster than me. My encounter with Volkov had effectively demonstrated werewolf speed. I knew I'd only get one chance at escape. I needed to bide my time long enough to find the right opening, one where I could either incapacitate her or at least catch her by surprise. At the moment, she was hyper-vigilant, and the door to the outside was a long way from where I sat.

I figured if she had wanted to kill me immediately, she would've driven me somewhere much more remote than this house. I didn't suffer any delusions that she was going to let me walk away from this; she'd gone too far to risk letting me go. I was as good as dead in her mind, but bringing me here meant she wanted something from me first. Something that would hopefully buy me enough time to try to get free. For now, at least, I was going to be patient.

Ruby walked over to the window first, glancing out the curtains and scanning the yard. Satisfied, she crossed the room toward the pocket doors that separated this room from the next. The doors opened with a creak. Ruby looked over her shoulder at me to make sure I was watching before she moved into the next room, stepping over the prone body on the floor. My scream didn't make it past the duct tape. Ruby watched my reaction, her eyes hard.

I might not have known the name of the man lying on the dining room floor, but I recognized his face: Wolfsbane. The room swam. I had to close my eyes briefly before I could look at his body again.

Unlike Jack, this man's death had not been quick. He had claw marks up and down his arms, and his shirt had been shredded, the blood spreading outward from each rip in his dark t-shirt. Looking at the cuts Ruby's claws had inflicted on Wolfsbane's body, I understood why the police had never recovered a murder weapon for Jack. She hadn't used her claws on Wolfsbane's neck, though. It looked as if it had been torn out with teeth.

The photo of Ruby mid-change flashed into my head, and

I knew she had taken her time with this kill, that she had enjoyed it. Nausea rolled in my stomach.

I tried to quiet the voice in my head that said this was my doing. I didn't know how Ruby found him, but I had no doubt that I was the beginning of the trail. Had I not contacted him, not met with him to get the evidence he'd offered Jack, he would still be alive.

But there was nothing I could do for him now. I forced my eyes away from his body to take inventory of the room.

My best bet seemed to be the small daggers hanging low on the wall. If I could grab one of them, I could hide it under my leg until I got another stretch alone. Then I could use it to cut through the tape. I stood up, but before I could take more than a step toward the wall, I heard Ruby coming back. Quickly, I sat back down, keeping my eyes focused on the window and not the knives I so desperately wanted to get ahold of.

"All alone." Ruby paused next to Wolfsbane's body. "As you can see, Henry here wasn't very cooperative. Had a real attitude about my kind. He was a geneticist, you know."

I hadn't known that, but it explained the evidence he'd claimed to have.

Ruby glared down at him, then looked at his wall of weaponry. "He thought we were abominations to be studied and disposed of." She snarled and kicked his leg. Then she turned her attention back to me. "But a pretty little thing like you, you're going to be a lot more cooperative, aren't you?" She waited as if expecting me to nod.

I sat stiffly, looking her directly in the eye. If she wanted me to talk, she wasn't going to get anything from me until she removed the tape from my mouth. She smiled and crossed the room to the weapons display, running her fingers over one of the revolvers while watching me.

"Nah," she said. "Too quick." She picked up one of the blades, balancing it in her palm before trading it for another. Ruby finally settled on a long bone-handled knife, the kind you might gut a fish with. I blocked out the visual that knowledge dredged up.

She tossed the knife into the air and caught it effortlessly before crouching down in front of me. She trailed the knife along the inside of my thigh. "I'm going to remove this tape. If you scream, I'll shove this knife in your leg. I'll miss the femoral artery. You won't bleed out, but it will hurt like a son-of-a-bitch. You got me?"

Slowly, I nodded. Ruby moved the knife to her left hand and pulled the tape off my mouth, her lips curving into a smile at my sharp intake of breath as it ripped free. As much as I wanted to scream or bargain with her, I waited for her to speak.

She passed the knife back and forth between her hands. "I want the photos."

"I don't know what you're talking about."

Ruby brought the knife to my face, using the side of the blade to force my chin up until we were eye-to-eye again. I tried not to flinch. "Oh yes, you do. And you'll give them to me one way," she sliced the knife along my cheekbone just deep enough to cut the surface, "or another."

She stood up and left the room, returning a second later with a dining room chair. She placed it a couple feet it in front of me and sat down, the knife still in her hand.

"I need to thank you, though. I knew Jack was meeting with someone to get enough evidence to break the story, but I didn't know who." She gestured to the dead body in the next room. "That is, until you led me right to him. I would have never found our friend Henry, here, without you." She tsked. "You should have minded your own business, made your little costumes, and left Jack's story alone."

I knew that repeated denials were just going to make her angry, but I also knew that she would kill me the second she got what she wanted. I needed to keep her talking to buy myself some time. I doubted she'd risk removing the tape from my hands or feet, so I twisted my hands back and forth as much as the binding would allow, trying to loosen the tape while I spoke.

"I'm not sure what story you're talking about," I said. "I just wanted to know what happened to Jack."

"You didn't even know Jack," she snapped. "Why would you care what happened to him?" I started to answer, but she didn't give me the chance. "Doesn't matter. What matters is that you and Henry were going to go public with Jack's story. That means you have the photos he took of me."

"I wasn't going to go public with the story," I argued.

"Liar." She lifted the knife to my throat. "You're going to tell me where the originals are."

I called her bluff, leaning into the knife, feeling the edge breaking my skin. "If you were going to cut my throat, you would've already done it. Like you did to Jack."

If I hadn't been watching her so closely, I may have missed the pain that flickered in her eyes before she hardened her gaze again. It wasn't much, but it was something I could work with.

"Did you love him?" I asked.

"Doesn't matter," Ruby said. But she leaned back in her chair, taking the knife with her.

"What he did to you wasn't right." I forced sympathy into my voice. "He betrayed your trust."

She laughed. "You know nothing about me or about my relationship with Jack."

"Did you let him take those photos, Ruby?"

She stood abruptly and knocked her chair over. Her jaw was clenched, her knuckles turning white where they were fisted around the knife. I was afraid I'd pushed too far, too fast, but then she took a step back, fighting to regain control. After a few measured breaths, she walked back over to the wall of weapons.

"Henry had quite the collection, don't you think?" This time she added a pair of brass knuckles to the knife she held.

I wasn't the kind of girl who got in physical fights, so I didn't have a frame of reference. But even I knew those were going to do real damage if she hit me with them. I scrambled to think of something to say that would buy me more time.

Ruby laid the knife on the chair and threaded her fingers through the brass knuckles before tapping them against her other palm. "Last chance before I mess up that pretty face," she said, taking a step toward me. "Where are the photos?"

I was out of time. "Online."

She waited for me to elaborate, rubbing her fingers over the brass. "Where?"

"I need a laptop."

"No. Just tell me."

"It's more complicated than that," I hedged. "I made copies and set them up to auto-send to *The Kansas City Star* and *The New York Times* as well as several news stations."

She looked skeptical.

"I did. I push out the send date every few days. It's my fail-safe." I looked pointedly at the knife balanced on the seat of the chair. "My insurance policy."

"Well then, you can give me the log-in for your email."

"No."

She narrowed her eyes and leaned over me.

"You can hit me all you want, but I won't tell you. But if you get me a laptop, I'll give you the originals and delete the copies from my email, as long as you let me live."

"You and I both know you're not walking out of here alive." She bent her head to whisper in my ear. "But if you cooperate, I'll make it quick." Ruby straightened and pointed to Henry's body. "Trust me, you don't want the alternative." For a second, she let the wolf rise to the surface, her eyes flashing amber.

I swallowed. "I need a laptop."

She returned the brass knuckles to their place on the wall and grabbed the knife before searching the room for a computer. Not finding one, she pointed the tip of the knife at me. "Don't move." Ruby looked over her shoulder before disappearing into the dining room.

"Jack!" I snarled, putting all the force I could behind the command. Then I jumped up and rushed to the wall, reaching for the knife closest to me. My fingers just brushed against one when Ruby came back to the room. She moved unnaturally fast, slamming my head into the wall. I staggered, seeing stars, before she jerked me back and shoved me toward the couch.

Once I was sitting, she powered up the laptop she'd brought back and sat it on my knees. While I might not have gotten my hands on a knife, my call to Jack had worked. He was standing behind Ruby, his eyes flitting between the two of us as if he were trying to reconcile this woman with the one he knew.

I lifted my hands in the air. "It'll be easier to type if my hands are free."

Ruby shook her head. "You'll manage."

The computer was an old one, and it took its time loading. While we waited, I focused my attention on Jack. "Do you really think Jack would have exposed you?" I asked, risking her ire. "He cared about you. That's why he hid your identity in those photos."

Her laugh was bitter. "The only thing Jack cared about was breaking a story big enough to get him back to DC. He couldn't care less about all the lives he would have endangered, mine included."

"If he were here right now, he might be able to say something that would make you understand."

"I really doubt that."

I ignored Ruby, staring directly at Jack. For his part, he couldn't take his eyes off Ruby. His brow was pinched as he looked from her to me, his eyes catching on the knot I could feel raising on my forehead.

"Come on Jack, give me something to work with, here."

He moved around so that he was facing her, his gaze pleading, but she couldn't see him.

"Is he here?" Ruby spun and looked around the room, skimming right over the spot where Jack stood.

"No, but I could try to call him if you let my hands go."

Ruby twirled the knife and stared at me without bothering to answer. The computer ding snagged her attention.

"I didn't think she was capable of this." Jack ran his hand through his hair. When he spoke again, the grief in his voice was hard to miss. "She killed me." It wasn't a question. "Ask her why," he demanded.

The laptop wasn't password protected; the start screen pulled right up. Ruby was watching me closely, so I clicked on the browser icon. Typing with my hands bound together was slow and awkward, but I wasn't in a rush. The slower I went, the longer it would be before she killed me. My only hope at this point was to keep her talking, and I was relying on Jack to tell me how to do that. I repeated his question.

"Why did you kill Jack? Why not just get the photos from him?"

Ruby grew more agitated, pacing the floor. Although she couldn't see him, she passed right in front of Jack before pivoting. "I tried."

I didn't miss the look of guilt that flitted across Jack's face. "And he wouldn't give them to you?"

"Oh, he gave me the photos off his phone, but I'm not stupid. I knew he must have had them saved somewhere else. I tried to get into his laptop, but I couldn't figure out his password. There was no point in asking him." Her voice was bitter. "He wanted to get his story more than he cared about exposing me, even if it meant my death sentence."

"For what it's worth, I think he cared about you," I said.

Ruby stopped pacing long enough to glare at me. "You have no idea what you're talking about." She grabbed the knife and pointed it in my direction. "Now type. Email first," she directed me.

Since I'd been bluffing about the email, I clicked a couple times as if I were deleting emails.

"Show me," she demanded.

I spun the laptop and let her scan my outbox. Satisfied, she told me to pull up Jack's originals. I obliged, opening the photo sharing site and clicking to open each of the photos.

"Here are the originals," I said.

She spun the computer around to face her, grimacing as she clicked through the photo evidence of her change. "Delete them."

"Okay."

Hampered as I was, it took a couple minutes to delete all the photos. While I worked, I kept pushing, hoping to come up with something that would get me out of here alive. "Why would it be a death sentence for you when it's not your fault? Just tell them Jack got the photos without your knowledge. Surely, they'll understand."

She laughed, but there was no humor in it. "They're real understanding. I'm sure that works for you. Just say 'oops. I'm sorry,' and it all goes away." Ruby didn't bother tamping down her anger, each word rising with it. "But for people like me, there's no room for understanding. I have to protect myself."

As I watched, she began to shift, fine hairs popping out from her arms first before the telltale crack of bones realigning. The whole transformation only took about a minute, and as much as I didn't want to look, I couldn't force my eyes away. Her body shifted in stages. First, her torso, then her legs, and finally her head. She dropped to the ground, and her hackles raised. I watched her fingers turn to claws and her teeth sharpen into weapons capable of ripping the flesh from my bones.

She wasn't what I expected. I imagined she would be grotesque, but she was beautiful. Ruby's wolf was reddish brown, much like the woman, and her eyes glowed in the dimly lit room. There was something mesmerizing about looking into the flashing amber eyes of a predator.

Looking at her, I knew if there had been any part of Ruby I could have reached, she was long gone. The beast across from me was all instinct, and she was solely focused on me. Her lips curled back, baring her teeth, and she snarled.

When she shifted her weight back on her haunches, I knew an attack was imminent. I stood, tossing the laptop at her and scrambling to get behind the sofa. Ruby's wolf tracked my movement, her body lithe and ready for the kill. She was between me and the wall of weapons. There was no chance I could reach them before she went for my throat.

CHAPTER 25

I wasn't the kind of girl who could fight off a wolf with my bare hands. I wasn't even sure I'd stand a chance with a knife in my hands. I turned away from her and called on the only thing I had access to.

"Jack." My voice was low, fear filling it with a power I didn't recognize. On his own, Jack was useless, visible only to me. But as a man, he would've been strong enough to at least give me a fighting chance. Focusing on Jack's profile, I looked at the fine tendrils that trailed like gossamer threads away from his body. I knew it was his soul, and thanks to Meira, I knew I could control it.

"Now, Jack. Animate." I pushed every bit of power I had into that one command, looking from Jack to Henry. Jack's eyes widened, but then his soul sank into the dead body lying at his feet. Henry's eyes snapped open, fixing on my own.

A warning growl reverberated through the room. Ruby launched herself just Jack lurched to life, lunging between the two of us. Ruby's fangs sank into his arm, her jaw locking. He shook her back and forth trying to dislodge her, but his movements were uncoordinated and slow.

I didn't wait for her to let go, trusting Jack to have my back. I edged around the two of them and lunged for the knife Ruby had dropped when she shifted. Grabbing it from the floor, I put as much distance between us as I could, flattening my back against the wall of weapons. I flipped the knife around, so the blade was facing me, wedging it between my hands and sawing as best I could.

For now, at least, Ruby's attention was on Jack. She attacked his leg until it buckled, and he landed on the floor next to her. Ruby didn't waste any time going for his throat, latching on and rending what was left of it apart with her teeth. I heard the sickening crunch of teeth on bone.

Finally, the tape gave way. I ripped my hands apart, the blade nicking my wrist as I pulled. With one final twist, Ruby let go of Jack's neck and rounded on me. Her body was blocking the only exit, her eyes feral. I threw the knife, aiming for her broad chest. It sailed over her head, clattering uselessly to the floor behind her. She started to advance, but Jack's hand snagged her back paw, slowing her enough that I had time to reach up and grab one of the guns off the wall.

Ruby's teeth sank into the back of my leg as I came down with the gun. I gritted my teeth and grabbed a handful of shells that had been scattered across the table. Jack collided with Ruby, knocking us both to the ground. My legs were still bound together, making it impossible to gain my feet quickly.

Instead, I tucked and rolled, protecting my neck as best I could while loading the gun. I rolled onto my back and brought the gun up in front of me. Ruby lunged as I pulled the trigger, her body slumping across my own. She let out a high-pitched whine before she began to shift back to a woman. I struggled out from under her and scooted as far away as I could, training the gun on her as I went.

When she was done changing back into a woman, I could see the entry wound. The bullet had hit her left shoulder, high enough it missed her heart but low enough to slow her down. I didn't know if she had speedy healing abilities like pop culture claimed, but I assumed she couldn't heal as long as the bullet remained lodged in her body.

Ruby eyed the gun in my hand, and I saw the moment she decided she'd rather risk a bullet than be taken alive. She pushed herself to her feet with a groan. I chambered another round and pulled the hammer back, aiming for a kill shot.

"Don't make me do this, Ruby. I don't want to kill you."

Before she could move toward me, Jack wrapped his arms around both of her legs, dragging her back to the ground and pinning her there. Even though he was in Henry's body, I could see how much it pained him to attack her. He tried to soothe her, but her wolf had ripped out his vocal cords. All he managed was air whistling through what was left of his throat.

I didn't waste any time, moving around the table to where a land line was plugged into the wall. As much as I wanted to, I knew I couldn't call the police. And I didn't have Meira's number, so I dialed the only number I knew by heart.

"Where are you?" Craig's voice was strained, but I was grateful he'd answered on the first ring.

"I don't know." Although Jack continued to hold onto Ruby, I kept the gun trained on her as I searched the table for anything with an address. Finally finding a magazine on top of the stack of newspapers, I read the address off, and Craig repeated it to me.

"I'm on my way."

"Wait," I interrupted before he could hang up. "Ruby's here. She's shot." I swallowed, the gun trembling in my hand. "I shot her. She killed Jack, Craig. She was going to kill me." My voice trailed off.

Craig was silent for a second. "I'll be there," he said finally, disconnecting the call with a click.

At the sound of Craig's name, all the fight left Ruby. She stopped trying to pull away from Jack, resting her forehead against the carpet.

"You can let her go, Jack." He hesitated but eventually released her. For a long time, she stayed as she was. When she didn't make any more threatening moves, Jack crumpled, his spirit lifting out of the husk of the body he was in. He stood over her for a long time, his expression anguished. After several minutes, he looked at me one last time. I nodded, and he flicked out of existence, leaving Ruby and I alone to wait for Craig.

Craig didn't knock when he arrived, the crash of the front door busting open announcing his arrival. He entered the room and took in the scene, sizing up the situation. Ruby was now sitting upright, and she'd managed to get dressed, although the effort had caused blood to seep through the front of her shirt. I remained sitting with my back to the wall, the gun growing heavy in my hands.

Craig walked past Ruby and headed straight for me, bending down to cut the tape that still secured my ankles. I straightened my legs and flexed my feet as the blood rushed back into them. Craig covered my hand with his, easing the gun out of my grip. I kept my eyes trained on Ruby. She could've made a run for it with Craig's back to her, but she didn't move a muscle. Craig scanned me, his eyes lingering on the knot on my forehead.

"Do you need medical attention?" he asked.

"No." I'd have one doozy of a headache tomorrow, but I'd heal.

Craig stood up and crossed to Ruby, extending a hand to pull her to her feet.

When Craig moved to let go of Ruby's hand, she grabbed his arm. "They were going to expose us to the world." She glanced at me before staring at Wolfsbane. "I did it to protect us."

Craig sighed, but he didn't pull away from her. "No. You did it to protect yourself. You should have told Max."

She hung her head. "I'm sorry."

"I know," Craig said. He turned to me. "Meira is on her way. I'll wait until she's here before leaving."

"Did Meira tell you everything?"

"She told me enough." He was all business, patting Ruby down to make sure all the weapons were accounted for. Then he examined Wolfsbane's ravaged corpse. "Who is this?"

I gave him the highlight reel: name, relationship to Jack, circumstances of his death. The only spark of emotion on Craig's face was when I mentioned the story, a flash of anger that he quickly tamped down.

I looked at Ruby, who sat on the couch, her eyes fixed to the floor. "What will happen to her?" I asked, not sure I wanted to know.

Craig's voice was flat. "Justice."

"She was trying to stop Jack from exposing the wolves, you know." He didn't answer, so I pushed on. "She was afraid she'd be killed for the photos he took of her."

"You're defending her?"

"No. But killing her won't bring Jack back." He didn't

respond. I tried again. "I have the photos. There's no risk of exposure anymore. Call the police, turn her in," I pleaded.

"That's not how this works."

"Maybe it could."

He didn't respond. When I looked at him now, all I could see was the enforcer. It was etched in the rigid way he held himself and in the dead weight of his eyes. There was no trace of the man who had just checked to make sure I was okay before turning to Ruby, no resemblance to the man who comforted me in the weeks after Jack's death.

When Meira finally arrived, Craig led Ruby out without a backward glance.

The ride home was a blur. Now that the threat had passed, exhaustion took over, and I slept for most of the ride. When I woke, I was in an unfamiliar bed. The room I woke up in was homey, with its patchwork quilt and sheer curtains. I looked to the door as Meira came in, carrying a tray with two scones and a cup of tea, steam rising from it. I sat up, scooting back against the headboard.

Meira adjusted the pillow for me and set the tray down. "You need to eat." She reached out a cool finger and traced the cut across my cheek. I grabbed her hand to still it. "It's not deep," she said. "It won't leave a scar."

I shrugged. It was hard to care about a scar right now.

"What will happen to Ruby?" I asked, unsettled by the idea that justice in this world was served with such finality.

"Don't ask questions you don't want the answers to," Meira said.

"And Leon Matthews? You can't let an innocent man go to jail for something Ruby did."

She picked the newspaper up from the tray she'd carried in and tossed it to me. "See for yourself. The police have already cleared him. Jack's murder is once again an unsolved crime."

I relaxed against the pillows she'd fluffed behind my back. "I should go," I said, eyeing the tray in front of me.

"No, you'll stay." Meira waved me off when I tried to object. "We need to talk about why I brought you here."

"Didn't you bring me here to heal?" I asked, looking around the room in confusion.

"I mean here to Kansas City."

"But you didn't," I started, before realization dawned on me. "You sent me that magazine," I accused.

Meira nodded.

"And the funding opportunity? Was that you, as well?"

She didn't deny it.

"Why?"

"There's no room for mavericks in this world, Kali. Like it or not, you're one of us, and that makes you my responsibility." She looked like she wanted to say more but stopped herself. She looked at the tray. "Now eat, child. You're going to need your strength for what's ahead."

Meira had cryptic down to an art, but I couldn't find the energy to argue with her. Besides, she wasn't wrong. Standing one foot in this world had almost gotten me killed. Dozens of questions rambled through my head, but I pushed them aside for now.

I focused on the tray of food Meira had brought me. I recognized a peace offering when I saw one. Slowly, I lifted the scone to my mouth to take a bite, savoring the burst of wild raspberry on my tongue. Satisfied, Meira pulled the door closed behind her as she left me alone to get my bearings in an unfamiliar world.

Tomorrow, I'd ask the hard questions. I'd demand answers about who I was becoming and what I was capable of. One thing was certain. For the first time since Claire died, I was done running.

NOTE TO READERS

If you enjoyed this book, please consider leaving a review or rating on Amazon or GoodReads. Your reviews help new readers discover my books and are always appreciated.

If you'd like to be notified of new releases and exclusive content, you can sign up for my newsletter at lamcbride.com/newsletter/ and join my Facebook Readers Group at https://www.facebook.com/groups/lamcbridereaders

BOOKS BY L.A. MCBRIDE

KALI JAMES SERIES

Book 1: Fastening the Grave

Book 2: Threading the Bones

Book 3: Stitching the Talisman

Book 4: Gathering the Dead

RILEY CRUZ SERIES

Prequel Novella: Boneyard Thief

Book 1: Demon Relic Hunter

ACKNOWLEDGMENTS

Special thanks goes to my husband Chris, who believed in this book even when I doubted, my editor Sara Lundberg who helped make it the best it could be, and Susan Breen and her novel critique group for helping me kickstart a stalled novel. Finally, thank you to Lauren Adams whose pep talks and inspirational gargoyle gave me the courage to take a chance on this story.

.

Printed in Great Britain
by Amazon

52626691R00169